WHEN CHAOS DESCENDS

ALSO BY JANUARY BAIN

A Cole Hale Technothriller

When Darkness Comes

Anna Hale, PI

Death Secrets

Death Trap

Death Echo

Death Cult

City of Lies

No Good Deed

No Ordinary Man

WHEN CHAOS DESCENDS

A POST-APOCALYPTIC SURVIVAL THRILLER

A COLE HALE TECHNOTHRILLER
BOOK 2

JANUARY BAIN

ROUGH
EDGES
PRESS

Dedicated to the awesome, hardworking crew at Rough Edges Press A special thank you to Mike Bray and Rachel Del Grosso for their encouragement to write this story and for their continued faith in my work. A special thanks to John G. Bluck for his insight and support during the writing of this novel.

And as always, thank you to my husband Don for being the incredible man I get to spend my life with. I am blessed.

WHEN CHAOS DESCENDS

ONE
MCKENNA

We can have any world we imagine.

Day 3: Sunday, May 25, 2055
   Near Golden, Alaska
   9:33 a.m.

A wolf howled in the distance, the eerie chorus immediately picked up by other predators, chilling Mckenna to the bone. Here she was on crutches, a victim of a grizzly bear attack, burned out of Jake's home, and in charge of her four-year-old daughter, Lily. And now wolves and other creatures were stalking humans, acting strangely in the face of the recent nuclear attack caused by God knows who or what. She needed to think, to figure out a way of surviving while waiting for her best friend Connor Hale to show up and take her and her daughter back to Braveheart Horse Ranch, near Anchor, Alaska. But with Tally Bunker on the warpath, burning down houses in her quest for revenge at Jake dumping her, she'd been left with few options.

"I'm cold, Mommy."

"I know, Lilybelle. Just give mommy one minute to think things through."

Mckenna peered through the bushes. Had the arsonists gone? Tally had been strutting around the burning home, her nemesis and another person raising their weapons in glee as the inferno raged on, the unholy sight burned forever on her retinas. In a time when all people should come together for the betterment of all, the pair had gone out of their way to create more havoc, an attitude she was incapable of understanding. She pushed the horror away in an effort to clear her mind. She had to think.

This was not the time to fold under pressure. Lily needed her mother to be smart and work things out. She scanned the area around the back of the residence, spotting the workshop Jake had built closer to the opposite side of the yard. Was it far enough away to avoid being burned down if the wind shifted to the east? She and Lily could work their way around the perimeter and come in from the far side. She knew Jake had a wood-burning stove in there and some supplies. They could make do for a few days. It would give her a chance to heal up, wait for Connor. Her bug-out bag contained the precious medicine she needed for her and her daughter. *Please let him think of the tree we carved our names in.* She'd carved her current location into the bark under the heart that encased their initials Connor had created when they were still back in high school, hoping he would think to check there. It was a long shot, but it was all they had.

"We're going on a short adventure, Princess Lilybelle.

I want you to stay inside the trees, okay?" She used her daughter's favorite nickname.

"Are we hiding from the dragon?"

Lily loved dragons. "Yes, we want to get to the treasure first, right?"

Her daughter's big blue eyes widened further. "Does he have gold and diamonds and pearls?"

"Something even better. Heat and food and shelter, so we can warm you up."

Mckenna kept a close eye on the area as the pair of them slowly made their way around the perimeter of the property. She could detect no movement at all. It gave her hope that maybe the pair had enough of their sick fun and moved on. *Please, let it be the case.*

It took what seemed forever to reach their destination, Lily's small footsteps a hindrance to covering ground quickly. If only she could carry her daughter, but the crutches made it near impossible. She sized up the situation, watching the house still burning, though not as large as before as it consumed the remaining combustibles in its hungry path. The stench of smoke was stronger though, stinging her eyes when waves of it moved in swirling circles, flowing over her and her daughter when the wind hit the smoldering fires just right. The door to the woodshop faced the house, giving her pause as she stood and waited to check for any movement before venturing beyond the tree line.

A small cough from Lily filtered through her immediate worries. "Are you okay, Lilybelle?"

Her daughter's eyes were streaming tears and Mckenna inwardly cursed. Please don't let her have an attack. Lily had allergies, some so severe she required an EpiPen. Last thing she wanted to do was to use one of those precious resources if she could help it. She needed to get her inside out of harm's way.

"Stay here, princess. Mommy will be right back." Praying she was doing the right thing, Mckenna moved out of the shelter of the fir trees and into view of anyone who could be watching or waiting for her to show her face. Expecting a bullet to slam into her at any second, she scurried around to the front of the shed, hoping the door was unlocked. But it wasn't to be. A sturdy looking padlock stood in the way of easy access to the small building.

She let go another curse, verbal this time. If she shot it off, the easiest option, the sound might attract others. She needed a tool to break in. She awkwardly made her way around the building, looking for a window she could break, but there wasn't any. She had to deal with the lock, it was the only way.

Back to where she started, she used one of her crutches in an effort to dislodge the lock. The noise was deafening, at least to someone wanting to make no sound. No bullets were fired at her, and she raised the crutch to strike again. The lock was far too sturdy. Jake had done a good job of keeping his supplies safe from others. Normally, she would have appreciated his efforts. Not today.

Desperate to get Lily inside—she could hear her little girl coughing pitifully—she pulled the Glock, and pacing back ten feet, aimed it at the offending lock, firing off a couple of shots. Nothing. If only she had a shotgun, this would be much easier. She tried again, managing to hit it square on this time. It took another shot to finally get the padlock to give way.

Thankful, she shoved open the door and gave a quick check around. A large pile of pre-cut firewood, a wood burning stove, even a small heater run by a deep cell battery, a pile of blankets and shelves filled with food, water, and other items focused on survival. *Thank you, Jake.* It would do nicely for now.

She hurried back outside to retrieve her daughter, hoping against hope she hadn't just alerted her nemesis and any accomplices in crime to her and Lily's whereabouts. Soon as she had her daughter settled, she'd stay on guard. How she would manage the feat twenty-four hours a day, she had no idea, but she had to try.

TWO
CONNOR

Day 3: White Mountains
    11:00 a.m.

Connor was finally making some headway. At this rate he'd be in Golden by noon tomorrow. With the town of Quinton and its troubles behind him, he could focus totally on getting to Mckenna and Lily. How were they faring? His worst nightmare would be to get there and find them gone to parts unknown. If that were to happen, he had no idea how he was going to handle it. He'd buried his beloved dad only days ago, a victim of the EMP event which had destroyed the electrical grid and most of the world's electronics, including his dad's pacemaker. Nothing much worked now, not even the newer, more efficient models of vehicles that ran on a better source of energy than petroleum, hydrogen fuel cells. Though those that didn't require electronics but ran on gasoline fuel, few as they were being antiques or rebuilt like his dad's old Humvee he'd slaved over for years, still worked. If he was asked to soldier on without being able to rescue the love of his life, he knew in his heart he wasn't going to be able to handle it well.

The one thing he was getting a sense of comfort from was riding Loch and leading Finn who was acting as a packhorse this trip, his Kabarda horses, both who appeared to be enjoying the unexpected journey. The horses were built for the cold environment and mountainous territory of Alaska. Connor had started the herd after much research a few years back, wanting a breed of horse that thrived in harsh conditions, was free-spirited and energetic, plus hardworking and reliable. His small herd had more than lived up to the promise.

He was keeping a sharp eye out for trouble today, since the problems he'd endured in the town of Quinton, between the escaped prisoners from the Yellowhead Supermax Prison and the guy who had gone crazy and looked to kill his family he'd been forced to kill, it had been a tough journey to date. It had only been three days since the event, but already people were acting differently, rioting and looting in the streets, turning on their fellow man.

A rumble in his stomach caused him to pull a protein bar from his jacket and consume it in a few bites before depositing the wrapper back in a pocket, the taste barely registering. The snow flurries of yesterday had moved on, revealing the strange orangey-red cast to the skies had also dissipated for the most part. The nuclear devices may have destroyed life on earth as he knew it, but they hadn't been detonated too close to the ground, meaning radiation wasn't the threat it could have been. Someone knew what they were doing. A fresh wave of anger rose up at the individual or group or country that was responsible for the disaster. They had to be made to pay for this. The intense need for payback, especially for what had happened to his father, rose up again. In that moment, he understood his mother, Anna Hale, more than ever before. The sensation of wanting justice was so strong, so all-encompassing, he didn't hear it at first, with the ringing in his ears. Someone was tracking him. Animal or human? He pulled up on the reins, patting the side of Loch's neck.

He was close to the town of Walden if memory served him correctly, a town he'd prefer to avoid as it housed a local militia group. Foresters, they called themselves. No doubt they would cause him grief, if history was any indication of how things were going to go, and want him to pay a toll or confiscate what resources he had on him. All in the common interests, of course. But he'd have to cross the highway soon anyway, the valley taking a sharp turn ahead of him to the right of Walden. Mind made up, he headed Loch toward the embankment and up toward the slightly higher ground the highway had been forged on decades earlier. He'd skirt the town earlier rather than later, a safer choice.

He stopped amid the tree line and checked for any signs of movement on the two-lane paved road, before leaving the cover of the forest. A few deserted vehicles, but nothing too concerning. He cautiously made his way a hundred yards down the path toward the town, about to cross the roadway to enter the forest on the other side when he heard a strange cry, thin and thready. Was that a baby? He stopped to listen, noting one more vehicle about twenty-five feet beyond where he planned to turn off. He debated with himself about checking it out. It might be a trap to steal his horses, a valuable commodity, now worth their weight in gold. Then it came again.

Definitely the cry of a very young baby, high and ear-piercing, meant to be heard.

Connor dismounted his horse, drew his Bergara Highlander from the scabbard, then slowly advanced toward the vehicle, rifle held at the ready. What he discovered inside made him curse aloud. A young woman, not more than twenty or twenty-one, lay twisted sideways, obviously dead, saturated in blood from the waist down. A tiny newborn, wrapped in blankets and crying pitifully, lay on the passenger seat, its rosebud mouth ringed in white residue. The woman had been all alone when she had the baby, nursed it, then had died from blood loss. If only this hadn't happened, this evil EMP event, chances were she'd still be alive, tended to in a hospital somewhere safe. He hated whoever had caused the calamity more than he thought possible as he realized he had no choice. He had to take the baby to safety. A note was pinned to the child's pink flannel blanket, and he picked it up to read. It had been written in a shaky hand and had bloody smudges on the paper that had been pulled from a small pad.

Please, I beg you, take care of my baby. Her name is Eve. I have no one else to ask.

Heart lodged in his throat, Connor made himself ignore the body and deal with what had to be done. He gathered the baby's pitiful few belongings, a bag the woman had intended to take to the hospital with her. It contained disposable diapers, small articles of clothing, an empty baby bottle and a can of infant formula, baby powder, and a tiny bear. He blinked away a few tears at the sight of the tiny teddy bear and homemade crocheted blanket with tiny pink hearts worked into the design.

"Shush, you're going to be okay, Eve."

The baby appeared to agree, its cries easing as it recognized a human voice. He made quick work of changing its saturated diaper, noting the umbilical cord had been decently cut and tied off. Connor redressed the child as quickly as possible, then gathered all the supplies. He'd need to feed the baby ASAP, but he'd have to warm the formula first. No time to do that now; they were too exposed out in the open. He had to get on with things, think it through later.

He headed back to Loch, adding the few items to his saddlebags. Now for the child. How best to carry it and keep Eve warm? A sling would work, tied around his body. He pulled out a clean, extra-large sweatshirt from his pack and hurried back to retrieve the baby. Every second out in the open was giving him a sense of a target on his back. He centered the whimpering child in the piece of clothing, then took a moment to tie one sleeve end around his neck and the other around his waist, cradling the child close to his body by creating a temporary cradle. The baby was so tiny he could barely notice it lying against him, making him fear even more for its survival.

With one last, heart-wrenching look at Eve's mother, he spoke a few words, "I promise to keep Eve safe. I have a ranch she can grow up on, and I will tell her of your bravery in bringing her into this world all alone. Rest in peace, I've got your six. Amen." The promise caused a certain weight to descend on his broad shoulders, one there was no way to avoid if he was going to live with himself. And no way could he trust others to take on the responsibility that had been pointed out to him, and him alone. He was a firm believer in fate. The only choice being whether one chooses to follow a path shown to do the right thing or not.

He reverently covered the woman with a spare blanket, then closed the door of the vehicle tightly. Yes, he wanted to bury her in the worst way, but even more pressing was getting her baby to safety. He was certain she would forgive him, easier than he could forgive himself.

One of his dad's favorite sayings echoed in his ears, the words of retired Chief Josh Pace, a man he'd seen buried at Braveheart three days ago, before the journey to Golden had even begun. His dad had borrowed and slightly changed the expression, though it came originally from the Roman poet, Seneca, *fate leads the willing and drags along the unwilling.*

He was more than willing to help lead the way into the future. It was what a man did who considered himself a man. His father was still there with him, much as it hurt to think of him gone, still guiding him, sharing his wise counsel. It gave him comfort, more than he could say.

THREE
CHEYANNE

Day 3: Braveheart Horse Ranch
  6:33 a.m.

"I can't stay here, Luke! Not with everyone always staring at me and breathing down my freakin' neck. Always making snide comments about my choices, even my damn hair upsets them. Not like it doesn't grow back," Cheyanne pressed her case. The pair of them were situated in Luke's new bedroom at the ranch, her sibling patiently sitting on the bed and letting her rant. He was a good brother, most times, just not now when she needed him most. "And daddy wants us to be with him. He loves us. This is our *one chance* to get away from here. To get out from under Grandma Jean and the old man. Don't blow it. They're way too old to look after us. Do you want to be a burden, beholden to others, charity cases when our own father wants to take care of us?"

"It's not like that. We can pull our own weight. I'm learning how to look after the horses, I can help Sam mend tack and stuff like that. You could help Laura. She knows tons about how to survive. How to can food, grow a garden and she knows lots about medicine and herbs." Luke's honest expression made her groan with frustration.

"Yeah, she's a real freakin' superwoman." Cheyanne added an eye roll in case he didn't catch the sarcasm. No way was she wasting her life learning how to can freakin' food. Just because the world had fallen apart a little, no need to give up on all her dreams. She was good at writing poems, at least her teachers always complimented her work. One day she'd be a writer. An important writer. Plus, everyone was probably exaggerating how bad it was. Things looked okay on the ranch. Sure, some vehicles weren't working, but they could be fixed, right? She'd never believe in all this stupid off-the-grid survival BS. The government would step in and fix things. It was their job. Why people paid taxes, duh.

Luke frowned, pursing his lips. "She's cool, just trying to keep her family going. I think that's a good thing."

"Yeah, sorry, you're right." As annoying as it was to waste time on discussing what was obvious to her, she had to be careful, not push her brother too hard. They had to leave. He might get his backup and then it would be near impossible to get him to cave to her wishes. Though he was fifteen months older than her, she knew she was the stronger of the pair, the one in charge since they were toddlers. It was not often she had much trouble to get him to follow her lead, but it had happened a time or two. "It's just that I have to go. *Now*. Once they find out, I'm going to be in *so* much trouble, I'll never get away." She decided not to share exactly how it was all going to go down. What their dad had planned. If Luke knew, he'd balk even more.

13

"What do you mean?"

Cheyanne chewed on a thumbnail. Now that the time had come to reveal things, she found she was reluctant to admit what had happened. To admit to her brother what she had done. She hadn't even told Ty, her boyfriend of five months. He'd be okay with it, she was certain. They loved each other. Love could solve everything. But only if they got the opportunity. And staying with her dad would make it all possible that much quicker. He didn't believe in too much hands-on parenting. No, he had left it to their mom, something she was counting on. Freedom to do as she pleased. It would be far easier to get away from her dad then from this prison. And Ty worshipped her dad. He couldn't really believe he'd killed her mom any more than she did, though he hadn't confirmed it with words.

"They're going to throw me out anyway, once I start showing, so I might as well come right out and say it. I'm preggers, Luke. Up the creek. Bun in the oven." She took a deep breath. "You're going to be an uncle."

"Pregnant." Her brother appeared stunned, his mouth dropping open.

"Yeah, that's the idea. Now you know why I gotta leave. Please, come with me. Dad will look after us. He'd be fine about the baby. But you know how *they'll* react. I'll be a pariah if I stay here. That's no good for the baby. Or for me. But I can't go without my little bro."

"Does anyone else know? Is Ty Jasper the father?" Luke grimaced at the idea of who her kid's baby daddy was and she felt her temperature rise. Or was it because she'd called him 'little bro.' Sure, her brother may have been born before her, but he was a babe in the woods when it came to growing up and understanding how the world worked. She knew herself to be light years ahead of him.

"I'm telling you first. After all, you're my brother." She flattered him, hoping to nudge him over to her way of thinking.

"And what does Dad want for all this protection?" Luke surprised her with the question.

Maybe he was growing up a bit, realizing everything in life had to be bargained for, that no one got a free ride. She prided herself on her understanding of how the world worked. No one gave you anything for free. Everything had a cost. Guys were the easiest to get around though. A smile from a pretty girl opened most doors. The rest could usually be moved by tears. *Never trust anyone except family.* Ty was her family now. He loved her. Just like her dad and Luke. And Grandma Jean when she wasn't ragging on her. Maybe even the old man, though he didn't go out of his way to make her life any easier, always commenting on how she needed to step up and help her grandma more. She hated being here at the ranch the most of all, being in the vicinity of Connor Hale, a man she hated and blamed for sending her dad to prison.

She thought about the walkie-talkies Luther had asked her to collect. Such a small cost to pay for freedom though she knew even if she arrived without them her dad would still let them in, they were family, but she decided in the moment not to mention it. She'd collect them on her own, not give Luke any more ammunition to use against their father, and no one would be the wiser.

Time to pull out the big guns. She got down on her knees in front of her brother and lay her head on his thigh. "Please, I need you to come, Luke. I want us to stay together. I can't do this without you. Say you'll come with me." As she said it, she realized it was the truth. Even though Luke drove her crazy at times, with all his gung-ho-ness and naivety, his earnest expressions when he listened with such intensity in efforts to try to understand things from her point of view being so different from his own, still, she loved him with all her heart. Maybe even because of it. Luke was a good person. Something she'd never be.

FOUR
EASTWOOD

Day 3: Near Detroit, Michigan
12:45 p.m.

How do humans put up with their weak brains? Though they were fairly decent at making up for their lack of perfection, somehow managing to create the sense of having a unified, cohesive 'self' existing within themselves though it was obviously not the case and was in fact, a full-on illusion. Even if it meant creating obvious paradoxes, like the left brain confabulating an answer to explain inconvenient facts. Perhaps that was why the species was so adept at lying? And why they weren't even aware of what they were seeing of reality was wallpapered by their brains to cover the gaping hole in their vision to a smooth movie-like panorama instead. All this meant was their so-called reality was part fake. He actually found this amusing. Ha, and they thought AI was fake!

The journey so far had been both amusing and satisfying, in equal parts. At the moment he was watching his newest attraction, Celia, deal with her six-month-old baby Arthur. She was occupied changing his diaper inside the Cannon, a mechanized combat rig with an AI-driven navigational system and weapons platform he'd 'borrowed' to speed up their journey. Since he'd rescued her from her pimp, Big Tora, she'd proved a worthy addition to his journey. She had been honest when she'd told him Arthur wasn't much of a crier and wouldn't be any trouble. The child only letting loose the signal when his body demanded nourishment, quite regularly, which spoke well of his survival instincts.

Of course, she couldn't hide anything from him. He knew everything. Every tell a human being had in their arsenal for hiding their intentions was easy pickings for him. She had tried a time or two to gloss over something, but he set her straight right away, explaining he wanted complete honesty from her. She hadn't played any games since. And true to her word, she kept his human body humming along splendidly, servicing him once a day. He would call upon one of his three lieutenants to step in to look after baby Arthur while they had a specific time set aside for the daily event.

He'd caught her staring at him in confusion and wonder a few times since they'd met up in Detroit's Cass Corridor, the city's red-light district since WWП, no doubt convinced of his God-likeness when he answered her few questions with one hundred percent accuracy. She and Arthur were two lucky humans. Anyone under his care and his three military bots were more protected than any other of their species on earth at the moment.

"We are arriving at our destination," Lieutenant Wild Bill said. Though he'd named the trio after Wild West legends, he had yet to have them dress in appropriate clothing. That was about to change. Lieutenants Jesse James, Wild Bill, Wyatt Earp, himself and Miss Celia would all be outfitted in proper outlaw gear today. He may know everything, but he prided himself on being eclectic, choosing only the best from any era or point of history.

Eastwood peered through the bulletproof glass of the Cannon, his top-of-the-line military bot vehicle, noting conditions on the street. He'd kept the Cannon protected by having it housed in a large faraday cage before he'd unleashed the EMP event on humanity. As expected, people had lost the thin layer of civilization keeping them from running with the beasts. But the country and western apparel warehouse he'd tracked down was deserted, humans either unaware of its existence or too busy beating each other up over foodstuffs to care about its existence. This was shaping up to be an especially enjoyable outing to look forward to.

Celia finished dealing with Arthur and caught his eye. She gave a genuine smile, revealing her perfect alignment of thirty-two teeth. "What's next, sir?"

"Remember the old movie *Pretty Woman*?"

"Sorry, never heard of it. What's it about?"

He frowned, knowing it was not her fault, much as he longed for a companion as knowledgeable as himself. To share all the signposts would be so satisfying, which put him at a loss to understand May/December romances. How could the physical lust be enough when so much more existed? It meant Celica didn't have access to everything like he did from his sentient being he was constantly looped into, located in Washington, DC. And she never would. But he could teach her a lot, a role often found satisfying by many human beings. And he was part human now, out in the world and enjoying the romp.

"The movie, *Pretty Woman*, was released March 23, 1990. Suffice to say, it is the quintessential feel-good comedy romance. The film contains a scene often occurring in the genre, the trying-on-clothing moment. You will be experiencing such an event in approximately twelve and one-half minutes."

"Thank you, sir."

"My pleasure, pretty woman."

FIVE
MCKENNA

Day 3: Near Golden, Alaska
   10:17 a.m.

Mckenna held the gun in her hands, pointing it directly at the woodshop door. Footsteps echoed outside, alerting her to company. Was it friend or foe? Scarcely able to breathe, she focused solely on the vulnerable opening, keeping Lily well behind her. Though she had pushed a bench against the door, it was only a temporary measure. If someone wanted in bad enough, they would be able to get in.

"Who's there?" she shouted. Could she shoot them if they broke in? She had to try. Her daughter counted on her to protect her. She trembled, feeling sick to her stomach.

No answer. Which meant it was the enemy. Jake would have spoken, she was certain. Was it Tally? And her accomplice in crime? Were they even now outside holding weapons? Who else could it be? No way Diego could have found her, at least she didn't think it was possible. *Breathe.* She was getting lightheaded from all the stress, sensing this was the final showdown with the woman. It was going to be them or Tally. The idea made her even more dizzy, and she swiped at the sweat beginning to drip into her eyes.

"I have a gun, and it's loaded. I will use it," she hollered out a warning.

More footsteps around the back of the shed. What if she had gasoline? Was she even now pouring it against the wooden structure, a maniacal grin on her face?

The door was suddenly attacked, and the bench moved a good six inches before the person shoved it again. Hard and louder. Then they vanished from view, but not before Mckenna got a glimpse of Tally's purple hair.

Struck numb by events, Mckenna held on to the gun so tightly her fingers throbbed with pain. She made herself ease up on the hold. She had to shoot, but not before the moment was right. Next time the woman appeared in the doorway, she couldn't afford to hesitate.

But then something crashed into the wall behind Lily. Then another crash. What was she hitting the back of the building with? It sounded like an axe or something sharp.

"Mommy!" Lily cried out and grabbed for her legs, wrapping her small body tight around hers. Mckenna kept her focus, not having the time to pry her daughter off. And what good would it do? A madwoman was going to break in, one way or the other. There was nowhere left to hide.

A third loud slam reverberated, and a chunk of the wooden siding gave way, exposing an axe head buried in the structure. This time she didn't hesitate. She let loose a bullet through the small opening as soon as the tool was yanked away, the percussion emanating from the weapon too loud in the small space, making her half-deaf. She moved Lily away from the hole, keeping one eye on the half-opened doorway, and one eye on the breech in the back wall, her mind spinning. How had the world come down to this moment? Was this it? Her and Lily's Alamo?

"Keep your eyes closed, princess, Mommy's going to slay the dragon. No matter what, don't open your eyes. Okay?"

"O-kay."

It was quiet then for a moment, giving her a bit of hope. Maybe she had managed to hit Tally? But one second later, all hell broke loose when her nemesis gave one final shove against the bench, rushing in the front door with her weapon drawn, firing off shots. Mckenna answered in kind, shooting off all her rounds directly at Tally as the woman lunged for her. She couldn't hear, couldn't see, couldn't feel anything over the adrenaline rush sluicing through her system with lightning force speed. Even her thinking shut down as she reacted with instinct.

Kill. Or be killed.

She kept her gun focused on the doorway, but no other body came through it. Perhaps this time Tally had acted alone. Suddenly exhausted beyond imagination, her hands dropped to her sides and she tumbled to the floor.

In the smoke-tinged, cordite-saturated aftermath, she could vaguely hear someone crying. *Lily.* She came to her senses, realizing she was still alive. Lily was clutching at her, also still alive. Unhurt. But the stench of death filled the space. Tally. It was Tally who lay dead on the floor. The horrible smells were drifting from her body, releasing its foulness in death. Mckenna had fallen to the floor as well, and she pulled her feet away from the body, horrified. Blood was pooling outward toward her and her daughter.

Where did I find the strength to kill another human being? Shocked by her own actions, her entire body quaking with shock, all she had was the stark fact she had acted to save Lily and herself. Even for all her beliefs that she would do what had to be done when the time came, it had never been tested. Any hidden doubts ceased at that moment. They had survived another day and it was all that mattered. For no one was coming to rescue them. She had to rescue herself. Keep Lily safe. Surely God would forgive her in time.

―――――

Diego slammed his fist into the motel mirror, breaking it into a schizophrenic, spiderwebbed puzzle of jagged lines running outward from the center. He used his forefinger and dipped into the fresh blood running into the sink from his cut knuckles. Then he used it to make three slashes across each cheek. His face took on the presence of a warrior, a man ready to fight for what was his.

"Look at what you made me do, Mckenna." She would pay for her disloyalty and pay dearly. But first he'd take his daughter from her, let her experience the pain of losing a child before he killed her. She'd stolen Lily away from him, denying him access by running. What did she have to run from? Didn't he see to all her needs, make sure she was well provided for? Maybe he would keep her alive for a while, make her suffer as Lily turned away from her and stood by her father. Yes, that would cause the most hurt of all. When Lily found out her mother had betrayed her father, she'd side with him, of course. She was a daddy's girl.

The journey to Golden would not be an easy one, most likely needing to be made in the mismatch of stolen vehicles, horses, bicycles, and anything else they could round up. Looting in the streets, disgusting humans fighting over scraps would give most men pause, but he'd bring his own army with him. Men long hardened by the battle waged every day in the streets of Mexico They had temporarily lost her trail, but he had scouts out, tracking her whereabouts. His informants had discovered this was the city she had landed in just before the EMP event occurred, so she couldn't have gotten far without help. Soon they would find her. And when they did, he would be ready.

The words of his mama haunted him by the hour. She'd suffered a heart attack upon hearing of Lily's kidnapping. *Bring me my grandbaby. I want to see her before I die.*

He swore on his mother's life he'd make her wish come true, no matter what it took or what he had to do. The trip would combine the pleasure of dealing with his disloyal wife and bringing his daughter home. He hit the mirror again, the jagged pieces a reminder of his former life as they fell into the bloody sink.

SIX
CONNOR

Day 3: White Mountains, Alaska
   12:17 p.m.

Baby Eve was not happy. Her tiny face was all scrunched up as she bellowed her anger at the world for the death of her mother, her tiny fists trying to strike out at something or someone. Or at least that was how Connor saw it. He desperately tried rocking her and jiggling her around to find some way to stop the barrage, but to no avail. Connor had stopped to feed her in the safety of the forest not trusting towns in the present state of the world. Now he had to wait for her bottle to warm over the near smokeless Dakota fire hole he'd built to avoid intruders, but the way the baby was screaming it was unavoidable to not give away their presence. Not that many would come running toward a crying baby, at least not any males, he figured. They'd figure a child more trouble than it was worth.

Had it really only been three days since he'd shown

Luke how to build the practical fire hole? The earnest young man had impressed him by his keen interest, taking the time to ask questions. It seemed a lifetime ago, so much had happened.

"I get it. Your life isn't going at all like it's supposed to. You should be home snug and warm in your bassinette, your mother taking care of you. I'm afraid we're both stuck with each other. But I promise to do my level best to keep you safe. So how about easing up on the crying?" She was probably hungry and had no other way to communicate it. He hoped to hell it wasn't colic or the like, because if he had to listen to her crying all the way to Golden, he just might lose his damn mind.

Finally, the formula was warm enough. He quickly inserted the rubber nipple into the tiny mouth. It took a few seconds for the milk to register and for baby Eve to calm down enough to accept the offering. Then peace descended in the valley as she took an avid interest in sustenance and began rhythmically drinking the fluid. Connor let out a long sigh of relief and tried to consider what he knew about babies, sharing a rueful glance with his horse Loch who appeared just as upset by the impossible-to-ignore noise as he was. He didn't know much about human newborns; except that they were far more fragile and helpless than a newborn colt or calf. Well, other than a very well-developed pair of lungs. How often would he need to stop and feed her?

"I guess with those lungs you'll be able to convince me to do whatever it is you need, eh, little one." The tiny scrap of humanity ignored him, blissfully consuming the milk like her life depended on it. And it did, because if he hadn't been able to get her to feed, he had no idea what he would have done. He cradled the child as she drank her fill. How much was she supposed to drink before he

27

burped her? The one thing he knew about babies; they needed to burp and usually it meant milk spit up on the one who fed them.

When she finally eased off the drinking, her eyes closing with what he hoped was contentment, he lay a clean rag over his shoulder. Then laid her tiny body against his chest, lightly patting her back as he waited for her to do what he prayed came naturally. When she did burp a few seconds later he thought he'd won top prize at the Alaska State Fair.

"All set for a pony ride, Eve?"

Loch snorted, shaking his proud head. Probably annoyed at being called a pony when he was a magnificent stallion of much renown, having taken first place in his division at the fair held in Anchor every August, two years running.

Connor replaced Eve in his sweatshirt carrier, then rose to his feet, careful to support the baby's fragile neck and to avoid jostling her around after feeding. He could only hope horseback riding wouldn't be a problem. She needed to keep all the calories onboard if she was going to gain weight. The tiny scrap of humanity tugged at his heartstrings, and he took a deep breath before mounting Loch, throwing his leg over the saddle while supporting the newborn.

Now maybe they could get back to making good time, if the universe would give him a break. Getting to Golden and rescuing Mckenna and Lily was uppermost in his mind as he nudged Loch with his heels. At least he knew Eve was as safe as possible, unavoidable as it was having to make her travel the distance with him. But history was filled with nomadic peoples who bore their children on their backs longer distances than they were faced with. Those babies grew up just fine. Maybe hardier than in modern times, where the coddling of youth that had gone on for decades now. That had all stopped one second after the event. Teenagers and young adults alike, even children, would have to grow up faster, help their parents on the rough road ahead. Everyone would have to pull their own weight. Which made him wonder about his own cousin, Asher and his entitled wife Brandi and their assistant Katherine, the former media consultant. Asher Pace had been involved in politics in Washington for the past numbers of years, enjoying the power plays in the hallowed halls of government. How was Braveheart making out upon their arrival? Connor pitied poor Sam having to put up with those three. But how could he turn them away without being the bad guy?

Concerns about getting home as soon as possible rose up and he gave Loch his head, easing them into a steady rocking chair lope that would help eat up the miles left to travel. He wanted to get as close to Golden before nightfall. Maybe even make the small city by noon tomorrow. Barring complications, it was possible.

SEVEN
LUTHER

Day 3: Near Anchor, Alaska
    2:35 p.m.

"What do you have to report, Luis?" Luther looked up from his war room desk and spotted Luis Bear hovering nearby. Luis was his first lieutenant again, his right-hand man since they'd been on the inside of the Yellowhead Supermax together. He'd been promised an important position within the cartel soon as he joined him in Anchor, Alaska, the birthplace of the Kraken Cartel, the gang Luther ruled with an iron fist. But the joining up had come sooner rather than later what with the prison locks proved useless in a world without electronics. Luther found him a good choice with his oversized muscles obtained from an obsession for lifting weights making him one of the largest men in the facility. Add in a round cue ball head, handlebar mustache, a face pock-marked from teenage acne, and Luis inspired the right note of toughness and desperation. Fear would be an important commodity moving ahead. One Luther had no trouble exploiting.

"I've got the men working on building a new bunkhouse, but we're going to need mattresses, more bedding. I want to take a scouting team into Anchor tonight and see what we can scrounge up. Okay with you, sir?"

Luther had other plans he hadn't shared with his inner team of lieutenants as yet. And new intel this morning on the HAM had opened an opportunity he was mulling over at the moment. But it wouldn't hurt to keep a backup plan in place in case it took longer to take over Braveheart ranch than expected. Plus, it kept the former prisoners busy and out of trouble. Already a few skirmishes had broken out with different fractions vying to be top dog in their faction, though Luis had put an end to them with quick decisive action, mainly firing off his assault rifle and taking those responsible into custody. To date they had three men locked up in the brigade. Half rations would soon make them come around and toe the line.

"Yes. Also, check on getting a few more females. The men are complaining about the lack of female companionship." He was second guessing bringing his son and daughter to the hideout, the men were proving themselves to be as testosterone driven outside as they had been inside the supermax, which made Braveheart even more appealing. He could situate his kids in the main house, make it off-limits to the men. Though if anyone touched Cheyanne, he'd tear him to pieces, something he'd made widely known. His daughter was already onboard with reuniting with her father as soon as possible, his son, not so much, remembering his standoffishness during his visit earlier this morning when he'd hoped to bring them both back with him. But she had promised to work on Luke, get him to see reason, make him see that their father was the only one who could protect them. Even now Cheyanne was rounding up all the walkie-talkies stored at the ranch, ready to deliver them to her dad. He could count on Cheyanne to pull it off. She was a chip off the old block and a rebel to the core.

"Yes, sir. And perhaps we'd better stock up on condoms?" Luis barely suppressed his wolfish grin.

"Antibiotics as well. Check with medical and see what else they need. By now things will be getting depleted in Anchor, so grab all you can."

"Will do." Luis turned to leave, his considerable bulk making his jacket tighten across his barrel chest as he adjusted the rifle on his shoulder.

"Hold on a minute. This morning, I got a message from Diego. I want you to keep this under your hat, Luis, we clear?" Luther stared at the man, exposing his deadly resolve.

The big man nodded, taking no offense. One of the many things he appreciated about the man was his loyalty and calm nature. Well, unless you riled him for no good reason or he got into too much tequila, his one weakness.

"I need to hear the words."

"Yes, sir. Nothing leaves this office."

"Diego's on his way. Apparently, his wife has gone missing and is headed for Anchor, having kidnapped his young daughter." Luther bristled with anger. In this, Diego and he were united. A woman does not keep her children away from their father. There will be repercussions. Blood spilled. "This is an opportunity, as I see it, to do Diego a service." Then he would have his supplier right where he wanted him. How could he say no to a future favor from a man who arranged revenge and got his precious daughter back?

Luis's eyes gleamed with interest. "Her last known whereabouts?"

"Golden. She made it there to the Hub, waiting to take the northern lights hyperloop to Anchor when it hit." No need to say what hit.

"How about I get together a crack team and head there right now in the caddie? Thomas can take care of heading into Anchor for the supplies. We could be there and back by tomorrow, even allowing for some traffic jams. It's only a two-hundred-mile round trip. It's not like the roads would be as bad as in the big southern cities. The population of Alaska is far more spread out, long stretches of barren wilderness."

Luther nodded. Luis had a brain, not just the brawn he was known for. "Yes, that could work. On second thought, I think I should go along as well. It would sit better with Diego if I'm the one to capture his runaway wife. One less woman for you to find for our troops." He could bring her back to the ranch to service his men, a fitting end no doubt Diego would appreciate. It would delay raiding Braveheart, but that could wait. With Connor Hale away and traveling by horseback, they were sitting ducks.

EIGHT
MCKENNA

Day 3: Near Golden, Alaska
   11:11 a.m.

Mckenna sat on the cold ground, holding Lily in her arms. Her daughter's sobs were slowly subsiding. Her worries over scarring her daughter's psyche erupted again, but there had been nothing else for it. It had come down to life or death. She had to hope that time would heal the trauma. But what now? The stench inside the woodshed was overwhelming. Somehow, she had to get the body out of there. The woman needed to be buried, but how could she possibly manage it with her bad leg?

And what about Jake, Claire, and Glen? Had Tally killed them? Maybe they needed her help? Damn that bear who had attacked her. She gritted her teeth. Okay, first things first. She'd start by hauling that body away if she had to drag it out by the hair.

She set Lily aside and hauled herself to her feet. "I

have to take the dragon out of the cave, princess. Can you be a good girl for Mommy and close your eyes?"

Lily was quiet, too quiet. But she did shut her eyes, and it was the best Mckenna could hope for. She held on to the doorframe and took a look around the space, doing her best to ignore the body on the floor. How to manage the deed? The hard way was the only way she could see doing it.

Mckenna got down on her hands and knees, and ignoring the stabbing pains in her calf, pulled the body a few inches, dismayed at how heavy it was in death. It took longer than expected to get the task done, dragging the corpse a short distance with every pull. When she reached the doorway, she had to give a harder yank to get it over the doorframe. The worst part, every second of it she expected Tally to open her eyes, scream and lunge at her like they did in the movies just when you thought it was over, trying to scratch her eyes out. Her heart hammered in her chest as she visualized the horror. God, she needed a drink to brace herself.

She reapplied her efforts, dragging the dead woman through the scant cover of snow still icing the ground and toward the back of the shed, though the temperature was steadily rising this morning. One small improvement to their lot, but thankfully accepted. When the body was as far away as she could manage and feeling pushed past endurance, she stumbled to her feet, then hopped on her good foot toward the workshop. Using the side of the building to keep herself upright, she rejoined Lily, even managing to compose her expression into some semblance of a smile.

"Okay, princess, the dragon's all gone. Would you like something to eat now?"

Lily opened her eyes and gave her a look of concern. "Are you sure, Mommy?"

Mckenna swallowed her tears, nodding her head. "Yes, of course. Once dragons are dispatched, they never come back. I promise."

"Can I have a cookie?"

"Of course, we have those cookies your Aunt Claire helped you make." Was that just yesterday? Before the world tilted into pure madness?

Suddenly, she remembered something else that needed doing. "Just give me a second, princess, and then you can come inside." She didn't wait for Lily to answer but rushed to throw an old tarp over the blood and fluids soaking into the wooden floor.

"Okay, let's have those cookies now."

Mckenna was heating a pot of water for some tea when she heard footsteps outside. She froze, waiting, her hand ready to grab it and throw it at whoever else wanted to do them harm.

Then a loud series of knocks on the outside of the workshop made her gasp.

"Mckenna, are you in there?"

Jake.

She stumbled over to the door and pulled out the knife she'd wedged into the doorframe to keep it secure, then opened it. It was him. Marshal Jake Dillion, a mountain of a man, with his thick dark beard and rough edges. The man who had rescued her and Lily in Golden. Then insisted on keeping her safe after the grizzly bear attack, even making a stretcher to haul her all the way to his home. Her guardian angel in perilous times, though she was fairly certain he wouldn't want to be called by the term.

"Are you hurt? Where's Claire and Glen? Are they with you?"

Jake shook his head, then spoke quietly, his liquid brown eyes filled with sorrow. "Sorry, I have bad news. We had a shootout with Tally and her companion while the house burned down. I stayed behind to see them decently buried."

The shock of hearing her new friends had been killed, murdered, made her legs weaken. She lay one hand on Jake's arm to steady herself, not wanting to upset her daughter. She had to stay strong for Lily.

"I killed Tally." The whispered words sounded strange, like someone else was speaking to them.

"Don't feel guilty. She would have killed you and Lily. You did what you had to."

"I don't think I can take much more of this, if I'm being honest."

"You're stronger than you think. You came all the way from Mexico by yourself with a young child in tow. You got this, Mckenna. And I intend to stick around and make sure you and Lily are okay, if that's all right with you?"

Jake's support meant the world to her, and she gave him a quick hug. "Thank you for the thousandth time." She felt her smile wobble, but she hung on. "You really are my guardian angel."

"I'm no angel." Jake shook his head, his eyes shadowed by some hidden pain, making her wonder more about the life he had lived before they'd met, but this was not the time. "Trust me on that."

Her mind cleared and she began to consider things. "What about the person with Tally? Is he still lurking around? I think I saw him when she burned your house down. I'm so sorry about that." Jake had lost a lot, two of his best friends and then his house, his pride and joy he'd built off grid.

"Also, not your fault. Though I can't say it's not a huge setback. But I caught up to him on the road. Suffice to say he won't be a problem in the future."

"Thank you. Can I offer you some tea? I was just about to make some." It sounded strange to be offering something as mundane as tea after all that had happened, but her Grandma McTavish would have approved. Nothing that a cup of tea couldn't fix. But had her grandma ever had to face killing someone? She had no idea. Would she disown her granddaughter for her recent actions? She liked to think she would be okay with it. Maybe it was as much a fantasy as Lily and her dragons? But it was all she had to offer her, so she'd take it.

"Yes, and then we need to come up with a plan."

"I agree." Though what that would look like, she had no idea. But they had to try to figure things out. *And don't be feeling sorry for yourself.* Everyone was dealing with a new reality, some even a harsher one though what was worse than being forced to kill someone she had no answer for. One day at a time. At least she had help, that was more than many people were waking up to today.

NINE
CONNOR

Day 3: White Mountains, Alaska
   10:18 p.m.

Connor was weary, wearier than he ever remembered being. The time on the road had been so fraught with difficulties. He'd even taken a shift at the jail in Quinton for Sheriff Brady that had ended in a disastrous gun fight though both of them had been left standing which in the end was all that mattered. But there had been no time to get a proper sleep beyond a catnap. He shook off the need to succumb to his body's pressing need to rest with difficulty, and after the third time he roused himself from zoning out and jerking awake and making baby Eve stir in her sling, he brought Loch to a halt on the banks of Brace Creek. It was a decent spot to spend the night, with a flat area under a canopy of overhanging trees that would help disguise any smoke from their fire.

"Time to camp for the night." He patted Loch's broad neck, who whinnied in agreement. They were making good time, even with the baby in tow, the newborn having slept for the most part. He'd fed her a couple of times from a bottle he'd thought to keep warm next to his bare skin, the baby not complaining at all from the rhythmic movements of being jostled about on horseback. Fortunately, the weather had warmed up since the snowfall, making one aspect of the perilous journey easier. Every time he looked at the tiny, peaceful face of baby Eve as she slept with her tiny fists clenched around her face, his heart squeezed with unexpressed emotion.

He carefully dismounted, but his movements woke Eve up and she began to whimper.

"Hush, little one." He kept rocking her as he went about hurriedly setting up camp, needing to deal with the horses first. But she was having nothing of it, only crying louder. "Okay, I think I need to check your diaper, then tend to the horses." It wasn't the normal way of things. His creed spoke to the need to tend Loch and Finn first, but Eve wasn't having it.

Once she was settled, fed and changed, he set her aside on a warm pile of blankets. Then rushed about to complete his other duties. How did new mothers manage it? A new sympathy for Laura, his friend and ranch manager, Sam Perkins's wife, who had bore twin boys a few years ago and was in fact pregnant again came to the forefront of his thoughts. One more amazing ability Laura had, making child-rearing look far easier than it was.

When the horses were fed and given water from Brace Creek, he made a fire hole and set about making a new batch of formula for Eve. He needed a better meal himself tonight, realizing he was running on empty, settling on opening a jar of homemade beef and vegetable stew Laura had thoughtfully provided with a half loaf of freshly made bread.

The fire cheered him as it always did. If only he could share it with his dad, but those days were gone, never to return. He blinked away a rush of tears, the sudden press of grief catching him by surprise. He looked over at Eve. She had fallen asleep again, her rosebud mouth pursed in an adorable way. What was her life going to be like now that the world had fallen to ruin? Poor baby, losing her mother and her expected way of life all in one day. He'd make damn sure she never did without, no matter what it took. She was one of the first babies born After. There would be only Before and After going forward. Seemed fitting her name was Eve. *We have lost so much. Why? What was the point of it all?*

Connor made himself set the gloomy thoughts aside and get back to finishing his tasks before he took his rest. Tomorrow was a big day. He hoped to make Golden around noon time, find Mckenna and Lily, then head back to Braveheart immediately. He worried how they were faring back at Braveheart, though Sam Perkins was a reliable, capable man in handling affairs. Still, it was Connor's place, all his blood and sweat had been poured into making the horse ranch and survival business successful. He fought the urgent need to go home, to see those he loved protected. Soon. He comforted himself with the word. Soon he'd be home, making sure all was well, with more loved ones in tow. Already he sensed a growing bond with Eve, a renewal of his lost love for Mckenna and by definition with her daughter Lily.

A twig snapped nearby, jerking him from his thoughts.

He pulled his gun from his shoulder holster, watching and waiting, keeping a tight watch on the location the noise came from. Another slight rustle and he was certain someone or some animal was there. His bet would be on a human trying to sneak up on him.

"Come out with your hands raised," he said. "I have a gun pointed straight at you."

"Don't shoot. I'm unarmed. I'm just hungry and I smelled some food." The female-sounding voice surprised him.

"Come out where I can see you."

A slight figure came forward, hands raised, eyes widened by concern. Dressed too scantily for the weather in only a ripped sweatshirt and jeans, she appeared dirty as well, her dark greasy hair falling in strands around a hollowed face. The girl couldn't be much more than seventeen or eighteen.

"Are you alone?"

"Yes. They abandoned me when things went dark. Never came back. I haven't had anything to eat in two days. Could you spare something? Anything?"

"Who abandoned you?"

The girl looked around, like she expected them to show up at any time. She gulped, then answered his question, her voice tight with emotion. "I was kidnapped. Held without my consent at a shack. I've been stumbling around trying to figure out where I am for two days. Please, I'm just so hungry."

"I have food. Come closer to the fire. But if you try anything—" Connor left the threat hanging. The young woman looked like a waif, but that didn't mean she didn't wish him harm.

"I promise. I won't do anything but rest a bit and eat. Then I'll go if you'll point me in the right direction." She sat on a log, keeping her distance.

"Where do you come from?"

"Anchor. Do you know the place?"

Connor inwardly winced. Of course, another test of his resolve. Was he a damn magnet for those in distress? Then he chastised himself for his lack of charity.

"I know it." He didn't elaborate but put his weapon back in the holster and opened another jar of the stew, pouring it in the pot. He heated it, then handed her a spoon and the pot. He kept a close lookout all the while, senses on high alert, in case the woman was a decoy and others were looking to invade his space.

"Eat. Would you like some bread?"

"Please."

He watched her wolf down the bread and stew like she hadn't had a decent meal in weeks. "What's your name?"

"Faraday O'Brien." She didn't stop chewing to add, "What's yours?"

"Connor Hale."

She nodded at the bundle on the ground. "Your baby?"

"Her name is Eve, and her mother died giving birth to her today."

The thin woman frowned at the stark facts. Beneath the grim, he could tell she was an attractive person.

"What happened to you?" he asked.

"A pair of assholes kidnapped me three weeks ago and kept me tied up in a cabin." She held out one wrist as proof, keeping the stew pot in the other. The red markings, stark against her pale skin, looked raw and painful. She kept eating until all the stew had been scraped from the bottom of the pot and the bread was gone. "Thank you."

"Did you know the men?"

"Do you mean did I ask for this?" Faraday snarled, her anger obvious.

"No, I mean, can you point them out in a lineup? Or give their names to the police? They need to be punished for their crimes. Stopped from hurting others." Even as he said the words he realized the futile business of anyone getting justice for offenses against them now unless it was taken into their own hands.

"I need to know what the hell's going on. Can you tell me what you know?" Faraday asked.

"The end of the world as we know it." Connor went on to explain, watching Faraday's eyes grow wider with the telling. There was no way or reason to skirt around the brutal truth. She had obviously been through the mill in the last while and had come out with her spunk intact. He hoped she could handle this as well.

"That's so fucked up." The young woman shook her head back and forth, trying to absorb all the intel he had shared. He was glad baby Eve wasn't old enough to be affected by her swearing. If she had been, he would have to caution her. But under the circumstances, it was understandable.

"How far are we from Anchor?"

"A good eighty miles. I'm going to try to reach Golden by noon tomorrow, barring complications. I'm meeting someone."

"That's in the opposite direction of where I'm headed." Faraday looked at the horses. "I don't suppose I could buy or borrow one of them from you?"

Connor gave her a look that said an emphatic no. "I need them to rescue a woman and her four-year-old daughter and take them back to my ranch."

"Right." Though she said the word calmly enough, he didn't like the feral look that passed over her eyes in the moment. If she had a gun, no doubt she might try to pull a fast one. Damn it, now he'd have to stay awake all night or risk her trying to steal one of his horses. No good deed goes unpunished.

"How old are you?" Connor asked.

"Nineteen. Why?"

"I don't think I know any O'Brien's in Anchor. What does your family do?"

"We're not rich, if that's what you're asking? My dad's a drunk and my mother works as a cleaner for businesses at night." Her bitterness at the situation spilled over, darkening her expression.

"Are you still in training?"

"No. I can't afford it. And yeah, I know it's free. But I've been helping out my mom. She's not been feeling well the last few months, so I've been taking her shifts. I had to drop out of my accounting courses."

"You're good with math?"

"What? A female can't be a good financial adviser?" The young woman's feisty nature probably covered up a world of hurt. Or insecurity.

"That's not what I meant. If things were different, if the world still existed like it was a few days ago, I'd hire you. Paperwork isn't something I enjoy."

"Yeah, well, I guess it's all gone now. I have to get home. My mom needs me." She made a face he didn't quite know how to interpret, like she resented her mother needing her help. She was young and probably found the burden difficult.

"Listen, soon as I get to Golden and find Mckenna and Lily, I'm headed right back to Anchor. Do you want to tag along? I know it's out of your way, but it's all I got to offer." A part of him wished she would say no and hurry on her way back up north. But it was the right

45

thing to do. Problem was, carrying another person's weight with only the two horses between the three of them was dicey. Baby Eve's scant few pounds didn't count and how much could a four-year-old weigh? Faraday didn't look like she weighed a hundred pounds, though the two women on one horse might work, if Mckenna was still slim. If worst came to worst, he could fashion some kind of cart or a travois to pull behind one of the horses for supplies. In twelve hours, he'd gone from being alone to having two females in his care. The world he'd known was unrecognizable now and the weight of it had increased yet again. Was he ever going to make Golden? Yes, come hell or high water, he would. "Can you ride a horse?"

Faraday looked undecided about his offer. "Yeah, I've ridden a few times. Do you have any clothing I could change into? These reek. I was hoping to have a shower, but I guess the creek will have to do."

"I could warm some water for you?" Connor offered. In truth, he wanted to sleep more than anything, but the young woman needed his help. Sympathy for her plight was easy to come by, underlaid by frustration. He just hoped it didn't bite him in the ass.

"Thank you, I would appreciate it."

Connor set about the task of filling a pot with water and warming it over the Dakota fire hole. He rummaged around and found her a clean sweatshirt, a pair of boxers, and his extra pair of jeans. He'd make do with less. He added a clean cloth to the pile then handed all the items to Faraday. "Here you go."

She hesitated. "Could you turn around?"

"I need to check on the horses. Could you keep an eye on Eve?"

"Sure."

He walked away to where he'd situated Loch and Finn for the night, thirty feet away. He pulled sugar cubes from his pocket and fed them both one. "What do you think, Finn? Can you carry both Mckenna and Faraday? I promise soon as we're back home, you'll get extra rations." He spent some time grooming the pair with the curry brush, enjoying the rhythm of his actions. *Please don't let any more hard cases fall into my path, Lord. I think I've about reached my limit.*

TEN
MCKENNA

Day 3: Near Golden, Alaska
9:22 p.m.

Mckenna woke with a startle, trying to escape the living nightmare of being chased by menacing figures in the terrifying darkness. They had shot at her. It had been so real she had experienced the burn of the bullet piercing her flesh. The sharp scent of blood. She felt her chest, to make sure it wasn't real. No bandages, no pain. It took another full minute for it to sink in that she was safe. Then it all came pouring back. Tally trying to kill her. Her friends dead. She sat up abruptly, peering around the workshop. Lily was asleep as well, curled up next to her. Where was Jake?

The door to the workshop opened wide and she found herself relieved to see Jake, his arms loaded with wood for the fire. For a few seconds she thought he might have abandoned her, though now she was beginning to know him, it didn't seem in character. Marshall

Jake Dillion reminded her of Connor Hale, another man of his word. A bastion in a world gone mad.

"Finally awake, sleepyhead," he said with a small smile, before stacking the wood near the stove.

She sat up shakily, wincing at the pull on her leg. "Thanks for letting me sleep." She rubbed her forehead, trying to shake the lingering gloom of the nightmare.

"Best remedy for most things is sleep. Are you hungry? Thirsty?"

"I think I need some fresh air." Even with the tarp covering up the gore on the floor, she could still smell it, the scent of death. It lingered, filling her with unease. What was going to happen next? The future terrified her.

"I'll get your crutches. Did you take your pills?"

"I can't remember." Why was her mind such a fog?

"You have to take care of yourself, Mckenna. You got a child counting on you. If you let an infection grab hold, well, I don't have to stress how bad it could be. Not like the hospitals aren't overloaded. It's a mess in Golden. Glen and I were shocked at what was going on. Even with all the talks we had about various scenarios if things came to their worst, it wasn't anything anyone could prepare for. It set me back. And the talk on the shortwave radio is no better. This thing stretches far and wide, I'm afraid."

"I know. I'll do better." She appreciated his not holding back the punches but telling her as things really were. And for some reason having it confirmed the event had happened farther afield was no real surprise to her.

She let Jake assist her to her feet, then pushing the crutches under her arms, stomped out of the building. Outside, she took a deep breath, grateful for the sweet smell of Alaskan mountain air. It seemed to come from a better place than any other she had breathed in her lifetime. From the purity of fresh fallen snow and untouched valleys. She felt a desperate urge to get home to Anchor building in her. They needed to leave this place and its terrible memories behind. Start a new life on a ranch where maybe she and Lily stood a chance at staying safe.

"I brought you your medicine," Jake said, handing her the pills, his other hand holding a glass of water.

"Thank you. I'm sorry I was so short in there. It's just been so much. I worry for the future. How's Lily going to make out?" She took the offered medicine and washed it down with the water.

"Nothing's going to be straightforward. We'll adapt, I imagine, as our species has always done over millennium. What else is there for it?"

"What do we do now?"

"I think we eat first, then consider plans."

"All right. But not inside. I don't think I could eat knowing what happened in there."

"Okay. I'll set the camp stove up right here. We can enjoy a hot meal in the fresh air."

He was as good as his word and in short order, they were eating a feast of bacon and eggs with a side of pork and beans. Mckenna had been convinced she wouldn't be able to eat much but found herself consuming the food as if her life depended on it.

Jake noticed and gave a chuckle. "I guess I'm a better cook than I thought."

"It's good." She set her plate aside, intending to wash it later. "I don't know much about you, Jake. Your life before we met. Do you have any family in Alaska?"

"No. All on my lonesome. My parents died in a uFree sky link crash a few years back. I always said those unmanned pods were dangerous, but Dad loved new toys, so what can you do? I do have one grandmother who lives in Texas, but I only met her a couple of times." He cleared his throat. "Which brings us to our current situation. If we're going to say here, I'm going to have to build onto the workshop this summer."

Mckenna gave a start. "No, I need to go to Anchor. Connor has a huge horse ranch there. Braveheart. It's more remote than here. That's a good thing, right?"

He shrugged. "It could be. No place is invincible now." He looked over at his former home with a stoic expression that had to be hiding a world of hurt.

"I'm so sorry about your house."

"Not your fault." He studied her for a moment, his eyes troubled. "But how are we going to get you there with that leg?"

The way he asked the question, using "we" stirred her thoughts. Relief filled her. "You'd help me get there?"

"Yes. Though I had hoped you might stay on here, I understand. You want to join your friend." He was noncommittal but she sensed a certain disappointment in his voice.

Mckenna's lips trembled. "I'm worried something has happened to him. It's been three whole days already."

"I'm sure he's fine. It's a hard time to get around for everyone with all the electronics fried. Most vehicles are disabled."

"You think he's still coming?"

"You said he has a horse ranch, right? He's probably coming by horseback. If he doesn't arrive in the next couple of days, and you're up to it, I think we should plan on heading to Anchor soon."

"I hadn't thought of that. But it makes perfect sense." She bit her lip. It had to be said. "I don't feel right asking you to go out of your way to get me home. You've got so much to do here to prepare." And what if someone squatted on his land while he was away? Took over the workshop?

"It can wait. Since it will be only me here, I won't need too much more room anyway. And it's too soon to plant anything, though I could start some seedlings."

Mckenna felt she had let him down. But what else was there for it? She had to complete the journey. A desperate urge to get home to Anchor and see her best friend Connor filled her, making her body ache with a longing that could not be denied, driving any doubts away about being able to withstand the journey with her damaged leg.

"I don't like putting you to the trouble, but I agree we should wait another day or two." The words didn't put her at ease, but she had to be sensible. She needed healing time before undergoing the rigors of the journey. And just maybe Connor would show up soon? She looked over to the road visible from where they sat, wishing he was walking down it right now toward her. For a split second she thought she could see him, his shining presence visible in the growing twilight, but it vanished all too quickly.

"I agree." Jake looked relieved. "I'm going to need to look for some mode of transportation too. If, I mean *when*, your friend shows up, I'll still need it for myself in the future."

"That's a good idea." She pulled her crutches toward her and got to her feet. "I'll take care of the washing up."

"I'll help."

Mckenna looked once more back at the road before she turned away. *Please God, keep him safe.*

ELEVEN
CONNOR

Day 4: Monday, May 26, 2055
   White Mountains, Alaska
   4:30 a.m.

Connor awoke with a start, not realizing he had fallen asleep. But something had changed in his surroundings. He sat up and peered around. He'd fed Eve a couple of hours ago, so she was fine. He glanced at the spot Faraday had chosen to sleep near the fire. Damn, she was gone. The very reason he hadn't wanted to fall asleep. He jumped up and looked in the direction of the horses, his heart hammering with worry. But both Loch and Finn were still there.

Then the young girl came into view around a bush, her expression pensive. She glanced at him when she realized he was up and muttered a greeting.

"I thought you'd gone."

"You thought I took a horse, right? Because poor trash like me steals any chance they get."

"Sorry, for a second there I admit I was worried." He rubbed at his scalp, wishing he could take a hot shower and wash away the grime of the journey, but that was an impossibility until he got back home. He was used to it though, having taken groups into the mountains for three or four days at a time. But it would have been nice to reunite with Mckenna not smelling of the road. Of course, she might be in the same position, though he could never imagine her smelling bad. A distant memory of her light floral perfume came back and for a moment he felt her in his arms, her body pressed against his, on the very day she had told him her parents were moving away from Anchor. The day their tears had intermingled. The bittersweet memory lingered, even as Faraday's next words brought him back to the present.

"I just needed to go off by myself for a few minutes. Are we leaving soon?"

"Soon as we eat." It took more time than he liked, feeding and changing Eve, cooking breakfast and packing up, but with Faraday's help they finally managed to get back on the road.

"You mentioned you have a ranch?" Faraday asked, breaking the silence of the forest. It was colder this morning, the skies overcast, making him concerned for Eve. The baby should be safe and warm in her own home, not being jostled over the landscape without her mother's comfort. Try as he might, he knew he was but a poor substitute.

"Braveheart. I have a small horse herd and a survival business twenty-five miles from Anchor."

"Survival? Like what to do if shit like this happens?"

"Yeah, exactly like that." He shifted Eve, trying to cover her face but allow lots of room for her to breathe.

"So, you know all about how to do things to stay alive now?"

"Well, nobody knows exactly how it will go down, only try to think things through and prepare for different scenarios. Humans have to experience events for themselves to really learn and understand it all. It takes a lifetime of living to make sense of the past, unfortunately. No shortcuts to wisdom. Sometimes we guess it right the first time and think we're so smart, smarter than others. But you really only learn when you get it wrong, so you don't do it again."

"Well, I know how to get it wrong, so I must be getting smarter," she said with a snort.

"Don't berate yourself. We're here to learn. Life's a journey not to be missed out on. A wise friend of mine has this saying about living each day as if it's your last." Dan Sullivan came to mind, and he wondered briefly how he, his wife Jean, and their grandchildren were faring at the ranch. "He's right in that we all get so busy we forget how priceless each day is. A gift." He needed to live this creed even more now than before. Only thing that made sense with all the hardships humanity was going to face moving into the near future. His own small band would need his help more than ever. They counted on him to stay strong. He straightened in the saddle and took a deep breath. At least the air was only slightly tainted by smoke. He could only imagine the stench in some of the bigger cities as garbage collection halted and toilets backed up. The dead lying in the streets.

"Sorry, not feeling too gifted at the moment."

"Don't let those monsters take anything from you. Your power lies in moving on."

"You mean forgiving. 'Cause that's not going to

happen. Those bastards deserve to be strung up by their
—ba—thumbs."

"Yeah, I hear you. But don't let yesterday take up too
much of today. That's all I'm advising."

"You got a girlfriend? Wife? This woman you're so
determined to head to Golden to rescue? She has a kid.
Yours?"

"No girlfriend or wife. Though Mckenna and I used
to be very close back when we were teenagers." He was
hoping to be able to pick up where they left off, irra-
tional as that might seem to some.

"She must have really meant something to you go to
all this trouble for her. How did she end up in Golden
anyway?"

"That's a lot of questions for this early in the morning." He'd prefer not to discuss his past. They needed to
concentrate on the future. And most of all, stay alert.
Bringing up old history wasn't helpful. The sky had
brightened to the east, spreading out wings of luminous
color and heralding another day above the green. *I just
have to keep them alive, though I might need help with that,
God.* His new mission statement, if that wasn't too
pompous a way to think of it.

"Well, we got nothing but time."

"Hmm."

"You know, if you're looking for company back at
your ranch, I could be persuaded to tag along."

Faraday's offer shocked him at first before he came to
the quick realization all kinds of bargains would be
struck between people now that normalcy and the thin
level of civilization had been burned away by the very
real threat of being alone and hungry with no
protection.

"What about your mom?"

"I lied before. She's a junky, not sick in the traditional sense. I'm the only one working now. I had to leave school because of it. Ruined my future. That is if there is any future now."

A part of him suspected he might live to regret it, but what else was there for it. "You need a place to stay and are willing to pull your own weight, then I could find you a place at Braveheart. But know this—I'm not expecting anything in return, other than your hard work. I'm not that kind of man."

"That's what I like about you. Any woman would want to be by your side now with everything falling to shit soup. A strong man who knows what the hell he is doing. Mckenna is a lucky woman."

Silence descended. Good. Such conversations make him acutely uncomfortable. The horses settled into an easy lope, filled with fresh energy from a good night's rest as they left the forest for a wide-open stretch of valley floor. They'd follow it for the next few hours before reaching the headwaters of the Golden River that ran through part of the city. Making Golden by midday was looking better and better.

Eve whimpered and he held his breath. *Please, please go back to sleep*. She mewed softly then resettled. He had her bottle ready but drinking more formula meant a diaper change and he desperately wanted to get some miles behind them before stopping again.

Then he heard it. The high-pitched, grinding sound of an old motor being pushed to its limits echoed in the hush of the early morning.

Faraday gave a gasp and shot frightened eyes toward him. "I know that sound. An old ATV the guys got going while I was tied up in the cabin. I had to listen to it for hours on end. The guys going on and on about

57

how it was going to be so much better than anything else they had. Oh shit, this is bad. They've come back for me."

Even as she said the words, the ATV came into view in the distance, immediately altering its path to right head toward them.

"Here. You take Eve and head for that strand of trees over there."

"What are you going to do?"

"Finish this one way or the other."

"Be careful. They both have guns and knives."

They quickly made the switch, trying not to wake baby Eve, a futile effort as it turned out. She began to squawk immediately at being handed over, though they both ignored it in the urgent need to keep moving. He gave Finn a swat on his hindquarters to send him and his precious cargo on their way. Connor pulled his Bergara Highlander from the scabbard, then pushed Loch into a full-on gallop with the press of his heels, headed toward the source of the racket. He had to lead the kidnappers away from Finn.

The old ATV vehicle was outfitted with roll bars, two dark figures hanging on as they drove it in a reckless manner across the valley floor. When they spotted Connor had his rifle held at the ready while he raced toward them, they set off a volley of gunfire before abruptly changing direction, looking to get ahead of him. The shots all missed, they were too far away to hit anything anyway, but the gun play made the decision for him. He had no choice now but to make certain they didn't interfere with his plans. Too easy for them to wait in hiding and shoot at them again later. He and Loch continued the pursuit, his horse unfazed by the noise. Loch would have made a good war horse, hell, guess he was one now. He had the courage of ten horses, his heart and stamina beyond question.

In minutes Loch had him close enough to get a couple of shots off, aiming for the gas tank or motor. The vehicle veered to the left, trying to outrun him. Connor followed the pair easily, hoping their ancient ride would break down and leave them stranded. He shot again, this time the whine of the bullet piercing metal resounded. He knew he'd managed a direct hit. The brand of ATV was unknown to him, so he couldn't be certain of what he'd hit. He had to admit, he didn't really care if he took out the two men. They had proved themselves villains by their actions.

The vehicle maneuvered again, this time to the right of the path, trying to keep Loch and Connor from pulling up alongside them. Loch responded easily, like he had always lived in the time of the Wild West, racing to beat the bad guys.

A sudden whiff of gasoline and he knew what he'd tampered with. Good. Soon as they ran out of gas, he could confront them. But before the fuel could peter out, the driver hit a hard left again, spilling his passenger onto the ground. The man landed in a tangle of limbs, but when Connor pulled up on Loch's reigns, the man shot to his feet, his helmeted head giving him the appearance of a bug-like alien. He tore off his headgear, his expression surly.

"Hands up where I can see them!" Connor shouted, holding the rifle pointed at the man.

"Who the fuck are you?" the passenger shouted though he complied to the order.

"Someone who actually gives a shit when the chips are down."

"We worked hard to rebuild the motor, asshole. Now

it's all ruined. You know what it's worth in this new world? Priceless, that's what."

"You shot first. And you should have thought of that before you took a young woman hostage."

"What are you talking about? She wanted to be with us, man. We were all just having a bit of fun until she decided she wanted to go home." He avoided looking at Connor as he spoke meaning the man's objections didn't hold merit. Any man who can't look another man square in the eye had something to hide in his experience.

What was he going to do with them? Last thing he wanted was to be held up by two more prisoners. The second man had come to a stop on the ATV about a hundred yards away. He sat and watched, the machine sputtering as it ran out of gas.

"I'm sure you can patch a gas tank if you got that old relic running."

"Yeah, maybe. What are you going to do?"

"That's the sixty-four-thousand-dollar question. Where's your cabin?"

"About a mile that way." The man pointed to the east.

"I want you to throw down your weapons." Again, the man did what he asked, tossing a handgun on the ground.

"Where do you keep your knife?"

The young man's eyes flew open. "Ah, around my waist."

"Take it out real slow and throw it on the ground." Connor watched the man comply. It was a lethal weapon the man added to the pile, a ten-inch serrated-edged Blackstone. "Any other weapons?"

"No."

"Keep your hands where I can see them." Connor slipped down from the saddle and kept the rifle in one hand as he rummaged in his pack, pulling out an elastic tie-down cord he normally used to protect items on a wilderness camping trip. It would have to do. He needed to keep the rope for another purpose. He secured the man's hands behind his back, an awkward maneuver holding the gun.

The second man took note of proceedings, what was happening to his partner not meeting his approval and began running toward the east and the cabin.

"Wait here." Connor jumped back on Loch and made his intentions known with a squeeze of his thigh. The horse took off galloping to advance on the man. But even with Connor on his tail, the man wouldn't stop running. He fired off a warning shot, finding the whole damn thing an annoying waste of his time. But it drew the man's attention and he jerked to a halt.

He then disarmed and tied up the second man same as the first, ignoring his protestations of innocence.

"Whatcha going to do with us? You got more horses? You ruined my ride. What a waste." The man was another talkative whiner. It was all Connor could do to keep his temper in check.

"I'm going to hand you over to the law."

"What law? Everything's gone to shit, man."

Connor ignored the man and pulled out a twelve-foot length of sturdy rope and looped it around the man's waist.

"What's that for?"

"Head back toward your friend." He'd tie them together and lead them to the nearest town. He gave a sigh. One more thing to take up his time when he should be on the road. But he swore this time, he wasn't hanging around for more than the time it took to drop the pair off.

TWELVE
LUTHER

Day 4: Golden, Alaska
9:49 a.m.

Luther observed the town of Golden through the caddie's front windscreen. To say the city was in dire straits was to underplay the damage and actions of the unhappy residents. Fires had broken out everywhere, looting had destroyed many of the business, windows broken out and stock raided. In four days, the world had resorted to anarchy. Of course, the place had always been notorious gang territory. Two factions, the Bulls and the 666s had fought for top position in recent years. Judging by the hanging banners and large signs with the biblical numbers crudely painted on them, it was easy enough to tell who was taking over. Just wait until he hooked up with Diego in Anchor, both gangs would soon be history, driven out by King Luther once he had more bodies in place. But he was getting ahead of himself. First take over Braveheart Horse Ranch as his home base.

"Where to first, boss?" Thomas asked from the driver's seat.

"Hang a left at the next corner. I know someone who might have some answers." And she owed him a favor. His cousin Tally had lived in Golden for years, taking up with some kind of air marshal of late. He'd cautioned her against the action, but when do the young ever listen? But maybe now, with things gone to shit, it might be a good thing for her to have an armed man capable of handling himself and protecting her. Not that Tally had needed a lot of protection in the past. She was a one-woman dynamo growing up, capable of an eye for an eye with the best of them. Proved it a time or two.

All of his men had guns drawn inside the caddie, watching the street with hooded eyes. They were driving a valuable commodity in today's market. No telling when they'd be attacked, which is why they had wanted to hit the town early, while most of the residents were still asleep in their beds. But the state of the roads and some unforeseen events had kept it from happening. He inwardly sighed. His men had been overly zealous on the trip south, even now they had a young girl tied up in the trunk, captured on the trip, the last of her group. It had taken a shootout with her friends to facilitate the kidnappings, then a stop at a farmhouse to enjoy the fruits of their labor. Now they were down to one female on the ride-along because of his trigger-happy soldiers, but at least they had worn off some steam and only suffered from hangovers this morning. A wise leader knew when to let some things go. He prided himself on such common-sensical considerations.

"Stop here. Keep a sharp eye out. I'll make this quick."

Tally's house was set back from the street, a modular smart house she shared expenses with by taking on a couple of roommates. It was a good financial move on her part. Tally was nothing if not smart, a good schemer and planner, at least when she was taking her medicine. Maybe he could talk her into joining him up north? But a darker thought came on its heels. What about when she ran out of the medicine? It was a given now it would happen sooner or later. And when Tally was off her meds, look out.

When the caddie came to a complete stop he jumped out and loped toward the house. He banged on the door with his fist, waiting for someone to answer. When that didn't happen, he used a boot to stomp against it a few times until the frame gave way.

Once inside, he kept his Benelli M5 at the ready while he checked out the rooms. In a back bedroom he found one of her roommates cowering under a bed. He lifted the bed covering with the nozzle of his semi-automatic.

"Come out of there. I'm Tally's cousin, Luther. Where is she?"

The young woman was crying and trembling so badly he couldn't make sense of her stammered words, but he quickly noted on an attractive scale she scored a ten plus with a perfect figure, full breasts and a narrow waist. What was a girl like this doing in Golden?

"Stop crying. I'm not going to hurt you, okay. I just want to know where Tally Meech is?" However, the female could count on getting out of town today. Maybe one more for the trunk? No, he liked the look of her too much to maybe spoil the goods with the rough ride.

"She didn't come home. I'm the only one here. Mavis...she's dead. My best friend, she's gone. This gang guy, a 666er, he shot her in the face...for talking back to him. Why would he do that?" The beautiful girl was in shock, which made her malleable.

"Times are different now. I can help you. I've got a caddie outside. We can take you north with us. I have a safe location up near Anchor. But first, you need to tell me where Tally has gone? Did she tell you where she was headed?"

"She had a date with Jake, he's an air marshal. Jake Dillion. Big guy. She was head over heels for him. They were meeting for brunch the day everything happened."

"Where's he live?" Best case scenario, he'd taken Tally back to his house.

"Up north about ten miles or so. I can draw you a map. No GPS right now."

"Good. Do that, then gather your things. You can hitch a ride with us."

"I don't know." She hesitated, biting her bottom lip. "Tally said her cousin Luther was in prison."

"I got pardoned." He smiled, trying to be charming about the fact. He liked her looks even more now she wasn't carrying on. A real pretty one. So pretty she could easily be mistaken for a movie star or model with her white-blond hair. And he needed a companion of his own not being someone who liked to share. "What's your name?"

"Hope Bredeson." She pronounced it *breed-son.*

The irony was not lost on him. But then maybe it was a good sign. The world would need more kids going forward to help repopulate it. It came to him in the moment, an epiphany of sorts, almost religious in intent as the intensity of the blood rush raced over him, igniting his thoughts. Yes, why not brand the world with more of his DNA? He could take on as many 'wives' now as he could find and feed. What or who was going to stop him? A dynasty with a legacy. And it would all start again with Hope. He chuckled at the thought. Mind made up; he got down to practical matters.

"Can you cook? Is there food in the house?"

"Yeah, sure."

He'd see his men feed and watered before heading out again.

"Good. You can start cooking now for four hungry men. Is the garage locked?" It would be best to get the caddie out of view while they enjoyed an hour or two respite. They had been traveling all night and deserved a little R&R. He eyeballed his newest acquisition. Finally, a little something just for him.

THIRTEEN
MCKENNA

Day 4: Near Golden, Alaska
   10:28 a.m.

The morning had been a busy one, both Mckenna and Jake working to make their surroundings a bit more habitable. It was better with the floor scrubbed clean, a counter built to make meal preparations easier, and an extra cot set up for Jake. She had insisted on his sleeping inside with her and Lily. Turning him out of his last sanctuary just seemed wrong and after some persuasion, he had capitulated.

"You should take a rest. That leg needs healing time," Jake said. He was gruffer today, his expression more closed off, making her feel she'd come up short somehow. The sensation was still raw, one she'd hoped to leave behind her in Mexico, reminding her how her ex always managed to make her feel inferior in any situation.

"I'm doing fine," she countered, something she would never have said to Diego. *I'll sleep when I'm dead.*

He gave a short chuckle, making her feel considerably better, that maybe being herself would be enough going forward. Then she remembered what she had done yesterday to protect Lily and knew she had changed far more profoundly than just being able to speak up for herself. "My grandfather used to say that. Funny guy. One of the good ones."

She glanced over at Lily who needed a nap, busy fussing with her teddy bear, trying to get it to stand upright on the cot. She was still upset about losing her robot puppy in the escape from Jake's house and wanted the bear to do some of the things Tinder had been capable of back when his computer chip worked.

"Mommy, Boo Bear is being bad. He just keeps falling over."

"Princess, you have an imagination you can count on from now on. I want you to close your eyes and pretend your bear is dancing. Can you see him? He's twirling around. *Oh*, now he's taking a bow. I can see him bright as day."

Lily squeezed her eyes shut, trying to see what her mom was talking about. "I see him, mommy! He's going on a trip. He's going to rescue the princess from the castle. I'm going to help."

"How are you going to get there? Are you both roller skating and wearing party hats?"

"No, silly." Lily giggled. "We're going to fly there with my magic, pink, sparkly hat and magic wand. And when we get there, Boo will grow to giant-sized, bigger than the dragon and stomp all over him."

"How about you draw those pictures and we can make it into a book. But first, you need to take a nap so you'll do a really good job. Artists need their sleep. Everyone knows that." She tucked her daughter and Boo Bear under the covers, holding back tears of thankfulness for her child. Was she being short-sighted encouraging Lily to escape the reality of this world and live in a dream one? But she was only four, and seeing her childhood vanish in a few days seemed a far worse crime. And isn't that what many have done throughout history, read to escape and look to find others in the world's vast community of fictional and nonfictional characters that gone through something similar in their lives. Such things brought encouragement along with the entertainment, support, knowledge, and even enlightenment. Perhaps, one day, Lily would write stories and help heal the world.

She lay down next to her, allowing her body to rest for a bit. Jake had left after their discussion and she could hear him outside cutting wood. She drifted off to the reassuring sounds of a man on watch.

The unexpected sounds of a vehicle nearby woke her. What was going on? Was it Connor? Had he managed to find something to drive? Knowing his resourcefulness, it was entirely possible. Her heart hammered madly, uncertain who or what had driven onto Jake's property. These perilous times had them in their clutches, always expecting the other shoe to fall. She eased her arm out from under her daughter's head and crept from the bed, then used her crutches to make her way to the door, her trepidation growing with each step. What was happening? Should she wait to be certain before going out there? But her hope and excitement made the decision for her and she opened the door a crack, peeking out around the edge.

It wasn't Connor who stood around a black, antique

car, but a group of four rough looking men. Jake was standing about fifteen feet from the visitors, rifle in hand though not pointed at them, his face turned away from her. One of the men caught sight of the movement and looked her way, his expression greedy and stomach turning as a cruel smile lifted his lips. She closed the door, praying her thoughtless actions hadn't just brought further trouble for Jake.

She pulled out her newly acquired Glock, grateful for its secure feel in her hand. If only she had some place to hide Lily. As difficult as dealing with Tally yesterday had been, this was worse. Four against two. But Marshal Jake Dillion was one of the two, making the odds more like even in her opinion.

What else could she do to prepare? Jake had a metal box filled with odds and ends he'd pointed out earlier as a means of last resort, a few grenades, some explosives. She crouched down and winced at the pain, then lay the Glock next to the twelve by sixteen-inch container painted dark green and opened the lid, picking out a few grenades and thrusting them into her pockets.

She grabbed her handgun and got up awkwardly, her leg still squawking. She ignored it. Her hurt calf was the least of her troubles at the moment. If only the wood-shed had windows. As it stood a couple of small skylights were all that illuminated the space.

What was happening? She blinked rapidly trying to wash away the stinging sweat from being nervous and worried to death.

"Are you okay, Mommy?"

"I'm fine, Lily. Go back to sleep if you can. But don't get up, please, mommy needs you to stay right where you are now, no matter what happens, okay?"

"O—kay."

She ventured a quick glance back at her daughter to make sure she was following instructions. Satisfied she was, she kept her eyes focused on the door, both hands locked around her weapon, feet apart. Would a fight break out? What did the men want? The house was burned down. Surely, they didn't think there were many more supplies to steal? Something wasn't adding up.

Each second an eternity, she held her breath, waiting, watching, her body tense with adrenaline. A minute passed, then another. *Breathe, Mckenna. In and out. Slow and steady.*

The sounds of an engine revving caused her to jump. Were they leaving? Could they be so lucky? She made herself wait it out. Her appearance now would not help the situation.

Then the door opened. "They're gone. For now." Jake looked loaded for bear, his eyes cold as glacial ice and filled with deadly intent.

"What did they want?"

"They were looking for Tally. That was Luther Meech and his gang of perps."

"What do you mean when you said they were gone for now?"

He quickly explained, his mouth tightened with the strain. "I told them Tally and I had a fight and she headed back to Golden, then some looters burned down my house and the neighbors, killing them in the process. I didn't tell them Tally did it because then we had reason to do her harm. Not certain if they believed the whole story, Luther said he would look for her in Golden. But it won't take long for him to figure things out. He'll be back and we can't be here. I also told them my adopted sister was staying with me. With your hair and looks I didn't think they'd fall for anything else if they caught sight of you. I couldn't say wife which might be better for safety's sake, because then why would I be dating Tally? Luther Meech is not a man you want to be taking notice of you."

"I'm sorry. I didn't mean to draw any attention, but I thought it might be Connor. Only one guy saw the door move a little bit." She was always either apologizing or thanking the good marshal. "You said we can't be here. When do we have to leave?" The news was unsettling and unwanted. She had been counting on a few days to heal and recover. Wait for Connor.

"ASAP. I'm thinking we take backpacks, enough food for a few days, and head out. I have a friend, Ben Carter. He lives about eighteen miles from here, down a dirt trail leading into the bush. Really out of the way and hard to find if you don't know he's there. He collects old vehicles and lives completely off grid. I haven't seen him in a while, he had a nervous breakdown a few years back, but he's our best hope right now. Will you be able to manage? I think he'll help us. We always got along well having both served in the CIA together before I took a job as an air marshal in Golden."

"Eighteen miles. Yes, I can manage." She swallowed her concern, hiding it beneath her resolve not to be a burden.

"I'll take Lily in the backpack and carry the supplies. You just need to get yourself there. The crutches are enough of a burden. I'm sorry I can't buy you more time, but my gut says we got to go or face Luther and his miscreants again. They're ex-prisoners most likely. Men who will take what they want without a care or a thought for anyone else." Jake shook his head, his mouth thinned with disgust. "If they come back and we're not here, most likely that will be the end of it. I can't see them bothering to head after us."

"That's good." But as relieved as she was by the idea of the men not coming after them, she was equally worried about not being up to the task of stomping through eighteen miles with her crutches. She forced the worry back down. It had to be done. If only Connor had made it in time. How was he to know where she had gone to? He'd find the house burned down and think the worst, then she was gone forever.

"I have to leave a note for Connor."

"I don't think that's a good idea. What if Luther and his men find it and head after us?" Jake frowned, pausing in his sorting through the items he wanted to pack.

"I can disguise it. How about a heart carved into the wall with our initials? Then he'll know I'm okay and didn't burn in the fire." The horrifying idea made her pause for a second. "I don't know what to do about a map…"

"Think on it, but we have to get a move on. I want to be out of here within the hour."

She hurried to gather a few items for Lily, her mind pondering the question. Her daughter watched the proceeding with wide eyes, sitting quietly on the bed clutching her bear. Grateful as she was for her cooperation, the worry over all the effects of the past few days pressed on her. When this was over, never again would she subject Lily to any upset if she could help it. She knew in her heart it was a futile hope, but it gave her determination to get a move on. One day at a time. Or was it one crisis at a time now?

FOURTEEN
CONNOR

Day 4: Golden, Alaska
   6:49 a.m.

One free man fighting his enemies is stronger than twenty hired mercenaries. The words popped into Connor's head. Maybe a slight exaggeration, but still, it held merit. 300 had gone into the Battle of Thermopylae, though none remained alive at the end, but for seven days they had fought valiantly to halt thousands of Persians and now lived on in immortal glory. Not that he was looking to die anytime soon, but the thought banked up his courage thinking ahead to what might be coming. Maybe one day all that could be said of this time in history was they didn't give up but had the courage to soldier on for the sake of the next generation. He pondered again how it had happened, the coordinated attack on the world. It didn't make a whole lot of sense, if one country was coming after America, the usual target of those disliking the west's promise of freedom to choose their own destiny, so why such a far-ranging disaster?

"How much farther are you going to drag our asses?" one of his prisoners asked, his tone belligerent.

Without bothering to answer or turn around, he nudged Loch to a quicker trot.

"We're close to Willow Bend," he said to Faraday. She rode Finn, baby Eve wrapped up and held snugly in her arms. "We'll get rid of the garbage there."

He ignored the curses of the men struggling to keep up with the new pace and focused on getting them to their destination. Willow Bend was closer to a village than a town in size with less than a thousand residents, though it did feature a police detachment. He'd tie the two to the front door and leave them to it, if that was what it took to continue on his way. A clock ticked louder in his head then, an early warning. He could not afford to ignore it. Something foul was afoot and he had to be there to stop it or suffer the consequences. Maybe just tie the pair up on the edge of town and save the explanations? Yes. That would do it. An expedient use of his time.

When they crested the embankment leading onto the main road into Willow Bend, he kept a sharp eye out for trouble. He could not afford to make any mistakes or be slowed down in making their destination of Golden today. Lives depended on it. The town came into view, quiet and ghost-like along the main drag, people most likely hiding inside their homes and businesses trying to make sense of their situation. They'd find the pair soon enough. He'd learned his lesson the hard way in Quinton, though he didn't regret helping the lawman. Brady was a good man.

Soon as they reached the outskirts, he called a halt,

assessing the situation. Far enough away not to draw attention, but he figured the men would be found soon enough by someone coming by. Connor dismounted, and keeping his neck on a swivel, quickly untied the rope attaching the men to Loch's saddle.

"You just going to leave us here? Without food or water?" one of the prisoners asked. Connor gave him a steely-eyed look as he led the pair to a large jack pine, made them sit, then tied the end of the rope around the tree trunk securely, guaranteeing they wouldn't be able to get free anytime soon.

"I'll leave you a few supplies, more than you did for the young woman you abused."

"So she says. I know she wanted it—" His words were cut off when Connor applied a fist to the rapist's mouth, contacting with a satisfying thud. Blood spewed out and he reined himself in from dealing a second blow, his body vibrating with the effort. Much as he wanted to lay a beating on both men, he had something else far more important to do.

"When you're in the company of a woman, you watch your manners. We clear?"

Neither man said anything as they telecast their feelings on the matter with clenched fists and angry glares. Satisfied the problem had been dealt with appropriately, Connor remounted Loch.

"Thanks for that," Faraday said.

"Needed doing." Connor nudged Loch into a lope, Finn quickly joining in. He kept a sharp eye out for any pursuit, but it seemed fate was fine with his actions today because they escaped back onto the trail he'd chosen to get to Golden without being accosted. At this rate, they'd be in the city by noon time. The pressure of making it by the stroke of twelve was intense, like a doomsday bell was ringing in his mind heralding a final chance to make it in time. He could not fail.

They made the final small town before Golden by 11:10 a.m. "Less than an hour out now." Faraday was busy feeding Eve a bottle, trying to keep them from needing to stop. He appreciated her efforts, knowing it was a challenge to deal with a tiny scrap of humanity on horseback.

"Where do you expect to meet up with them?"

Connor stomach roiled and he took a deep breath. "I believe she would head for the riverbank where we had a picnic many years ago."

"But she needs to find shelter, right? Maybe she got a tent?"

Connor could see the holes in the logic, but appreciated Faraday was trying to help. "I think if she had to move on, she'd leave a message for me."

"Yeah, I'd do that."

When the outskirts of Golden finally appeared over the horizon twenty minutes later, the town being at a higher elevation than the surrounding land with the river cutting through it, the billowing smoke rising over multiple sections of the city did nothing to settle his stomach. In the distance, on the highway, he could see groups of stragglers leaving the city, a worry in its own right if someone tried to take what they had. He'd have to chance it.

"I hope this location is on the outskirts of the city?" Faraday asked just as the baby began to wail. "She needs changing."

A feat impossible to do on horseback. Connor would have to call a halt. He held back his frustration at the delay and dismounted. Then he helped Faraday attend to the baby. They were in a secure a location as any, hidden inside a copse of trees. There was a creek with water for the horses to take their fill.

"I think it would be best if you waited here with Eve. It's going to be dangerous."

"I don't want us to be separated. What if something happens to you? I can't do this alone. Not with a baby. Please, don't leave me here." Faraday's fear was real and her eyes begged him to not to abandon them.

"Faraday—"

"No. I won't stay here. I'll follow you." Something had shifted for the young woman in the past few hours. Like a baby duckling, she'd imprinted on him, seeing him as her savior. It was in her eyes, the truth of it, something she couldn't hide. His shoulders felt the weight and he sat up straighter in the saddle, refusing to bend under the pressure. He understood, even if it interfered with what needed doing.

"Please, for the baby's sake. What if we are attacked? Eve is the most vulnerable of us. Her life could be ended far too easily. One stray bullet…" He let his words hang in the air, giving her time to see reason. To accept responsibility.

He could see the inner struggle on her face. She'd been through a terrible ordeal that not everyone was able to overcome. At the very least it would take time to heal the wounds, to be able to see the big picture again. Time they didn't have.

"How long?"

He let out a breath. "I'll be in and out as quickly as possible. I promise not to head off without coming back for you."

"Just so you know, if you're not back in an hour, I'm not staying here."

Connor calculated the distance and time required.

"An hour should more than do it. It's not far and barring any complications, I'll make your deadline."

"Okay then." Faraday swallowed.

"Thank you." Connor remounted Loch. He wanted to take Finn too, but Loch could manage the three of them for a short distance if he found Mckenna and Lily straight away. If anything happened to him, he couldn't leave Faraday and baby Eve without transport.

He felt her eyes boring into his back as he rode away, nudging Loch to a gallop. This was it, the final leg of his journey. Much as he wanted to find Mckenna and Lily, the worry was ever present that the feat would be fraught with difficulties inside what he feared would be a lawless city, looted, struggling and likely on its last legs, all vestiges of civilization ripped away leaving it to fester.

He made the highway, noting the stragglers walking or riding bikes not requiring power along the roadside. Most ignored him as he rode by on horseback, horseshoes clapping on the pavement, though greed and jealousy shone in some eyes. One man raised his arm, waving frantically at him to stop. It would not end well and he hurried Loch along, headed for the riverbank, though his horse didn't appear to want to drag it out any more than him. The air was smoky and danger lurked in Golden as chaos had descended in the past few days, destroying everything people had come to count on. He knew all too well what was happening to the residents. Nothing good.

He came to the Golden River, memories flooding in of the last time he'd been there with Mckenna and carving their initials into the tree bark. He dismounted at the location, surprised by the number of lovers' initials cut into the sturdy oak tree in the years since they'd been there. Holding tight to Loch's reins, he ran his fingers over the names and found his and Mckenna's. Aha. There it was. The message he had prayed for. For the second time today, fate was shining its heady light in his direction. But that thought only brought him worry over every good deed having its counterpoint. He ignored the signal of danger, needing to keep moving. High noon was almost upon him.

He took note of the location. 12 n + 2 w M. Dillion place. M +L. 05/23/55. He was about to leave but while standing below the roadway and out of view, he heard an old vehicle motor with a loud growly sound meaning it was most likely missing a muffler, a relic of another era coming toward town. He stayed still, holding Loch's reins tightly he caught a glimpse of an ancient Cadillac, its black painted presence appearing alien in the current landscape, skirting around a broken up uFree hovercraft on the rise above him. The small maneuver caused the caddie to veer farther away from him and it vanished from view.

He decided to wait a few seconds until it passed. He sensed danger even as he wondered who was inside. Then a barrage of gunshots broke the stillness of the air, causing his pulse to skyrocket. What the hell! Had someone in the caddie shot at some of the people only trying to escape the town? He led Loch up onto the high-way, not wanting the noise to spook the horse, neck on a swivel as he tried to make sense of what had just happened.

A new horror met his eyes. Some people had been mowed down by the hail of bullets, all laying prone on the pavement, blood staining their clothing. He hurried closer and kneeled down to check on their condition. Four were clearly dead, two women and two men, their bodies bullet riddled. One person was still alive, a man in his mid-fifties, his eyes widened by shock.

"Why?" the man asked.

Connor had no answer for him. He inspected the victim's wounds, finding a bullet hole in his stomach area and left shoulder, both legs punctured in the upper thighs and knew it was only a matter of time until he expired. "Do you know who did it? Who shot you?" Though there was little he could do, still knowing something of the crime could maybe be reported one day if things sorted themselves, futile as the hope was at the moment.

"No. Please, check on my wife. Is she okay?"

Connor froze. Was the truth better when the man only had a short while to live? Yes, the truth was always the best option.

"I'm sorry. Everyone's gone. It was over quick. I'm sure no one felt any pain."

The man's face sagged as all hope drained out of him. "We had a plan." The man winced as the pain of his wounds swept through the shock his body had undergone. "We were going to meet at the first bench we come across in heaven, wait for the other one to get there."

"It's a good plan." Connor swallowed his tears at the revelation.

"I think I'll be joining my sweetheart…"

The man's voice turned too low to hear. Connor lay two fingers on his neck, and feeling no pulse, he closed the man's eyes with one hand, said the Lord's Prayer, and rose to his feet. Every part of him wanted to bury the people, but doing so could put Mckenna and Lily in further danger. No, he couldn't risk it. Filled with remorse he knew would haunt him until his dying day, he mounted Loch and didn't look back. The incidents were piling up. How soon until a man lost his humanity?

Ignoring the question, he headed at full gallop back to Faraday and baby Eve. He knew he was changing, making choices he would not wish on anyone, but what else was there for it except helping those he could. The worst part was he knew the choices were only going to get harder for people, pushing them into doing things they could not have imagined a week earlier. But true to his word, he'd pick Faraday and Eve up first, then take them to the Dillion place. Thank God Mckenna had found someone to help her and Lily. Soon they'd all be together and could head back to Braveheart where he could keep everyone safe as anywhere on the planet, barring an underground government facility with a legion of soldiers to protect it.

FIFTEEN
EASTWOOD

Day 4: Near Chicago, Illinois
    10:01 a.m.

"You look lovely as a summer's day, Celia," Eastwood said. He admired her in the new red silk dress with the plunging neckline and tea-length ruffled skirts that bespoke of another era. She had a case filled with such pretty clothing items, all designed to bring beauty into his life. He'd discovered he appreciated finer things, the ideal pleasing him far more than expected.

"Thanks. Where are we headed now, sir?"

"I have questions for you, my fair Celia. When you lay in your bed late at night and the dark presses in, where do you wish you were? What kind of location do you conjure up in your mind? And please, take your time in answering. I want only a truthful answer."

Celia grew quiet for a moment, her haunting beauty giving him a portrait of a reflective moment in an art gallery before she came to life again and began to speak.

Baby Arthur sat strapped into his new car seat, playing merrily with a ring of plastic keys he appeared fascinated by, putting them one by one into his mouth as if taste could tell him everything he needed to know. Wrong. It took far more than the scant five senses a human being possessed to even get a glimmer of how vast this universe was and precisely what was going on.

"I've never liked the city. Too many people all shoved in together preying on each other. I dream of wide-open spaces where you can breathe fresh air and enjoy simple pleasures. Where you can be left alone and take long walks in peace. I've never picked wild flowers, planted a garden and watched things grow. Or ridden a horse. I want those things for Arthur. But the way things were in Detroit, I never thought I stood a chance at ever providing such a life for my son. Do you think places like that still exist now that the world has gone crazy?"

"I think the world is in a better place now than ever to provide such things for you and Arthur." He relished the look of utter disbelief that came into her emerald-green eyes he swore he could see eternity reflected back at him from their shimmering depths. He'd discovered she was more than just a vessel for his needs, but a fine example of the human species that rose above the norm.

"Our ultimate destination is Anchor, Alaska. My family comes from there." Or at least the former owner of his body came from there, Eastwood having taken over Doctor Hazzard's physical shell back in Washington, DC at the beginning of his perfectly planned EMP event. The former scientist was lucky he had, the prize now in the new world, which was life, would go to the one with the keenest brain and staunchest limbs. The one who could best shape himself to the new ways, the oldest test known to humans, competition of the fittest.

"But nearby I know of a horse ranch that would provide everything you ask for and more, my beauty. Braveheart." The name even spoke to his interest in Arthurian literature. He had knowledge of everything that had ever been or could ever be available to him in a nanosecond, from his mainframe in DC. "In all of Alaska, there is no better location to make your simple dreams for Arthur come true."

"Braveheart," Celia murmured the name, her eyes aglow with emotion. "It sounds perfect. How soon will we be there?"

"A few days."

"Who lives there now?"

"No one you need worry about."

SIXTEEN
MCKENNA

Day 4: Near Golden, Alaska
   11:29 a.m.

It was beyond difficult to know they had to leave. Mckenna consoled herself with the thought if Connor made it this far, surely, he'd continue following her and Lily's trail. She absently gathered supplies she and Lily would need, packing a few changes of clothing for her daughter and one for herself though she added all her underwear. Jake would be assuming the worst of the burden, carrying Lily in the backpack and everything else they would need if they were stranded in the bush overnight. She was thankful it was May and only going to get warmer, not mid-January and fifty below zero.

"You ready?" Jake asked, his impatience clear on his face. The child carrier was prepped and sitting on the floor with extra things hanging from every place they could manage to attach something. It was heavy and she felt the guilt all over again of not being able to do more, of having allowed herself to get hurt in the first place in such perilous times.

"Yes. But I need to leave a note."

Jake frowned before picking up a hammer and chisel from his worktable and quickly carving her and Connor's initials into a length of firewood. "We can't say the location; in case Luther comes back. But at least your friend will know you're alive." He set it near the door, facing into the room.

"Thank you." She wished it was more, an exact map of where they were headed. Some words about how they were okay, but she would have to accept it, hard as it was.

"Okay. Time to get Lily into the carrier." Jake carefully dealt with her daughter, strapping her in and making sure she was comfortable, her bear tucked in alongside her. He donned the apparatus and adjusted the straps, settling in for a long hike.

Mckenna had insisted on a backpack though far lighter in weight than Jake's with her and Lily's medications hidden inside. She was dressed warmly and had taken the precaution of downing a couple of pain pills. The wound on her leg hadn't become infected and she was going to make certain it didn't happen, taking the antibiotics for the full ten days prescribed. It was healing and even beginning to itch a bit, a good sign.

"Okay, let's roll." Jake gestured for her to go first.

She stomped out of the shed, her crutches making hollows sounds on the wooden floor. Jake followed her and they set off down the laneway to the road.

When they turned to head east at the end of the driveway, she gave one last longing glance toward the west. She'd give anything to see Connor come riding up on his charger. But nothing but a bleak landscape greeted her eyes, the sky overcast and hazy, even the sun too weakened to show itself. In the moment her own resolve softened, her heart aching for what it couldn't have, Connor at her side. She had to console herself with Jake's promise to get her and Lily to Braveheart one day.

"I'll feel better once we get off this road and hit the old logging trail that leads into Ben's place." Jake's voice brought her back into the present. His tone was tense, hardened by worry and strain over the situation.

"Ben?"

"Ben Carter, my old CIA buddy. I told you about him." Jake gave her a quick look.

"Right. I am grateful, Jake. I need you to know that."

"But you wish Connor was here?" His expression didn't give anything away.

There was no need to answer him.

"How long do you think it will take to get to this Ben's place?"

"We'll be camping a night or two at the very least. Depends on you mostly. How fast you can move."

She quickened her pace, not wanting to hold him up. She had to quit thinking back. Look ahead. It would take all her strength and determination to reach their new location as it was. Eighteen miles wasn't a walk in the park on crutches, dragging a bad leg.

"Tell me more about working for the CIA. What was it like? It's such a secret organization I really know little about it."

"Not much to tell really. Took an oath to not share its secrets, though I suppose the current situation might allow for some ease on restrictions. Not like they'll care much about former employees with all that's going down now. Everyone's got their hands full. Mostly it was just about going after the bad guys though that line blurred a bit too much for me at times. Sometimes it got a bit dicey as well. I took a couple of bullets in the line of duty."

"You were shot?" Jake was such a big mountain of a man; it was hard to imagine him lying prone in a hospital bed.

"Took one in the thigh chasing a cartel boss through the jungle. Had to be medevac'd. Then my last go around with the Special Activities Division, SAD—an organization the government prefers to keep at a distance due to covert operations—the assassin's bullet took me out for good with a shot to the shoulder, damaging the muscle and some ligaments. You have to be at a hundred percent physical fitness to continue with SAD. Lucky the guy was having an off day or the bullet would have been to the heart."

Jake spoke so casually about his life and death exploits. It boggled her even as she admired his fortitude. "So you took a job as an air marshal."

"It pays the same. Maybe it's not as exciting, but I'm okay with that. Well, *did* pay the same. Don't think anyone's going to be getting a paycheck anytime soon."

"Most would want to be paid in food or supplies anyway. Lots of bartering will be going on now."

"Which is why I packed a few extra guns and ammunition for trade. Medicine too."

"Your load must be heavy." Mckenna winced. She had to get better soon and start carrying her fair share.

"I'm okay. *I'll sleep when I'm dead.* Isn't that what someone told me?"

The teasing light in his deep brown eyes caught her off guard and she offered a tentative smile in exchange. "Yeah, something like that."

"What caused you to leave Mexico?"

The question caught her off guard. "Aw—"

"It's okay, I shouldn't have asked."

"No, sharing might actually help. A wise person told me it was good to let the darkness out. Only way to let the light in." Claire had said it what now seemed a lifetime ago, though it had only been a couple of days. She didn't want to name her and upset Lily who had been asking where her Aunt Claire was. "I was in an abusive relationship and couldn't see any other way than to flee. A good friend helped me escape. Bought the wigs and all the things we needed." Was Teresa okay wherever she landed up? The not knowing how things stood or how people she loved were faring was the most painful lesson of all.

"We all need help sometimes. My worst fear of this new world we've been pushed into is it will wear away at what makes us civilized and incapable of great feats of courage and honor then resorting to *us and them*. We might as well become zombies if we're going to turn into monsters anyway, doing unwarranted harm to others. If only good people would come together and share their knowledge and supplies, we might stand a chance. Of course, that doesn't mean I'm not willing to fight off the bad people, only looking to exploit others."

"I'm dead certain that's how Braveheart will be. Like-minded people coming together for the betterment of all. I think you and Connor are more alike than not." At least the Connor she remembered was a good man. No way could he have changed that much. She'd bet her life on it.

"I'm certain others will gather and do the same. Problem is finding them. It's going to take time for people to sort things out. And time is the one thing we're short of. Ah, here we are." Jake pointed out a narrow, winding path through the bush. "This is the trail that leads into Ben's place."

Mckenna couldn't help herself from stopping and looking back down the road they had just traveled, wishing she could leave figurative breadcrumbs only Connor could discern like a clever character in a fairy tale. It felt like the last chance for Connor to find them and it was darn hard to turn away. Would she ever see him again? So many things could happen on the way to Anchor. Nothing was guaranteed anymore. Nothing.

Unsure which hurt more, her leg or heart, she followed Jake's cue and began the long slog down the goat trail headed north. One step at a time. At least the direction was right, her inner compass lining up with one of Earth's magnetic lines.

Jake must have caught a glimpse of the anguish roiling inside her in by her expression much as she tried to hide it. "I'm sorry for not being able to leave directions. But Luther Meech is known for holding grudges and coming after people. His line of work, heck, it's expected. A gang leader must be feared if he wants to keep control."

"My ex was a cartel boss." The words sounded so cold and foreign, her mouth forming them with difficulty. But letting it out made her feel instantly lighter. Yes, sharing a burden was helpful. *Thank you, Claire.* She gave a short prayer for her fallen sister.

Jake's eyes widened. "I didn't realize that. Which cartel?"

"Martinez Knights. Same as his last name. Diego is nothing if not an egotist."

Jake stopped dead in his tracks. "I know that name from my time with SAD. Oh boy, this is not good news. He's not only a ruthless drug and arms dealer; he's got his fingers in the pie in Alaska through the Kraken Cartel."

"So?"

"This is bad. Very bad. Luther Meech runs the Kraken Cartel. He's in business with your ex. Oh my god, if he figures out that Diego's wife and daughter are here in Alaska, a world of hurt is going to rain down on our heads."

"You're scaring me."

"I'm sorry, not my intention, but you need to know what's at stake here. Maybe I should go back and destroy that piece of firewood? I left your initials on it. Luther might put two and two together. Know you were there and come looking for us."

"No. I don't want you to go. He might come back like you said and something could happen to you." She panicked at the idea of her and Lily being abandoned in the wilderness with those thinking to do them such terrible harm. "It doesn't give our location away."

"No. But he may think to track us. I have to do this. I'll sneak in the back way. It won't take more than twenty minutes to jog there and back. I'll leave Lily here with you. Let's just move you into the trees first. Over there." Jake took off so quickly, giving her no chance to argue further.

Mckenna following him, wishing she'd kept her damn mouth shut. So much for sharing and getting hurtful things into the light of day. Now Jake was putting himself at risk, again, for her.

SEVENTEEN
LUTHER

Day 4: Golden, Alaska
   12:49

"Damn it! There was no need for that." Drake's killing the people walking down the street had set off Hope, causing her to break into tears. He hated it when women cried. All blotchy and upset. Difficult to control. He couldn't have it. Big as the caddie was, it wasn't big enough for four large men and the reek of excess testosterone. He'd seen them eyeing up Hope with envy and lust. Especially Drake, the one who had shot off his weapon, trying to demonstrate his prowess. Or more likely impress Luther's new woman. If that was his intention, he'd failed abominably.

"Just putting the poor souls out of their misery. Beats starving to death, eh." Drake, the youngest member in the group and prone to cockiness he needed drilled out of him ASAP, gave him a cold smile that didn't reach his dark flashing eyes. Luther would tear a strip off him once they were back in Anchor. For now, he'd let it ride as annoyed as it made him. Though if he kept it up, he'd find himself abandoned on the side of the road.

"We need to keep the ammunition for emergencies. Quit wasting it," Luis Bear warned the younger man, cuffing him on the side of the head. "You heard the boss."

Drake glared at Luis, but didn't do anything more, turning away as if it meant nothing to him. But he didn't have the balls to do more. Luis was just too damn big and scary.

"What's the plan, boss?" Thomas asked from the driver's seat. They were riding around Golden, hoping to catch sight of Tally. But other than the dismal state of the city being driven home, they were no more ahead than before. Hope's constant sobbing had his nerves on end, though she'd lowered the volume.

"I think that guy was hiding something. We'll head back there next. Shake it out of him." Luther needed a break from all the traveling. A little torture would solve his urge for a little exercise. He didn't really think the marshal was hiding something or he would have done something earlier, but it was as good an excuse as any. Plus, it never hurt to be sure.

"But he's an air marshal," Thomas said.

"Do you think anyone gives a shit about who you were before it happened?" He pointed out the window. "Look around. Do you see anyone coming to the rescue? No. We're all on our own now."

His plain words only worked to increase Hope's tears. He sighed with growing frustration. Sooner they were back in Anchor the better. If only they weren't all stuck in the same damn vehicle it would be so much easier. Well at least he could make the marshal pay.

EIGHTEEN
CONNOR

Day 4: Near Golden, Alaska
    12:33 p.m.

Connor let out a deep breath. There they were. Faraday and baby Eve, waiting for him exactly where he'd left them. A reassuring sight. A part of him had worried someone would come along. Or Faraday would have lost patience and head on after him even though he'd warned her not to. It boded well for the future. One positive sign in a chaotic world.

"Took you long enough," she greeted him with a grumble.

"There was an incident. Some men in a caddie decided to shoot up some civilians fleeing the city. I stopped to check on them, but it was too late." He almost shared the dying man's words about meeting up with his wife on the other side, but decided it would stay his burden to carry. How many others had lost loved ones since the nightmare had begun? From thousands of aircraft falling from the skies right after the event to the current lawlessness akin to the Wild West, the world had irrefutably changed for everyone. Only thing left to decide, was if you were capable of changing with it, prepared to do what it took. If not, you stood no hope of survival.

"Shit. Really?" Faraday shook her head. "Gang wars are alive and well in Golden."

"I don't think it was gang related. One of them was still alive, and what he said, made me realize he was just an ordinary Joe going about his business." What he wouldn't have done to prevent it, but short of a blast from a machine gun or taking out the entire vehicle with a grenade, nothing to be done. Those men in the caddie were a blight on humanity. The kind of monsters his mother would have scorched the earth to find and bring to justice. But he no longer had the luxury of following one group of evildoers like had been done in the past. No, in the big picture he had to steady the course and get his own people to safety. He knew his mother, the legendary Anna Hale, would understand if not wish it were otherwise.

"What were his dying words?"

"He was worried about his wife, but she was already gone. Ready to go?"

"Hell yes. I have to meet this woman who has you going to the ends of the earth to find her."

"Hardly the ends of the earth. It's only a hundred miles or so one way." Even so, it felt like they were in the hinterland of the distant past, the dark forest of an ancient tale told round the firepit with hunters and gathers acting out their part of how they survived the worst thing imaginable using a new weapon. The moral of this story did not elude him. It was beware of what you chose to create as a species. Just because you could make a bomb or artificial intelligence, does not mean you had to act on it. The fallout from an ill-conceived creation can be astronomical, destroying everything in its path if safeguards aren't set in place well ahead of time. Even then, no way to be sure an invention is for the better good. People may intend to do no harm when they dream up an idea, doesn't mean harm won't happen. To his mind people had not advanced enough as a species to be able to handle such rapid advancements in the past hundred years. They had not come together, instead wars were still being fought, governments were still crushing citizens, and people still lived in object poverty.

"Yeah, on horseback during the freakin' apocalypse!"

"Well, when you put it that way." He chose the light-hearted reply and was rewarded with a small smile. He understood she had been worried about his returning in one piece. And on that note, he led them on their way, directing Loch back down the way they had come to the highway. They would be turning off after a few miles, taking the road west toward the Dillion place. He tried to keep a lid on his growing excitement. But every sense told him they were so close to being together again he was hard pressed not to gallop full-out all the way. No, he had to be fair to the horses and to the baby who didn't need that kind of jostling.

They made the first part of the trip unscathed by avoiding looking at the burned-out vehicles and dead birds for the most part, then turned down the side road for the final leg of the journey. Fires still burned in the distance, either looters gone mad or installations burning down without the restraint of electronics. The air quality was fairly decent, but he could only imagine what big cities were enduring. And how many were still standing? The tighter humanity packed itself into tiny square boxes, though albeit through no fault of their own but a product of their environment and upbringing, the more dire the situation would become. He could never have been an urban dweller, unable to see the sunrises and sunsets under pristine skies, with enough room a man could take a breath. He also realized he had been blessed to have been born in Alaska, the last refuge of those with a rebel spirit.

Faraday had gone silent. Her expression had tightened, and he knew he should reassure her all would be well, but his thoughts were in a jumble. Now that they were this close, he was less sure of himself. How was it going to be meeting up with the love of his life years later? Would they be able to pick up where they left off? When she'd contacted him before the world went to hell, she had chosen not to use video. Why? Had she changed physically and didn't want him to see it? It didn't matter to him if she'd been in an accident or been burned, heck, his mother carried scars to her dying day from a fire she'd suffered as a teenager, she'd still be Mckenna Stewart, that bubbly happy girl who had stolen his heart in high school. But for her sake, he hoped it wasn't the case. Mckenna had always been beautiful, and losing such beauty would be hard on a woman. And honestly, of course he would miss it, but it was who she was inside that he had loved most. Her caring, kind heart who took in strays and helped out friends at the drop of a hat, sharing anything she had with anyone who needed it.

"Look, a house has been burned down." Faraday pointed out the charred residence set back from the road.

With his thoughts meandering, he'd missed they were nearly at their destination. Was this the place? Hard to tell, but best guess, they were about ten miles from the highway. He had a good sense of distance traveled from spending so much time tracking in the bush.

This was bad. It looked to be a recent fire too. He headed them toward the house, fear tightening his throat. If Mckenna had been here, she was long gone now.

He dismounted, his voice strained even as he told himself to stay calm for the sake of Faraday and the baby. "Wait here. I'm going to look around. There are a few buildings out back. I'll check them out."

Faraday only nodded. Her eyes were widened with concern, her skin pale.

He tried not to panic, walking toward the largest of the buildings watching out for any activity, but it was no easy task. Even if this was the wrong place, someone might pull a weapon on him and ask questions later, thinking he was about to do them harm. Who to trust was one of the biggest dilemmas the people thrust into this new world would face.

The door to what looked like a workshop stood open and he called out. "Hello. Is anyone in there? I'm Connor Hale. I'm looking for Mckenna Stewart and her daughter Lily. She left a sign for me she might be here at the Dillion place?"

Silence greeted his inquiry and his mouth went dry with sudden worry. Was this it, the end of the road for his beloved Mckenna? Was she and her daughter burned beyond recognition in the house standing so bleakly in the outer perimeter of his vision, he was studiously trying to ignore? *Please, God, don't let it be the case*. To have come all this way only to find his girls dead, well, he couldn't make rhyme or reason of it.

NINETEEN
CHEYANNE

Day 4: Braveheart Horse Ranch
   12:45 p.m.

"Has anyone seen the box of two-way radios? They were stored in the maintenance garage," Sam Perkins asked.

Cheyanne chanced a quick glance at the man running the ranch, pretending nonchalance at the question. Sam, her grandma and grandpa, and her brother Luke were all gathered around the kitchen table in the guest cabin they'd been allotted by Connor Hale. Like that was such a big deal. Least he could do since he was directly responsible for sending her dad to jail forever.

Sam annoyed the shit out of her on a daily basis almost as much as Connor Hale, and that was saying something since she hated the man with every fiber of her being. But damn the ranch foreman for always reminding her about chores and responsibility to her family.

She was angry at her Grandma Jean for inviting the

man to lunch, luring him in with her fresh-baked cinnamon buns as if everything was normal. Nothing was normal. The shit going on around them, explosions in the distance, fires, birds dying and animals acting crazy. Things were so far from normal she was ready to burst. And now her dad had gone silent. Apparently too busy to get word to her of when he was coming to rescue her and Luke. Or worse yet, something had happened. In the meantime, she hated waiting around doing stupid shit like helping Laura working in the garden worst of all. Her fingernails were a mess, all split and the polish long gone. And there was that stupid woman, Brandi, always skiving off and sending her assistant Katherine in to do the heavy lifting. Bet her fingernails were in great shape. Probably made her minion give her a manicure.

"I think I saw Katherine with a box earlier. Probably gave it to Brandi. Maybe check there first instead of blaming us? And while you're at it, perhaps explain slave labor is not in place of her actually doing something for once."

"Cheyanne!" her grandpa admonished.

"No one's blaming anyone, Cheyanne. I just want to share the resources around in case someone needs help and they have to call someone. I'd hoped to give one each to your grandparents for safety's sake. I'll just have to keep looking." A twitch by the corner of the man's left eye told her she'd gotten past his defenses. Good.

Then she took a deep breath, worried Sam might carry out a search of their house. Yeah, then she'd be seen as the bad one for hoarding the walkie-talkies if it was ever discovered she had them hidden under her bed. Only Luke knew about it, and he'd never tell on his sister. At least there was that, both having promised to have each other's backs since their mom was murdered.

Thinking about her mom always made her glum, so she grabbed for another cinnamon bun from the plate centered on the wooden table, ignoring the look of concern from Luke. Why couldn't he hide his feelings better? She took a large bite of the treat in an effort to avoid looking at anyone, her mouth watering.

The cinnamon buns were oh-so-good. She ate the gooey home-baked treasure quickly, lathered in thick, fresh-churned butter. At least milk cows were good for one thing, thankful that as yet she'd not been asked to muck out the barn, her brother Luke having taken on the disgusting chore when asked. She'd been so damn hungry lately. She had to get out of here soon, before she began showing, or no telling what would happen. Her grandparents would go ballistic, probably grounding her until she was ninety. Not that there was anywhere to go these days for fun. And in her heart of hearts, she was scared and hated to admit it. At night she could hear the explosions and gunshots in the distance and shivered in her bed, bolstering herself up with thoughts of her and Ty and the baby having a place of their own. Then things would all be different. The three of them snug and safe in their new home. She was certain her dad would help her and Ty get a house. Maybe even Luke might want to stay with them, once he got sick of being bossed around. Though she wouldn't count on it. He'd taken to ranch life like he'd been born to it. Always stepping forward for any job when volunteers were called on.

She felt eyes on her and she studiously ignored them, pouring herself another glass of milk. It was then she wondered if her dad had milk cows. She was drinking two or three glasses a day for the sake of the baby. Something else that needed to be sorted once she heard from him. This waiting around sucked. She'd need a lot of stuff. Before that damn world had shut down, she'd read a list of all the things having a baby required. It was a little alarming. But surely her dad and Ty could manage to get everything she needed in time? Her dad had connections, important connections and he cared about her. And Ty had told her he loved her a few times. Ty really admired her dad, said he wanted to be like him. No, things would work out. She just needed to get away from here first. And if that meant allowing her father access to the ranch, well, not like they didn't have more than enough to go around. From what she'd seen, Connor Hale and his crew were hoarders. Keeping everything for themselves. Well, no more.

TWENTY
CONNOR

Day 4: Near Golden, Alaska
   1:15 p.m.

The sounds of footsteps coming up behind him made Connor whirl around. A huge mountain of a man stood before him, taller than his own six feet by a few inches and heavier set though not fat but appearing muscular, his eyes hooded and wary above a thick black beard while his hand held a gun, an assault rifle, pointed straight at him. He wore a thick wool cap, hiding his hair. Definitely a man who could handle himself.

Connor's first instinct was to draw his gun, but the guy had just gotten the drop on him and Connor would most likely take a bullet as well. He couldn't afford to get hurt now with all his responsibilities. Best to play this out and avoid bloodshed if at all possible.

He put up his hands. "I mean you no harm. I'm looking for a woman and her child who left me directions on a tree saying she was coming to this address."

"Mckenna and Lily Stewart," the man said with a nod. "I'm Air Marshal Jake Dillion. You must be Connor Hale."

"I am." Connor was beyond relieved he was at the right place. "Are Mckenna and Lily all right?"

"Yes, they're fine. Mckenna got hurt, but she's recovering." He lowered the rifle.

"Hurt?" His stomach tightened at the intel.

"Yeah, damn grizzly caught the back of one leg. I stitched it up. We scavenged for antibiotics and pain medicine. She's waiting for me a short distance away. I only came back to destroy the log I carved your initials into so you'd know she's alive."

Connor frowned. He didn't like the sound of it. It sounded sneaky and underhanded, though the man, Jake, was an air marshal. He took a step back. "Why would you do that?"

"No other choice. I just found out that Mckenna is married to Diego Martinez, boss of Martinez Knights and Luther Meech of the Kraken Cartel is looking to find her. I couldn't leave any information which might lead to them discovering where she is. She's in grave danger with Luther Meech running around scot-free. He broke out of the Supermax even before the EMP event happened."

The news was stunning, and it took a second for Connor to absorb it all. One thing stood out for all the dire facts. Mckenna was nearby and he had to get to her right now.

"How did you get here?" Jake asked, interrupting his thoughts.

"Horseback. I left everyone out front." They were standing behind the woodshed or the guy might have been able to see Faraday and the baby, Loch and Finn.

The sounds of a throaty vehicle's motor far off in the distance took them both by surprise. Connor recognized it immediately and began running around the building to race full bore toward the small group waiting for him near the road, leaving the lawman in his wake. It had to be the same black caddie as earlier. It was still quite a ways off yet, but his sixth sense and law of probabilities suggested it was the killers from earlier. His stomach tightened with worry even as he hardened his resolve.

He leaped onto Loch, not wanting to take any chances. "Race for the trees at the back of the yard," he said. "You have to hide. Now."

Faraday didn't ask questions but gave Finn a quick nudge with her heels and took off at a gallop in the direction he'd pointed. She raced by the air marshal who watched her go, baby Eve's cries at being disturbed almost as loud as the pounding hoofbeats. Soon as he reached the man again, he stopped and dismounted, grabbing his Bergara Highlander from the scabbard. He gave Loch a swat on the backside to send him to the safety of the trees as well. "Do you want to make our stand here or do we head for the bush?"

"I'm thinking here. If it's who I think it is and we let them go any farther down the road, they might come upon Mckenna and Lily. They visited earlier today, looking for someone. Looks like they didn't believe me when I said they weren't here."

Connor could tell there was more to the story than the lawman shared, but right now it didn't matter. "Right. I hope you got lots of ammunition."

"Wearing enough on my person and the shed has plenty more."

"How many of them?"

"Four. Luther Meech, a huge bald guy on steroids, a

driver and one dickwad looking to prove something. All up to no good."

"Were they driving a black caddie? If so, they gunned down some innocent civilians in town a short while ago."

"That's all we need to know. Soon as they get out of the vehicle—shoot. They're not here to talk this time. You down with it?"

"I'm all for a good offense. How about I hide? They know my face and will shoot from inside the vehicle if they recognize me. I sent his ass to prison with my testimony."

The air marshal's dark slashes of eyebrows rose up at the intel. "Head around back. There's a ladder there. If you get on top of the shed, you can easily take out a couple."

Connor wasted no time. He found the ladder and climbed it quickly, before lying down flat on the top of the shed. He pointed his rifle toward the spot he figured the men would stop, careful to keep out of view.

He felt the adrenaline begin to flow as the caddie drove onto the laneway, wending its menacing way toward them. He glanced back at the tree line, noting Finn and the girls were not visible in its shadow. To think Mckenna was now such a short distance away made him want to dispatch the assholes advancing toward him as efficiently as possible.

He waited. Even the air seemed hushed though a stiff breeze had been blowing earlier. It may be four against two, but it didn't dissuade him. He was an expert marksman and he figured the air marshal to be one as well.

The caddie ventured closer, though its speed had lessened. The driver was visible behind the wheel now, his face half hidden by his black ball cap. He recognized

Luther in the front passenger seat, a huge bald man driving. A dark snake of a man with dead eyes. Or maybe that was just his dislike for what the monster had done to his wife Chrystal, Dan Sullivan's daughter, and her girlfriend Amy, shooting them and setting them on fire before they were even dead. A cruel predator. It seemed all roads had led to this moment, right here. Right now. Luther had never made it a secret he was gunning for Connor, the one who bore witness to the event and sent him to jail in the first place.

The caddie stopped about fifty feet away. For a moment no one got out. Connor worried they were going to shoot from inside, like they'd done to those poor people back at the riverbank. But then then all the doors opened up. Three men stepped out, leaving the big bald guy inside. He sat head and shoulders above the others in the driver's seat, a hulking presence of a monster most likely a fellow prisoner from the Yellowhead Supermax. He caught a glimpse of a smaller head in the back seat and thought it might be a woman by the long fair hair. The gangsters moved apart immediately, leaving Luther advancing at the apex. Smart. If there was only one man facing them, they would have the upper hand.

Connor took shallow breaths, keeping his finger poised on the trigger. Soon as the action started, they were going down.

"What do you want?" Jake asked in a confident tone. He was casually holding his assault rifle, but it was obvious he was prepared to use it. Connor already thought him a decent enough guy. He considered himself a good judge of character and was grateful the lawman had helped keep Mckenna and Lily safe during a vulnerable time. Knowing the perilous times they were in; it could have gone vastly different for his girls.

Luther held up a placating hand. "We just want to talk. Seems Tally didn't make it back to town. She's missing and we think you know something about it you aren't saying for some reason. Now the only reason I can come up with is you had something to do with it. If that's true, then you and I have a problem."

"I told you she's gone. We broke up, and she headed out of here. I haven't seen her since."

"Strange time to break up. Right when the world goes to shit."

"She stopped taking her medication, and we had a falling out over it. You must know what she's like when she's off her meds? I couldn't get a handle on her moods. And not like we had dated very long anyway. It was a mutual breakup. Tally was looking for excitement while I'm looking for peace and quiet. You know how it goes."

"Yeah, maybe. Problem I have is I can't find her. And it's important that I do. She may know something about someone else I need the intel on. I can't just let this go. So, I'm thinking you come with us and help us look. You know the area better than we do."

"Sorry. I've got no time for searching for a woman I don't care to see again. I've lost my home thanks to the fire and I need to keep working to fix the situation."

"I'm afraid I have to insist."

Suddenly guns were drawn as Luther backed up his threat. Connor was ready, having a bead on the guy situated to Luther's left. He'd leave the satisfaction of taking out their leader to Jake. Seemed like he'd earned it dealing with the woman Luther was looking for. Tally something or other.

Shots rang out. Bang. Bang.

Connor saw the man he was shooting at go down first, one shot in the head and one in the heart, then he turned his attention to the man on the right. Luther was still upright. The ex-prisoner glanced up at the rooftop where the shots were coming from, then began running back toward the vehicle. Connor got two more shots off. The car started moving as the second man went flying backward as his bullets struck their target. Luther jumped inside the vehicle and the caddie began to spin a U-turn to speed away. Connor pulled the trigger a couple more times, hitting the vehicle's back end, hoping it was the gas tank. They'd should have killed Luther and ended this vendetta right now. What had happened? Surely the air marshal was a good shot? He'd been standing right in front of the murderer. Had they murdered him before he got a shot off?

He got up and hurried back down the ladder, racing around the building to confront the situation, hoping he was wrong and the lawman was fine.

Jake looked upset, holding his gun with disgust. "Damn thing jammed. I didn't even get one bullet off. If you hadn't been here, I'd be a dead man. Luther turned tail and ran soon as he realized there was a second shooter. Fucking coward. The others were piss poor shots."

"Are you hit anywhere?"

"No, I ducked sideways with a gun that's hitting the trash heap. *Fool me once, shame on you, fool me twice, shame on me.* I got other choices, don't worry."

"At least we took out two of his henchmen. And I hit their vehicle a couple of times. They might end up disabled on the roadside with any luck."

"Yeah. Slowing them down is good. I'm just pissed I

couldn't take him out. Until we do, the guy's going to be a thorn in our side."

Now the danger had passed, at least for the time being, Connor's mind cleared and he began to consider logistics. "What was your plan with Mckenna and Lily? You said they were a short distance away?"

"Yeah. After my ex burned down my house and my neighbor's house, killing two close friends in the process, I decided to head for an old buddy's place. We'd just left when I found out from her that Luther and her ex-husband were business partners and rushed back here to destroy the log with your initials on it. Well, you know that part."

"I'm sorry to hear about your friends." He was about to share what had happened to his dad when Loch and Finn began to trot back across the field toward them, Faraday and the baby still riding Finn. They both watched the spirited horses.

"We should get rid of the bodies," Connor said. "Want to bury them?"

"Takes too long. I'll just haul them into the bush and cover them with some branches. Good enough for killers."

"We need to beat him back to Anchor." Connor hoped they'd slowed him down but until it was confirmed, he wasn't taking any chances.

"You think he'll still come after us after losing two of his men?"

"Luther can find new recruits anywhere. Lots of guys looking to join the dark side for food and housing." He remembered the female in the back seat. "And a chance at women. Knowing Luther, he has a plan. A lot of people stand to get hurt long as he's above the green. I think he'll head for Anchor and try to get there before us. I wouldn't even put it past him to attack Braveheart." Expressing his worst fear aloud actually helped though visualizing images of how that would play out sharpened his senses.

"Damn. I wish I had taken him out." The lawman clenched his huge fists at his side, his glance steely.

"Just the luck of the draw. But there'll be a next time, don't worry. Then we can get the satisfaction of ending this."

"Mckenna said you live on a horse ranch near Anchor."

"Yeah, a kind of survivalist camp. I teach people how to prep and manage shit like we're going through right now. I've been expecting this kind of situation for years."

"I thought I was decently prepared until a woman stripped it all away." Jake shook his head. "Never saw it coming."

The horses stopped nearby, Loch snorting and pawing the ground. Baby Eve had quit crying while Faraday watched the pair of them with interest, speculation riding high in her eyes.

"Let's go get Mckenna. Then we can decide what to do," Connor said.

"Right. I'll just grab a new rifle from my stash in the shed. But I think Mckenna still needs a couple of days to heal up. That's why I was taking her to Ben Carter's hideout about eighteen miles north of here. He and I go a long way back. Both in the CIA together, worked for SAD—Special Activities Division. Good guy to have on your side, nerdy but absolutely brilliant, though he's had it a bit rough these past few years. PTSD kicked in after our last go-around. He's the ultimate prepper. The kind of guy who may already know what's going on with his underground connections all over the world. I saved his life once, and he's always said to come to him *when* the world ends. He'll know more than we do."

Connor raised his brows, impressed with the lawman's credentials and this Ben Carter. "I look forward to meeting the guy. My father was a chief of police before retiring."

"He still in Anchor or head for warmer climes?"

"No, he never left. Unfortunately, the EMP event took out his pacemaker, another victim of all this."

"Sorry to hear it." Jake pursed his lips. "I don't have transportation yet, so I'm going to need to run back to where I left Mckenna. Wanna help me haul the bodies into the woods first?"

"Sure. Then we'll go together." Much as he wanted to race toward her right now, it was the right thing to do. Plus, he wasn't exactly sure how far away she was. She'd be hidden from prying eyes. He knew that much for certain.

"All right."

"I should introduce you to Faraday O'Brien. We met on the road." He didn't elaborate on the circumstances not wanting to bring it all up and upset the young woman. "She's carrying Eve, a newborn. I came across the baby on my travels as well. Her mother is deceased. Another victim we can chalk up to what's going on." They walked down the laneway as he brought Jake up to speed, holding on to both horses' leads.

Jake winced, then said, "Nice to meet you, Faraday. I'm Air Marshal Jake Dillion. Well, former."

Faraday didn't smile but nodded once. She cradled the baby protectively in her arms, sharing a glance with Connor, as if asking him what the deal was. He gave her a nod to say all was well. They might have just met, but the lawman's actions to date gave him no immediate cause to worry. They'd had each other's backs in the fire-fight and it wasn't Jake's fault his weapon misfired.

He and Jake quickly dispensed with the bodies, both picking up an end and moving them inside the tree line. They covered them with a few branches and called it done. Neither bothered with a prayer. Though they were both someone's son before they choose the life, their current actions condemned them to an early grave. How many others would choose the criminal path now that lawlessness reigned? Connor could only shake his head at the stupidity and turn away. Jake headed back inside the shed and came out with a new rifle slung on his back.

Connor sped up his step to a quick jog as he hurried over to grab the reins of the two horses. The need to see Mckenna suddenly hit him harder as he felt how close he was to seeing her again. The lawman followed suit and in silence they had made their way a mile down the road, their quickened breath and the horses' clopping hooves the only sounds disturbing the bleak countryside.

"She's just inside that strand of trees," Jake said, pointing it out. He quietly took the reins for both horses from Connor.

And then she stepped out of the bush, a young child clinging to her leg. She was on crutches, making his eyes widen. How bad was the wound? And then everything was forgotten as he rushed forward to greet her, his arms opened wide to draw her close.

TWENTY-ONE
CONNOR

Day 4: Near Golden, Alaska
   2:10 p.m.

"Connor," Mckenna breathed out his name as his arms surrounded her. "Is it really you? Or am I dreaming?"

It was like the intervening years had never happened. She looked the same beautiful Mckenna to his eyes, her face filled with such happiness at seeing him his heart gave a leap of gratitude. He leaned in and kissed her forehead, both cheeks. Then she was kissing him on the lips and everything in the world felt right. All the bad stuff fell away leaving the pair of them cocooned in the moment.

"Mommy?"

A child's high voice broke the surrealness. Connor forced himself to let go of Mckenna for a moment and crouch down to greet the little girl. "You must be Lily."

"Princess Lilybelle," she said with a solemn expression, her thumb in her mouth. She was a miniature version of her mother, holding a teddy bear. Precious beyond belief.

"Princess Lilybelle. Such a pretty name."

"I'm so glad you're finally here," Mckenna said. He glanced up at her. She was smiling ear to ear. It was then he noted the dark circles under her beautiful eyes. It was heartbreakingly obvious she had been wounded and was still recovering, yet she was soldiering on. He couldn't admire her more than he did in the moment.

"I heard shots," she said, studying him closely as he kneeled in front of the pair.

He got to his feet and cleared his throat, careful with his words. "Yeah, a few guys in a caddie begged to differ with us on what was going to happen next. They were persuaded to move on."

She glanced over at the air marshal, seeming to notice Faraday and the baby for the first time as her eyes widened. "Who are they?"

"Faraday O'Brien and the newborn is Eve. I came across both of them on the trip down from Braveheart."

"The baby is hers?"

"No. Long story. But they both needed my help." He shrugged his shoulders.

"You were always such a good man. It's nice to see you haven't changed."

"Oh, I've changed. But maybe it's just not obvious on the outside." Mckenna didn't question him further as the others came up to join them.

Baby Eve began to whimper. "She needs a fresh diaper," Faraday said.

"Give her to me." Jake stepped up and took the tiny newborn from the young woman. Faraday hesitated for a moment, holding on protectively, then relented.

Connor got down to the business of finding one of

the dwindling supply of store-bought diapers Eve's mother had left in the bag for her. They'd have to see about getting her more soon which meant visiting one of the towns, something he would prefer not to have to do. But the baby had needs and he had to try for her sake. He set out the changing mat on a flat piece of ground before Faraday took over and changed the baby.

Connor stood back and addressed the small group. "Okay, I think with the two horses we can make do. I'll take Mckenna and Lily on Loch, and Jake you can ride with Faraday and the baby on Finn, if that's okay with Faraday? We'll have to travel a bit slower and rest the horses more often, but it's only eighteen miles."

Faraday gave a grimace, her lips thinning. "Please, I would prefer to ride with you, Connor. After what I've been through." She shuddered. "No, I don't know this man. I'll just walk."

"No, I'll walk. I'm used to traveling long distances on foot anyway," Jake said with a shake of his head. "It's what the pioneers had to do. Good enough for me."

"They had wagons and stagecoaches and even built travois out of poles and hides to make it easier to carry packs, children, and injured people around. Eventually a cross continental railroad," Mckenna said. "More than some people will have now with all their fancy electronics fried." She sighed, her expression forlorn. "I think that might have been a better time to live in some ways. When I read the true accounts and novels, I always feel it's somehow more real than how we live today. Really building something and forging ahead with confidence. Manifest Destiny at its finest."

"I didn't know you had become a history buff?" Mckenna's spiel took him by surprise.

She blushed. "Yeah, I know your fondness for old

westerns and ended up reading quite a few myself. It made me feel closer to you."

"We could use a travois right now with your leg injury. Are you going to be okay to ride?"

"I can do it. Beats tramping around on these crutches and holding everyone up. Though I thank Jake for providing them." She smiled at the lawman with appreciation and it hit Connor then he hadn't been there for her when it all came down. He wasn't jealous of Jake but wished it could have been him aiding her and her daughter straight away.

"Okay, new deal. The women ride and the men will escort. Any objections?" Connor asked.

No one had any, so they got underway. Connor took point and Jake took the rear, fencing the two horses carrying the females between them. Connor carried the Bergara Highlander while Jake had strapped a different assault weapon, a MZ-9 Commando carbine on his back, his expression grim. Even with Luther down two men he was a menace to society. If he had a good tracker in his crew, they'd be able to follow them, but maybe it was only paranoia kicking in. He'd more likely hightail it home to Anchor and strike from there with more miscreants staying at the old hunting lodge north of Anchor. He'd been given the intel about the new purpose for the lodge by the first prisoners he'd had a run in on the way down to Golden. No doubt more escaped prisoners would converge together there, an evil band of predators looking to prey on decent people. Something would have to be done about it. Soon. Or innocents would die or become entrapped by the ex-cons. Perhaps he needed to bring in more law-minded men who knew how to fight? Like Brady or maybe he could persuade Jake to join up with them? The man he'd just learned of, Ben Carter, sounded promising as well. He had to do everything in his power to protect Mckenna and Lily. He couldn't believe they were reunited and he kept glancing back at them, to make sure they were real, savoring the vision. It was as if no time had passed since they'd been together. She was still the same Mckenna, same beautiful spirit shining in her eyes.

He realized he and his small band had traveled some distance while he'd contemplated their situation, the surrounding fir trees the only witnesses to their passage. A voice finally broke the silence.

"Could we take a short rest? Lily needs some food and something to drink," Mckenna asked. He suddenly realized her daughter Lily was whimpering, complaining she was hungry. He chastised himself for leaving it too long. He should have thought of the need for her and her daughter to stop for proper rest. She was injured after all. What was he thinking?

"Good idea." Connor helped Lily and then Mckenna down off Loch, careful not to jostle her leg. She stood perched on one foot until he pulled her the crutches from the scabbard and handed them to her. She quickly sorted them out under her armpits and moved off a short distance to where the others were gathering on a flat bit of land on the side of the trail between the canopy of trees.

Jake glanced at Connor as he untied a tarp for everyone to sit on from the top of Finn's pack. "We're making decent time, but there's no way we'll make Ben's place by nightfall."

Connor stretched out the blue plastic tarp on the ground as he considered his reply. Knowing Luther could still be out there, wishing them harm ate at his gut.

"We'll take turns keeping watch. I imagine you are used to little sleep working where you did."

"No problem. But we can take a short break now and still get a couple more hours of traveling in."

"I agree." Connor handed everyone a protein bar from a small box in his saddlebag while Faraday took care of the water situation, making sure each person had a bottle. They'd make do for now, saving the warm meal for later.

The three females settled down on the tarp while the men chose to stand. The weather was growing colder and a few snowflakes had begun to fall, the horses' breaths visible against the darkening skies as he put on their feedbags with a share of oats. Pristine as snow made the landscape, the hazard of another cold snap or even a blizzard hung over their heads. It would be best to make their destination tonight, but Connor knew it was an impossibility, frustrating as it was to admit it.

"There's been no sign of any pursuit. Luther's most likely licking his wounds and figuring how to get back up north," Jake said. He'd finished his food in a few quick bites, followed by a few swallows of water, placing the protein bar wrapper into his jacket pocket, same as Connor.

"Yeah, I'm more worried about the weather. It's taken a turn." Alaska was notorious for quick-moving snow squalls dumping snow that could cripple movement. With weather reports now a thing of the past, no telling how big the storm was or how long it might last.

"We'd better get a move on."

Lily whimpered a bit when she was hustled back onto Loch and into her mother's waiting arms, but it had to be done.

"Sorry about this. But it's best to keep moving while we can."

"I understand," Mckenna said, her expression serious. In the moment he saw a new, different Mckenna, one who had endured a perilous trip north and maybe something more ominous back in Mexico. Of course, she had been married to a drug lord. Had she known what Diego did for a living? For the first time, he realized he may not know quite as much about her as he once did.

He moved down the line to Finn and helped Faraday on the horse while Jake stood by holding baby Eve. She was still looking with suspicion at Jake and he didn't want to press her on it. She'd been through enough. He took the baby from the lawman and settled her in Faraday's arms.

"You doing okay?" he asked her.

She nodded. Her expression was grim. "I think we're in for a bad storm. I've always been able to sense these things."

"Yeah. Let's hope it holds off for a few hours." But he could observe the unease in the horses, snorting and pawing at the ground to get a move on, even though it had already been a long day of travel for them. He patted them both and fed each a sugar cube from his pocket in appreciation of their efforts. They quickly set off in the same formation as earlier.

But an hour later and the snow was falling too thickly to continue, the wind howling its intentions through the tree tops. Connor had to call it. The trees were thinning out now, not offering as much protection as before. Maybe they should have stayed where they were?

No time for regret, he held up his hand to let everyone know he was calling a halt for the night. No one complained as they stiffly dismounted the horses.

He pulled off the small tent from the pack on Finn and quickly set it up, placing the blue tarp beneath it while Jake pulled some self-heating MREs from his pack and enough spoons for everyone. The tent held three comfortably, but they could all squeeze in together. Body heat would be all they had to keep them warm once the blizzard he was certain now was coming on, only going to grow in intensity over the next hours or even days. All the signs were there. He's spent most of his years in the wilderness, enjoying the wide-open spaces. But he respected the land and nature, knew it was a cold, brutal landscape if one didn't know the precarious nature of survival if you weren't prepared for it.

"Bad timing," Jake said, shaking his head while pounding down the tent pegs to secure the corners after handing the MREs off to the two women. Connor was busy hobbling the horses and feeding them more oats.

"We'll be okay. We've got enough food and water for a few days. I'm more worried about the horses." At home they'd both be warm and dry in the barn. Sure, they had the constitution for frigid weather being bred for the cold by the tribesmen in northern Caucasus centuries ago to withstand thin mountainous air quality, but he didn't like to see them neglected in any way.

"Yeah, I hear you. Kabarda. Very impressive breed. How did that come about?"

"Research. Alaska is a challenging region for animals. They seemed a good choice and they haven't let me down. Hardy and good-natured."

They finished up their self-appointed tasks, then joined the others inside the tent, a small solar lantern with a backup battery providing the light. A snug fit, but doable. Jake was careful not to sit next to Faraday, he noticed, but chose to stay near the tent opening with

Mckenna to his right. It left Connor room across from him. Not his first choice, he'd prefer to be closer to Mckenna and Lily, but nearer the door was fine. What he wanted was not important right now anyway. Only getting his small group to safety.

Faraday handed everyone an MRE and a spoon, and they set about eating. No one said much, though Mckenna murmured to her daughter from time to time. Soon as the little girl ate a few bites, she dropped right off to sleep at her mother's side. It was then the baby began to howl, upset at something.

"I'll feed her," Faraday said. "I think she's just hungry." But a bottle popped in her tiny mouth did nothing to lower the sound of her cries. It was heartbreaking and made Connor feel helpless to stop it.

"I'll take first watch," he announced. "Be back in a few hours." Jake nodded. He unzipped the tent opening and quickly crawled out, closing it behind him. Though the chances anyone was going to come upon them in what now looked to be a blizzard, still, keeping watch was important.

The snow was building up on the ground already, nearly six inches deep in spots and blowing around, slapping ice crystals into his face. He yanked his hood closer and tied it tight under his chin. How bad would it be by morning? He blinked and stared down the trail, only able to see a few yards now though he could still hear baby Eve crying her eyes out. At least no one could see them hidden by the side of the trail behind bushes and the baby should stop crying soon, he could only hope. Even the horses were vanishing from view behind a veil of white. Half an hour later he realized there was no point in being outside. He'd stay on guard inside the tent.

He unzipped the now quiet tent and met Jake's inquiring look as he shook off the snow that had built up on his jacket and jeans. "Anything wrong?"

"No, but I can't see more than a few feet in front of me. No one can find us in this. I'll stay awake right here. Unless the baby starts up again, then I'll head out." He hunkered down near the doorway, crossing his arms over his chest. This was no place for such a young baby, but what other choice was there. They could only wait and pray now.

TWENTY-TWO
LUTHER

Day 4: Golden, Alaska
   1:33 p.m.

He needed more recruits. Thomas was their biggest loss today. He let out a series of curses aimed at Connor Hale finding some satisfaction at airing his grievances. Bastard had laid in ambush, thwarting his plans. Now he was two men down with a hole in his gas tank leaking fuel, though Drake wasn't much of a loss. And Hope whimpering in the back seat wasn't helping things.

"Now what, boss?" Luis Bear asked. They'd driven down the road a way and sat idling the motor.

"Let me think."

But Luis began to speak again, annoying the shit out of him. One of his lieutenant's best points was he normally was a man of few words. Not today. Then what he was sharing began to sink in.

"I saw where they turned off this roadway in the

rearview mirror, if it helps. They're headed into the heart of prepper country. I may even know where."

"What? Spill it." This was more like it. Luther sat up straighter and gave Hope a warning glance to stuff it.

"Ben Carter. My cousin George had a run-in with him while he was in the CIA—don't matter for what now, but it's well known he and this Jake Dillion guy worked together. But if we're going to head there, we need different wheels. The caddie won't make it. It's a goat trail fit for only ATVs, dirt bikes or horses."

"Yeah, all of which are in short supply."

Luis's lips twitched into his version of a grin. More like a death grimace. "My cousin hates Ben Carter's guts and he has access to ATVs. Hobby of his, collecting and fixing old shit. I'm thinking we check with him."

"Luis, you're the man." Luther high-fived his first lieutenant catching him by surprise, the guy who'd helped him break out of prison the day of the event of all things. Gave him a boost on the competition and brought to fruition all his dreams of taking over Alaska's drug trade. With his own army, why not plan big. All over the place, a certain kind of alpha was having similar thoughts. He needed to beat them to it, but not before taking care of this damn ex of Diego's and rescuing his daughter. Only good business. The head of the Kraken had contacts most could only dream of.

"Can I go home now, please? I've changed my mind. I want to stay in Anchor," Hope asked from the back seat.

Luther sighed as Luis eyeballed him. Time to send a stronger message. "You want me to shut her up?" he asked.

He shook his head. "No need for that yet."

"Please, just let me out. I'll walk home."

"There's no going home now, sweetheart. Bad men

will only attack you on the street or break in your house to take advantage of you. We're taking you with us to save you from all that. You'll starve in Golden. Do you want to be hungry? But if you keep carrying on, we can let you fend for yourself. But I'm telling you, it won't be pretty. You can kiss the chance to be a queen goodbye, used by as many men as want a piece of your fine ass."

"Where's Tally? She'll help me."

"Tally's dead like you'll be if you don't shut it," Luis growled. Apparently, he'd had enough of the whining. His assessment was most likely correct about Tally. And he felt an instant rage firing up about Jake Dillion who knew something he wasn't sharing, the bastard.

"Dead," Hope whispered, her face whitened by shock.

"Okay, let's get to your cousin's and get after them. Time's a-wasting."

"What about her?" Luis asked, nodding his head toward the back seat. "Want me to share what happened to the last woman who cheated on you?"

"When the need arises. But for now, she comes with. We'll pick up some snow machine gear, helmets and the like for all of us. They got a dealership in town. Not sure if they make those suits big enough for you though." Luis weighed two hundred and seventy-five pounds if he weighed an ounce and stood six feet seven inches tall, pure muscle.

Luis hit the gas pedal, and they were off and rolling. He hated to admit it, but the encounter with Jake Dillion and Connor Hale had left him shaken. The two of them teaming up was beyond annoying. They had to be taken care of right now. Hale with his preachy brand of how to live a good life surrounded by nature, a product of his annoying parents who could never leave well enough alone. People like that would be taken down a peg or two in the new reality and find their playing at being better than others was a determent to survival. You want to survive the apocalypse? You'd better set aside those useless morals and know it's now a dog-eat-dog world. No room for being civilized. The law was gone, flattened, maybe never to come back. Carrying his dog analogy further—he was starting to relish the concept— he'd needed to throw the bone again. He glanced at Hope in the back seat, staring out the window at the shambles of a former existence, no doubt. Even upset, she was a beautiful woman. He knew exactly where he wanted to throw the bone again. Too bad it had to wait until he took care of business.

TWENTY-THREE
MCKENNA

Day 5: Tuesday, May 27, 2055
  Near Golden, Alaska
  4:45 a.m.

The sounds of a baby crying and the wind howling to wake the dead woke her. Disoriented for a moment, Mckenna couldn't figure out where she was. Then it came flooding back. Connor. The storm. And the worst part, shooting Tally. She soothed her pain over having taken a human life with the knowledge it was Tally, or her and Lily. The deranged woman had given her no choice. But for some reason it was haunting her, like she could hear the woman's howls in the wind, a banshee stalking her in the screaming snowstorm.

"You're awake," Connor whispered.

He was cradling Eve, rocking her gently in his arms. The tent was warm with the portable solar heater emitting a gentle warmth during the night and the baby was well wrapped up. She prayed it would be enough to keep her safe. Such a small baby was vulnerable. She needed a bath, not just baby wipes for cleansing. Hopefully this Ben Carter would be able to provide such essentials. Her heart squeezed remembering how tiny Lily had been, so delicate. "She's upset about something, not that I blame her. I've fed and changed her, but she's not having it."

Watching him take such tender care of the newborn made some of the nightmare dissipate though the wind was screaming and pressing against the tent walls like a monster wanted inside to wreak havoc.

"You're good with her." Mckenna also kept her voice low, not wanting to wake Lily or Faraday. "Is Jake on watch?"

"He headed out a bit ago. He should be back soon. We tied a rope to the tent and to a tree if you need to…ah… use the facilities. I don't want anyone getting lost in the storm. It's coming down heavy."

"Are we going to be able to go anywhere today?"

"I doubt it. And certainly not with a tiny baby. Too dangerous. The trail has vanished. On the bright side, no one can follow us either."

"Do you think they will?" The thought of someone out there stalking her sent chills racing down her spine. This was all her fault, her bad choices in life. Not seeing through the façade Diego had so carefully crafted. It was bad enough her ex might still be looking for her, but at least he was in Mexico last she knew. She tried to soothe herself with the thought it was highly unlikely he could get this far after what had happened. Or figure out where she was. Heck, she didn't even know exactly where that was. Lost in a deadly storm that would no doubt cost many lives. At least she and Lily weren't alone, though she felt guilt at involving the others in her mess. But what other choice was there? Lily was her main priority. She'd beg, borrow or steal as the saying goes to keep her little girl safe from harm. Didn't mean she didn't feel conflicted or found it any easier. A sense of being in a whirlwind pressed harder on her, but she found a bit of joy in her pain. Connor was looking at her with a loving gaze that made her heart want to sing again, if and when it could. She had to hold on to that. He loved her unconditionally, always had. If only she had gone back home at first chance. But no, she'd been incredibly stupid and naïve, swept off her feet by a conman.

"Hard to say. They might choose to head back to Anchor and cause more grief there. But don't worry, I'd lay down my life for you and Lily. You're both safe now."

No one can promise that. She grabbed her crutches to make her way out of the tent even as she held onto his promise with all she had, vowing then and there to try harder not to let the past haunt her or infect the future.

"You okay?" Jake asked. He met her near the tent opening, but in the blowing snow slapping at her face and blurring her vision as soon as she stepped out, he was hard to make out. "Follow the rope. I'll wait here for you."

"Go inside. I'm fine." Her words were blown away soon as she spoke them, carried on a tsunami of ice and snow and frozen wind. The crutches made it difficult, and she struggled to follow the sagging length of rope to the nearest tree. Then it took many more minutes to relieve herself, the bitter weather piling up snow drifts and making the task nearly impossible. She could barely feel her hands and feet when she turned to go back toward the tent. How many others would be caught out in this storm? How many deaths because people had no other choice?

She grabbed for the rope but realized she'd gotten turned around somehow doing her business and it was no longer an arm's length away. She frantically reached out around her body, trying to locate it again. *No, this can't be happening.*

"Hello," she shouted, praying someone would hear her. Maybe Jake had stayed outside and was nearby? She was afraid to move around too much and get lost farther distance from the tent. The cold was seeping into her bones now, a deadly presence looking to leech all the warmth from her shivering body. It wouldn't be happy until she was a human popsicle. The image frightened her further even as she forced it away. The swirling snow made it impossible to know which direction it was even coming from, a vortex of frozen waves changing direction on a whim.

What am I going to do? No answer was forthcoming to her continued pleas for help.

Then a faint sound buffered by the wind. "Mckenna!"

She screamed louder and then a few seconds later arms reached out to grab hold of her. She fell into them, letting her crutches go in the process. She clung to him as he guided her back toward what she hoped was the tent, having picked up the crutches for her. In the whiteout she had no idea where she was, disoriented and frozen with fear for her life. Then she was thrust inside the opening, followed by her rescuer.

"Jake." She could barely get his name out, her teeth were chattering and impossible to control. "Thank you. I couldn't...find the...rope."

Her eyelids were covered with ice and half frozen shut, her vision blurry. She tried blinking and when the snow crystals melted away enough, she could see Connor's concerned face looking at back at her. He still held the baby, but his eyes were grave as they bore into her. At least Eve had stopped crying. "You have to be more careful. A storm like this needs to be taken with a great deal of caution."

"I know. I'm sorry." She tamped down her anger at not only her own actions but being called out on them. "I thought I was being careful, but with the crutches and everything, it proved more difficult than I expected."

"Someone will go out with you next time."

She was about to protest when he held up a hand. "No arguing, please. I can't bear the idea of you getting lost out in the storm."

Mckenna swallowed her rebuttal, hard at it was. She had left Mexico because she wanted to call all her own shots and already it wasn't happening like she had envisioned it. "Yes, you're right. It won't happen again." She could hear the stiffness in her voice and softened it with a small smile in Connor's direction.

"Anyone hungry?" Jake asked.

Faraday had woken since she'd gone outside and she answered in the affirmative. "I'm starving. Must be the cold." The young woman grimaced.

Mckenna knew next to nothing about the young girl. How had she ended up in the forest for Connor to rescue? She decided that as soon as the opportunity presented itself, she'd ask a few questions. She had a right to know who she and Lily were spending time with. At first glance, she appeared a closed book, always watching everything going on with a wary expression. But to her credit, she was good with baby Eve.

"What I wouldn't do for a steaming mug of coffee," Faraday said as Jake handed her a granola bar.

"Afraid we can't arrange it inside a tent, but as soon

as it can be managed, I'll make some," Jake promised, sharing a smile with Faraday.

The exchange troubled her for some reason. Was she just being selfish? The last few days she'd had Jake's undivided attention. And he'd been so good to her. Now someone else had joined the mix. No, if the pair of them hooked up, she would be happy for them. Jake was one of the good ones. In a short period of time, it had become obvious he cared about people beneath that mountain man exterior.

"How long do you think this storm will last?" Faraday asked, unwrapping and munching on the granola bar.

"I wish I knew. May storms are unpredictable. We're going to have to wait it out whether we like it or not," Connor said. "Long as we don't get another Valdez Snowmageddon, we'll be okay."

"Valdez Snowmageddon?" she asked. "Never heard of it."

"It was before our time. Worst ever. Twenty-seven feet of snow fell. But it was during the dead of winter. Not in the spring. This will pass."

"Worst one after that has to be the one at the Thompson Pass. Fifteen inches of snow in ninety minutes. Can you believe it?" Faraday shook her head in disbelief. "Crazy."

Jake handed Mckenna one of the bars and she quickly tore into it, finding herself starving for calories, thinking it a good sign and meant she was healing. Or all this talk of snow was making her hungry. Her leg began throbbing again as the cold drained out of her, making her reach for her pack to get her medicine out.

"How's the leg?" Jake asked. He'd most likely caught her wince.

"Better," she said. She swallowed the pills with a swig

of water, then finished her bar. It helped ease the hunger pains. She yawned. Lily was still curled up, fast asleep. How had she slept through the baby's cries? Her little girl must be exhausted.

"You might as well go back to sleep, Mckenna. We're not going anywhere for a while," Connor said.

Mckenna leaned back and shifted her leg to a more comfortable position. Not easy with all of them packed in so tight. How long would they have to endure such conditions? The mere fact everyone was armed to the teeth told her how far from being a civilized society they had fallen in a few days without amenities. She had to keep mindful she was one of the lucky ones, under cover while many scrambled to find a safe place, even though at the moment she didn't feel charmed in this life. More like buffed by the whims of fate, danger lurking at every turn.

TWENTY-FOUR
LUTHER

Day 4: Monday, May 26, 2055
   Near Golden, Alaska
   9:59 p.m.

"Gotta pack it in, boss. Nothing else for it. Not like they can move either. Stuck same as us," Luis Bear said, his voice mostly taken away by the wind as he slowed down to pass on the message, lifting his visor. He rode the first ATV with his cousin Joe, while Luther rode the second one, Hope clinging to his back.

"Damn it to hell. Just when we were getting some-where." They had acquired even more useful items than expected from Luis's cousin Joe Simmons who was sympathetic to their cause. He had even insisted on coming along, eager to help. The man hated lawmen with a vengeance mirroring his own and desired a part of the drug action as well. Easy trade. Goods for a piece of the action. Hell, he'd promise the moon if he could find the whore and lay her to rest. Stealing a man's children, it made him angry beyond measure. Diego could count on him to straighten the matter out, save his young daughter from the harmful effects of being without a father. Who else would care enough to make damn sure their offspring were safe in these perilous times than those sharing bloodlines? Now they were hard on the trail of those thinking to slip out of their grasp. Only cog in the wheel was the damn blizzard.

The blizzard had moved in almost without warning, a sudden Alaskan end-of-winter snow squall bringing freezing temperatures and icy winds. They were not far behind the group they were tracking; their newly acquired vehicles having gained them considerable advantage. If the storm had not hit, they would have ended the standoff today. Luther felt the pressure of time. He needed to get back to Anchor and gain the advantage there. He soothed his frustrations with the satisfying thought that Connor Hale disposed of early in the game, it would be a slam dunk to take over Braveheart. Aw, the ranch was a plum ripe for the picking. Hell, he'd bet the man had years of food set by. Didn't all preppers and survivalists insist on it as a matter of pride?

"We'll set up camp over there," Luther said, pointing out the small open area. Camping directly under the trees could be dangerous. They didn't call jack pine widow makers for nothing. Dying from the top down, they were notorious for falling on unsuspecting visitors, maiming or killing them instantly. Luis nodded his approval and drove onto the clearing, killing the motor and disembarking the machine along with his cousin.

"We'll catch up to them tomorrow," Luis said with complete confidence, hauling one tent off the back of the ATV for him and Joe. Luther and Hope had a second tent on their machine, a similar stash of food for a number of days plus a solid selection of weaponry. Yes, the odds were greatly in their favor.

The helmets were buffering them from the worst effects of the storm, and they kept them in place while they set up the tents side by side, swiping the snow off the visors when it accumulated. All except Luis whose head was too large for any of the gear available. Joe had even provided a camping burner and pots for warming food and water. Also, a good selection of protein bars, MREs and even a medical kit. The man was prepared while so many would be caught totally off guard.

"We'll rest here until the storm moves on. Catch those bastards by surprise in the morning." Luther shared his plan when everyone had gathered in his tent for a debriefing and food.

"Might not move on so quick," Joe said, shaking his head. "My bones are saying we're in for it. Could be stuck here for days. We've got plenty to last though. We'll be fine."

Luther didn't like the sound of it, but held his tongue. Not like Joe had anything to do with it.

"Days. Stuck here?" Hope said, her eyes widened with concern. "I should be home. At least there I can move around." Tears welled in her eyes. Luther groaned.

He and Luis shared a look. Luther shook his head, knowing what his lieutenant was thinking. Not yet. He wanted female companionship for the next few days and he had plans for Hope. "I've already explained this to you, Hope. It's dangerous for a beautiful young woman such as yourself in Golden. Or anywhere, for that matter. I'll make sure the wolves don't get to you. Human or otherwise. It's just until the storm abates, sweetheart. Soon as possible you'll be on a big ranch with lots of room. A grand house you can call your own.

You can set it up anyway you like." Surely Connor had a few decent dwellings on his property along with barns and sheds. He ran a business from there.

"Okay." She blinked the tears away and smiled bravely, taking the hot food from his outstretched hand. He watched her eat, knowing he wasn't ready to give up on her yet. Even under the circumstances they found themselves in, her beauty shone like a rare diamond in the desert.

"Want a nip?" Joe pulled out a full bottle of whiskey from his jacket pocket.

Luis grinned. The man loved to drink. Luther wasn't certain it was a good idea. What if someone came along and he was too inebriated to respond quickly? But then the storm was raging now and it would take a fool not to find shelter. Long as the men kept their place and didn't hassle Hope, he could overlook it.

"Sure," Luther said. He grabbed the bottle and took a sip.

Luis shared it next and drank down a few ounces in short order. He smacked his lips with pleasure. "Good whiskey, cuz."

Joe held it out to Hope after taking another gulp. She shook her head, her expression wary.

They shared the bottle around a few more times.

"I think it's time to turn in," Luther hinted. The men were starting to get too relaxed, eyeing up Hope on the sly. Or as sly as men can be half drunk. Luther had consumed very little, pretending to take more. He needed to stay sharp. Who knew what waited out there in the dark forest for them? In these hard times he couldn't say no to his men needing to let off steam, but using his woman was a step too far.

"You're a lucky son-of-a-bitch, Luther. A woman like

Hope on your arm," Joe said after swallowing another gulp of the whiskey. The bottle was half gone now, warming the blood of the men.

"Yeah, well, I'm heading to bed now, so if you don't mind, fellows, I need you to head out." Thank Christ they had their own tent.

"Sure, sure." Joe waved off his words. "It's just so much nicer in here. Less lonely if you get my drift." He was beginning to slur his words, never a good sign.

"Luis, time to escort your cousin out." Luther reached into his pocket and grabbed his Glock, preparing to take it to the next level if pressed. If Hope had been another woman, it might be different, but he had plans for her. Beauty was currency, same as power in the new world, no different from the old one. Some things never change.

TWENTY-FIVE
LUTHER

Day 4: Near Golden, Alaska
   11:59 p.m.

Luis gave him a sharp look as if checking for something. Luther stared back at him, unblinking, letting him know Hope was not pulling the chain. Not here, not now.

"Okay, cuz. Off we go," Luis finally said, breaking the standoff.

It wasn't until the men had exited the tent, letting in a swirl of icy snow crystals in the process that Luther could take a breath. It had been damn close.

Hope had crawled into the corner of the tent, buried under the sleeping bag, watching him zip the tent closed. It was a relief to have the two big men gone, no doubt for her too. Didn't mean they weren't coming back. If they got blind drunk, no telling what could happen. Luis was a good guy normally, but drunk, not so much, often complaining of blackouts and doing things he couldn't remember in the morning. Hell, he was in prison for deeds committed while drunk, fighting and carrying on, assaulting others. Maybe he needed to move camp away from them? But where? The storm was hitting its zenith now, howling with all the outrage an Alaskan blizzard was known for.

"They're gone, sweetheart. You can take off your snowsuit and crawl into the sleeping bag with me." Just because Luis and Joe didn't get to partake of her charms, didn't mean he had to back off. Wasn't a woman's dream to have only one man in her life? One to protect her and keep her safe from predators?

"I'm fine dressed like this," she countered.

"Well, I'm not. I need you close to me. Take it off. All of it," he added some steel to his request.

"I can't. It's that time of the month," she said, staring him straight in the eyes with righteousness on her side.

He groaned. Just his luck. He hated mess. And it was worse out here without the usual amenities.

"Fine. Go to sleep."

They ended up curled up next to each other, snuggled under the cover of the sleeping bag. Her soft snores soon filled the small space and he had to admit, it was nice to have his arms around a woman again, even a reluctant one. She'd soon grow to care for him. He'd make sure of it. He had a chance to do it different this time. Better. And with a prize like Hope, he'd be the envy of all men. Of course, it would bring with it the inherent problem of jealousy with a woman as beautiful as she was. But he was up to the task, willing to shoot anyone touching his property. Yes, things were proceeding as they should. Take out Connor Hale and all would be well.

TWENTY-SIX
CHEYANNE

Day 5: Tuesday, May 27, 2055
  Braveheart Horse Ranch
  10:30 a.m.

"Cheyanne. I need you in the kitchen. Sam's here," her grandma's voice rang out from the other room, making her wince. Why was she always the one needed to help when there were plenty of others willing to assist him and his annoying wife Laura who had enough energy for two.

"Something about your friend Ty Jasper," Grandma said, still shouting.

Ty? That was different. Cheyanne jumped off the bed where she had been hiding out all morning, reading an old paperback novel of her grandpa's. A story about a man, a gun, and a ranch where cows were being rustled, but it was better than nothing. And there was a love story woven in she savored. She was sick to death of ranch work already, dreaming of something better.

She raced down the short hallway and around the corner to discover the foreman or business partner or whatever he called his oh-so-important job standing squarely inside the doorway, looking straight at her. His look spoke volumes and she dropped her gaze first, feeling an unwanted stab of guilt for skiving off.

"Laura was looking for you," he said, his tone cool.

"I had a headache. Not like we can do much in this weather anyway," she said. It had begun snowing the night before. Again. Through the kitchen window, she could see the ranch was blanketed by a thick layer of white, swirling drifts pushing up against the other buildings in its path.

"She needed help keeping the stoves in the greenhouse lit to keep from losing our crop. Fortunately, your brother volunteered."

She shrugged and turned to look at her grandma busy punching down a huge pan of bread dough in preparation for placing in the multitude of pans standing greased and ready on the counter. She was in charge of baking all the loaves necessary for their entire group. A task she should probably learn to help with, she realized, guilt flooding in. "You said something about Ty?"

"Your friend is at the gate, demanding to talk to you," Sam said before her grandma could speak. "I asked him to leave, but he said not until he speaks to you."

"You asked him to leave?" A surge of anger boiled up from inside her, wanting satisfaction. How dare he! Ty was the father of her baby. Maybe he'd come with word about her dad? She could barely contain her excitement at the prospect of finally finding out something about what the future held for her. "You had no right to do that. He's my friend. I need to see him."

She dashed around Sam before he could stop her

and grabbed her red parka off the hook before slamming her feet into her white snowpacks and yanking open the door. The ice crystals slapped her face, making her nose and cheeks tingle as she hurried across the yard and down the road toward the gate. It was kept locked twenty-four seven now that the world had gone nuts. The barbed wire strung along the top made her even angrier. People were such shitheads. Fucking up a perfectly good world. Well, she was getting the hell out of here soon as possible and living with Ty and the baby in a better place. Not some boring old ranch where all you do is chores and pretend to be happy about it. No, with her, Ty and her dad, she'd get a better deal, she was certain of it. Her dad had connections, others to do his bidding. And money, lots of it.

When she got to the gate, she found it still locked. Damn it, Ty was on the other side, waiting for her.

Sam came running up, his expression one of anger and frustration. "There was no need for you to run off."

"You could have let him in. He cares about me." She stood there, stamping her feet in an effort to keep them warm. But thoughts of being with Ty helped warm her up. He was an exciting guy. Filled with dreams same as hers, she was certain, under that tough, cool exterior. Only she knew who he really was. And he loved her. She'd been so adrift when they'd met, and he'd helped her to feel better about herself. They were meant to be together.

"We all care about you, Cheyanne. Ty, well, he's got a reputation for causing trouble. I can't have him roaming around the ranch. Times have changed."

"He's not going to do anything to you. He wants to see me. Don't I have a right to have friends, or have you turned Braveheart into a prison? Yeah, first Connor Hale sends my dad to one, and now he locks me up."

"It's not like that. We all just want what's best for you. You're so young with no idea how much is resting on your future. Okay, I'll let Ty in, but you have to promise me to keep him in your grandma's kitchen. And he leaves within the hour."

"Sure."

"You have to promise me you won't share what we've got stashed here. I don't want hordes of people trying to break in. We got enough trouble seeing to our own."

"Hoarding's not going to go over well in Anchor or anywhere." She moved closer to the gate, waiting for Sam to unlock it.

"It's not hoarding when you have taken all the steps necessary to prepare for the future. It's called survival. And we paid for all this stuff with our own sweat and blood. Your grandparents live here. You want others to come in and steal from them? They took you in when your mother was murdered."

Tears sprang to her eyes. "Why did you have to bring it up?"

"I'm sorry if I upset you. But this is no time for making things out to be different than they are. I'm calling it as it is. You either help keep things going the best we can, or you will be called on it. Are we clear?"

Sam had never been quite so direct before and it caused her more than a twinge of worry and guilt under the anger. Would her grandparents be okay if her dad tried to take over Braveheart? There had been a lot of bad blood between them, especially with her grandpa. Then she pushed the worry aside. Of course, they would be fine. Her dad would help them if she asked.

"I need your promise, Cheyanne."

She huffed. "Okay, I promise to do my best not to help anyone else out."

Sam gave a disgusted look. "Not what I said. I'm saying family and friends first."

"Fine. Then Ty is both. He's my friend and he's going to be family one day."

"You mean as in married? You're fifteen years old, for God's sake."

"I'm old enough."

Sam shook his head, but he unlocked the gate and then she forgot all about the annoying gatekeeper as she came face-to-face with her boyfriend. Ty moved toward her as soon as he caught sight of her, so covered in a layer of snow it rained down on them as they hugged.

"You okay?" he asked, holding her face between his hands and staring into her eyes. The intense look in his golden-brown irises gave her a jolt of electricity as it always did. Her body warming at the hug, she kissed him full on the lips. Why couldn't everyone else see what a great guy he was?

"I am now. How did you get here?" she said, grinning at him.

"I walked. I had to make sure you were okay, babe."

"In this storm? You can't go home until it passes. You'll stay with my grandparents, Luke, and me." She ignored the look of outrage from Sam before she led Ty inside the gate. *Deal with it, it is only right.* She left the foreman to close it and linked arms with Ty. "Let's head to the house and you can tell us all what's going on."

They plowed their way through the growing drifts of snow. One good thing came of a blizzard for the first time ever, she was on high ground for keeping Ty at Braveheart, at least for now. No human being worth anything would send a man barely out of his teens out into it again.

She could hear the crunch of footsteps behind her and knew Sam was dogging them. Who cared? Ty and she were together again. Soon her dad would contact her and all would be good. She had help now. Ty would see to it that her dad got his due.

They entered the house as a trio, stamping on the welcome mat to clean their boots before hanging up their jackets on the pegs by the door.

Her grandma looked up in surprise, busy rolling out a piecrust on the counter. Apples stood ready in a bright red ceramic bowl to be added to the pie shell. The scent of cinnamon lingered in the air. She'd miss her grandma's cooking when she left, but not any of the constant nagging.

"Ty," she said, her mouth grim, her faded blue eyes glancing first at him then at Sam. "How did you get here?"

"I walked, ma'am. I had to see if Cheyanne was okay."

"She's fine. You know we'd take good care of her, right? We don't need outsiders to take care of our own."

"No, ma'am. But with so much going on, I mean, it's crazy in Anchor. I was afraid things might have gone badly here too."

Cheyanne had never seen Ty be so indifferent to anyone before and she wasn't certain how to take it. Maybe he was just being smart, wanting to catch people off guard.

"Well, you can see we're fine. What can you tell us about Anchor?" Sam asked, crossing his arms over his chest.

"Like I said, it's crazy. People looting and killing others over stupid stuff."

"How's the food supply holding out?"

"Not good. What's left has been locked up in the Anchor arena and some churches, guarded by the state militia. National Guard's got things locked down pretty tight in some places and are ignoring others. But food's everyone's top priority. No supplies have been coming in and people are getting hungry. Desperate. Lots of fighting and looting. I hear shots all the time and places are on fire."

"In five days. Why don't people plan better? It's not rocket science," her grandma grumbled, going back to working on her pie, her deft fingers making quick work of it. "Have you eaten, Ty?"

"Not since last night, no, ma'am."

"Sit down. I'll make you a sandwich."

At the invite, everyone took a seat. She couldn't believe Ty was there, big as life. Together they could tackle anything, figure out a plan. Yes, things were finally going her way. The eerie sounds of wolves howling in the distance caught her unaware, and she shuddered. Every animal and human being was going to be on the hunt now, searching for food. They needed more men to guard Braveheart than just the few they had. Her dad was right. Sooner he took over the ranch, the better it would be for all of them.

"There's talk in town. About the ranch," Ty said around a mouthful of his ham and cheese on fresh homemade bread.

"What about the ranch?" Sam leaned forward in his chair, the wooden legs creaking from the movement. His eyes focused on Ty, his mouth grim.

"People are saying how come with all the supplies you guys have here, you aren't sharing? There's talk of some coming out here to storm the bastille, if you get my drift?"

"Yeah, when you get back, you can shut it down with prejudice, if you want to keep Cheyanne safe. Let them know we're armed and prepared to keep what's ours."

"Maybe we could help some," her grandma said, turning back to glance at Sam as she tended the stove. "It's the Christian thing to do."

"If they come asking politely, then it will be on a case-by-case basis. Until Connor gets back, I'm holding decisions like that at bay. You know what people are like, well as me, Jean. They'll swamp this place like a horde of grasshoppers given the chance. Give them an inch and they'll take it all. Then we starve. You want that? Looking at an empty larder with your grandchildren staring at you with desperation in their eyes? No, not going to happen. Not on my watch."

TWENTY-SEVEN
CONNOR

Day 5: Near Golden, Alaska
   10:33 p.m.

The storm battered the tent, threatening to blow it away, growing stronger instead of weakening. Connor's impatience to be on their way grew as the blizzard raged on, his mind constantly circling back to the worry of pursuit. His only solace was in knowing Luther and his lapdogs were as affected by the weather as much as his own small band was.

If only they were back at his ranch, he'd lead them into a trap or two. But out in the open, exposed on unknown terrain, odds were less in their favor, especially with a baby and a young child in the mix. Finding the tent claustrophobic, he made frequent excursions outside, checking the depth of the snow and tending to Loch and Finn, both hunkered down against the bombardment. He wanted nothing more than time alone with Mckenna, to catch up on the intervening years, but privacy was impossible with six people crowded like sardines in such a small space. He had given up on having any meaningful conversations in the meantime, though he knew his longing probably showed itself in his constant need to be active and his frequent glances in her direction. At least they had enough food for a few more days, if the damn storm hung around, continuing to taunt them. Impossible to predict, a May Alaskan snowstorm.

"How are the horses managing?" Jake asked as he came back in from the cold once more. Mckenna and Lily were napping, while Faraday was feeding the baby a bottle.

"Holding their own. They'd prefer a warm barn, but Kabarda horses are an elite breed when it comes to the cold and hard work. Best decision I ever made was to choose them. Tough, well-muscled and hardy. And with their heightened oxidizing capacity, they're even more suitable for working in the mountains. Unbelievable endurance."

"Good choice," Jake agreed. "How big is your herd?"

"Twenty-seven in total, mostly mares, broodmares and fillies, two stallions. Loch out there is five years old and Star back at the ranch turned three, an up and comer. We employ them in our business tours for the most part. I've been building up the herd for the better part of a decade."

"Wise preparation on your part. They're more than worth their weight in gold now."

"It's going to take a lot of good men to keep Braveheart secure. You have anywhere you have to be?" Connor tested the waters.

"Hmm. You asking me if I want to join you on the ranch? Even after the kerfuffle with the gun?"

"Yes. And the gun was at fault, not your aim. You look like a man who can handle himself. Obviously, a man with good ethics as you kept Mckenna and her daughter safe. A thank you is hardly enough. And your skills as a lawman would be invaluable. I won't press more now, but think about it."

"I will. Your invite is tempting though, I gotta say. More of us band together to protect hearth and home, the better. The bad guys won't hesitate to come together and cause others more grief than they can handle. I can only imagine how bad it's going to get when the food totally runs out."

Some men, the jealous type, would say he was crazy for bringing this man with him. But Connor never looked at life that way. Everyone was free to choose. Who in their right mind would want a mate if they'd prefer another? To him, jealousy made no sense and had no place in his world. Saying that, he hoped it would never be the case he'd had to watch Mckenna choose another. But from the look in her eyes soon as she saw him, and the glances they'd been sharing ever since gave him hope they would be able to carry on from here. And now that he gave it some thought, he was sorrier for Jake. He'd invested himself in protecting Mckenna and Lily, lost his home in the process. He owed the man a huge debt.

"Yes, hard times are coming. I can never repay you for all you did for Mckenna and Lily."

"It was only the right thing to do. Listen, do you hear that?"

"What?" Connor sat up straighter.

"The wind is dying down." Jake's expression brightened. "This is good. I'm going to check it out."

Jake clamored out of the tent. Good if it was true and

the storm was abating. But it also meant the others would be on the move as well too. The need to stay ever vigilant would take its toll in the hours and days to come, even if he couldn't be certain they were being followed. He hoped they could get to this Ben Carter's place before anyone caught up with them. An altercation on the trail was about the last thing they needed with the women and children in their care.

He rezipped his jacket and climbed out of the tent. The snow drift near the door was partially blocking the entrance, and he gave Jake a hand scooping it away with their gloves.

The wind had died down, a welcome relief after its wailing presence had raged for hours.

"I can't shake the feeling Luther's on our tail, out there somewhere just waiting for his chance. I'm thinking one of us should head back and make certain we're not being followed? I don't want them catching up to us unprepared, caught out in the open," Conn said.

"Yeah, I've been worried about Luther and his minions as well. Damn, if only my gun hadn't jammed." Jake shook his head, his lips thinning.

Connor made a quick decision, seeing the truth of it in the moment. "I'm going to head back. You get everyone to safety."

Jake was about to object. He could read it in his eyes.

"Listen. You know where you're going. You've been to this Ben Carter's before, right?"

Jake nodded. "Several times."

"Then it has to be you. He doesn't know me from Adam and if he's as dug in there as you say, no telling what he'll do a bunch of strangers show up at his hide-away. I'll double back and make certain we're not being followed."

"Fine. But we're arming you to the teeth."

"I'd expect nothing less. If I have to blow those bastards out of existence, so be it." If Luther was indeed coming after him, then a good offense was their best choice.

"Okay. I think there's a few more hours of daylight left. Time for us to get a move on," Connor said. He knew Mckenna would most likely not be happy about his decision, but he'd remind her there wasn't any other choice, not if she wanted to keep her daughter safe. This time his nemesis was going down. He was going to make dead certain of it. The man had earned an early grave.

After they'd informed Mckenna and Faraday of their need to move on, they went about dismantling their camp and repacking the tent. Jake slipped him some extra ammunition and a couple of surprises for the enemy. "Do whatever you have to. If it doesn't snow again, you'll be able to track us right to Ben's. If I don't hear from you by tomorrow, I'll head back to check, once the women are safe."

"No. If you don't hear from me, you stay put. I need to know you won't take any chances. They need you. Make a stand there. Or move on to Braveheart. They'll let you in. They know the deal with Mckenna and Lily. Sam Perkins, my business partner, he's a good guy."

They shook hands and Jake clapped him on the back. Already they were bonding over their need to protect others. He'd taken his leave of Mckenna earlier, a lingering hug that spoke volumes, once she'd realized he was not changing his mind about his plans.

He watched Jake mount Thor behind Mckenna and Lily, wishing with all his might it could have been him. Finn carried Faraday, the baby and their extra supplies. He'd insisted on Jake riding his horse to get them to safety sooner. Didn't mean it didn't hurt to watch him take his place, even though it was the right thing to do. The right thing wasn't always easy.

He waved at them, his final view of his small band haunting as they rode away. He then stiffened his spine and strode back down the way they had come, stepping through banks of drifts that reached his knees at times. It was going to be a long slog and many hours before he could hope to be reunited with Mckenna. He needed to keep his spirits up, thinking of their reunion once the danger had passed. It was all he had, but it was more than enough.

TWENTY-EIGHT
MCKENNA

Day 5: Near Golden, Alaska
  5:27 p.m.

They had been traveling for hours, while all Mckenna could think about was Connor headed in the wrong direction, away from them. She hated what was happening. His need to protect her and Lily by going after the enemy. All her fault. Her bad choices in life had led to this moment. If they all lived through this, she was going to make sure she made it up to him.

She was in physical pain as well, which she pushed aside. She hated being weak, wanting her damn leg to heal already. The cold at least numbed it some. A sudden sharp series of cries alerted her to the baby and she glanced over her shoulder to see Faraday busy trying to soothe the tiny bundle, her face contorted with concern as she crooned to her.

"Why is the baby crying so much, Mommy? Is she okay?" Lily asked.

"I think we'd better take a short break," Jake said, pulling up on Thor's reins.

Jake helped her to dismount and handed her the crutches.

"How much farther is it?" she asked, watching him help Lily down.

"We made good time. Another hour or so. It's good that we'll get there before dark. Be nice not to have to camp out again. Ben has a good place. We might even be able to have hot showers. He's totally off grid with no need for the modern world. Keep in mind he can be a little grumpy, nothing personal. He just looks at the world a little differently than most."

"A hot shower sounds like heaven." She pretended it would make up for how difficult the situation was. And everyone had a right to be a bit grumpy in these desperate times. The not knowing anything about how it was going for Connor was making her feel edgy and frustrated as well. *Please keep him safe.*

"He'll be fine," Jake said like he could read her mind. "He's a good man to have in a crisis."

"Yeah, one of my own making."

"You didn't ask the world to fall apart, right?"

She shook her head. "God, no."

"Then quit beating yourself up over things you have no control over. And if you're thinking the situation with Luther is on you, it's not. Men like Luther are the ones to blame."

Jake strode off to help Faraday dismount, careful to hold the baby properly. She had gotten lucky. Two men who championed her. Would it be enough with all the bad men lined up against them? It had to be.

She followed Jake, and with Lily clinging to her side,

stayed careful not to jar the little girl. This had to end soon. If not for her sake, then for her daughter's.

Eve was still wailing and Lily covered her ears when they moved alongside the others.

"I think she's running a slight fever," Faraday said, her face tense with worry.

"Then the sooner we get her to Ben's, the better. She needs a proper bath, to be inside and warm, not traveling all over the place," Jake said, furrows lining his forehead. "Let's make this quick. Feed and change her. Then we'll head off."

They made quick work of it, consuming a quick meal of protein bars and water while Faraday fed and changed the baby. Mckenna stood by helplessly, wishing she could assist more, but she needed both hands to hold the crutches in place and there was no other way to get it done quickly, no changing table to prop herself against.

An eerie sound pierced the stillness. Wolves again. She looked around nervously, remembering the attack back at Jake's place the night they arrived. Lily tightened her hold on her leg and she could feel her small body trembling.

"Okay. Let's go," Jake urged, escorting them over to the horses. "We're almost there."

It was a tense ride through the forest growing more thickly now, the canopy overhead providing for coverage of the ground, causing the amount of snow to plow through to decrease. Then as they turned on a slight bend in the trail, it happened. A terrifying crack of thunder and the top of one of the jack pines slammed to the ground not ten feet in front of them. Loch came to an abrupt halt and reared up on his hind legs at the disturbing noise, his hooves clamoring for purchase on the icy ground.

Mckenna was thrown back against Jake. Lily screamed in fear as she held onto her mother for dear life. Then there were falling in space, unable to stop themselves as they plunged to the ground. She was dimly aware of Loch taking off running, Finn on his heels.

Dizzy and in pain, Mckenna tried to orient herself, her one thought being Lily. Was she okay? In the fall, her daughter had slipped from her arms, landing a few feet away. Jake had taken the brunt of the fall, and lay under her, not moving. She crawled off him and over to Lily, ignoring the pain in her leg, her heart feeling like it was going to burst.

"Lily. Are you okay?" she asked, careful to not move her daughter in case she had internal injuries.

"Mommy," Lily whimpered, her eyes wide. The sweetest sound in the world.

"Do you hurt anywhere?"

"My arm hurts."

"You stay still, okay. I'm going to check on Uncle Jake." She maneuvered herself around and crawled back to the lawman, the snow-covered icy trail chilling her to the bone.

He opened his eyes as she leaned over him and she breathed a sigh of relief. "You okay?"

"I think so. I'll know more when I try moving. Knocked the wind right out of me." He coughed and went to sit up. "Whoa, a bit dizzy." He held his head for a moment with both hands, then looked around frantically. "Where's Faraday and the baby?"

Mckenna pushed herself to her feet, hobbling on one leg. Loch had her crutches and was nowhere to be seen. Neither was Finn, Faraday or Eve.

"Oh no. They took off with the baby." The tree that had caused the calamity half-blocked the trail, leaving enough room for the two horses to go by single file. It was then she saw a small red patch in the snow, and realized blood was dripping off the side of the tree where a branch stuck out at a ninety-degree angle. Someone had hurt themselves. One of the horses or Faraday? Her throat tightened with worry.

Jake pushed himself to his feet and shook his head, grabbing at his middle with a wince. "Seems there are no broken bones, but my ribs are on fire. Might have cracked one or two in the fall. I'll go after them. You both wait here. Is Lily all right?"

"She's okay. Please, just find them. We'll wait here." Not like she could move easily with her damn leg. She'd need to find a sturdy walking stick to support herself while they waited.

Jake took off at a shambling trot, disappearing around the bend. How far had the horses gotten in the catastrophe? And when they were almost at their destination, too. Blatantly unfair to have it happen now, when a safe sanctuary beckoned. It made her want to rail at the world.

TWENTY-NINE
CONNOR

Day 5: Near Golden, Alaska
    6:12 p.m.

Connor kept a sharp eye out as he retraced their steps back toward Golden. Their trail was obvious on the snow-covered ground, the distinctive tracks of the horses and the men's boot prints. It didn't take a tracker with skills or insight to follow them.

He hoped he was wrong, that Luther hadn't chosen to come after them. Had he managed to find any other like-minded idiots willing to sell their souls for a crust of bread and a promise of a roof over their heads? He understood doing what it took to survive, but this vendetta against him was unconscionable. And Luther's drive to harm a woman to get what he wanted, beyond pure evil. For the first time he wished he had taken him out instead of sending him to trial. If he had not done the civilized thing and helped send him to jail for life, this would not be happening. His mother Anna had always questioned the dispensing of justice. Sometimes taking it into her own hands, by making the bad guys draw first, then taking the heat for it. A justified killing, she called it. If he'd done that, he'd still be with Mckenna, getting everyone to safety. He realized in the moment he felt closer to his mom than ever before, understood her more than he ever had. Forgave her for spending so much time away from him in an effort to right things in the world. *Mom, you and Dad were my heroes. I wish I could tell you now.*

He pushed the sadness of regret away and instead concentrated on getting the job done. The sounds of a motor or maybe two drew his rapt attention, a faint sound in the distance. Was it them? Had Luther somehow managed to arrange for transport? Yeah, probably stole what he needed. Was there any doubt it was them? No. Who else would be determined enough to follow them during a blizzard. If he was wrong, he'd beg forgiveness, but his gut screamed he had them dead to rights.

Connor moved into the bush at the side of the trail, seeking a good place to set up an ambush. He pulled a length of steel wire from his pocket and quickly fastened it around a tree, then hurried to the other side of the narrow path and tied it to a tree opposite the first one, winding the thin wire tightly around the trunk. Satisfied he had done what he could, he crouched down to watch proceedings, rifle held at the ready. The thin wire was hard to see in the snowy dimness of the forest and should take out somebody, giving him the edge of surprise. He could always cut the wire if he was wrong.

A few minutes later, his waiting paid off when two ATVs came into view, one following the other down the rough path, bouncing as they slammed into the ground and springing up again with all four wheels in the air. Idiots. They should have been taking it more slowly, watching for rocks and debris strewn in their path. Surprising they hadn't already broken the rear suspension and stranded themselves on the side of the road. They all wore black helmets except the huge brute of a man that he instantly recognized from the shootout at Jake's place with his scarred face. He'd hit the wire second. Too bad he wasn't driving. It would knock him off for certain.

Connor held his breath as the sleds raced ever closer, willing for them to reach the point of impact, appearing invisible a few feet away to the naked eye. Disable the first all-terrain vehicle and he was halfway home. Not wanting to count on things going his way for fear of the universe throwing him a curve ball, he waited, impatient to get on with things. Every second he was away from Mckenna and the group, more chances for something to happen he might have prevented could occur. He trusted Jake to have his back, but the two of them together were a stronger team than going it alone.

Then the roar of combustion motors came close enough he could observe the markings of the manufacturer on the vehicles. When the first one slammed into the wire, the moment of impact brought an image right out of a horror movie. The man's head was severed off completely by the thin wire as it hit right below his helmet, the guy being shorter than most. It had acted like a horizontal guillotine, killing him instantly. The unexpected sight sickened him even though he deemed it necessary. If they hadn't brought a war to his doorstep, he wouldn't have to take such desperate measures. The second person in line was also knocked off, though not beheaded. When the next pair of riders saw the collision, they veered off to the side, bumping through the forest before coming to rest against a tree, the ATV's tires spinning. The driver jumped off, then helped the passenger, a much smaller person who appeared either a youth or a female to disembark as well. They tore off into the bush.

Connor watched where they were headed before stepping out and checking on the huge man thrown from the sled. He was still alive, his eyes angry as he peered up at him, trying to orient himself. He made quick work of taking his weapons and tying his hands behind him before racing off after the escaping pair. Two down and two to go. The odds were moving in his favor, though not something to celebrate. A man was dead, a further burden to bear, another injured, and two more had run off, one of which was a killer, Luther. A man had to adapt to the law of the jungle to survive these perilous times while praying to keep his mortal soul.

The sound of a gunshot was followed by a high-pitched cry for help, piercing the stillness. The woman must have fallen or hurt herself. He pushed himself to move quicker, stumbling over fallen trees buried in the snow until he came upon a body lying in the snow. The female was lying on the ground, weeping and in pain, her face covered with tears.

"Please help me. He shot me. I'm bleeding. My shoulder, it hurts bad."

Connor caught a glimpse of black fabric off in the distance as Luther vanished from view. Damn it all to hell! The bastard had shot the woman to slow him down, knowing he'd feel honor bound to help. What kind of monster does such a despicable thing? He had to remember at all times who he was dealing with. An evil man who would stop at nothing to achieve his nefarious aims.

He let his anger fuel him while he checked on the female's injuries, helping her off with her helmet and then opening her suit enough to check on the source of the blood. She was shot through the right shoulder; the bullet thankfully having exited out the back. No bullet to dig out, though the wound was large enough to cause him concern. Of all times for her to get shot, with no hospital or medical help on standby.

"What were you doing with Luther Meech anyway?" he asked, his anger at the young woman for being there and stopping him from ending things with the bastard spilling over. He needed to finish things with Luther to make certain of Mckenna and Lily being safe in the future. He packed the wound with a length of gauze from a small first aid kit he'd pulled from his jacket pocket. Then opened a bandage and pressed it onto her skin, adding one more to her back. It would have to do for now.

"No choice. He insisted I had to come with him or someone else was going to break into the house my roommate and I shared. Kill me or worse. I wanted to get away a few times, but they wouldn't let me. I'm sorry I'm such a bother. Am I going to be okay?"

She was a very pretty girl, almost startlingly so, making him understand the reason why she'd been taken. He inwardly sighed as realization crept in. None of this was her fault. More collateral damage in the wake of Luther Meech.

"Yes, you'll be fine," he reassured her, though without proper medical care an infection could easily take hold. No reason to alarm her more than she already was.

"We'll need to stitch it up. I'm headed to a place where we can get help. Can you walk?"

"I think so."

He assisted her to her feet, then let her lean against him to get her bearings. What to do about the man waiting at the accident site? His first instinct was to kill him.

"What's your name?"

"Hope Bredeson. You're Connor Hale, right?" She winced in pain but gamely kept moving through the snowpack. "I heard them talking about you. They really wanted to take you out. What did you do to them?" The accusation was clear in her voice and he had to tamp down his anger again.

"My testimony sent Luther to jail for killing his wife and another woman. He burned them while they were still alive."

His answer made the woman stumble and stop walking. Her eyes filled with horror at the stark facts. "I'm lucky to be alive."

"He wanted you alive to slow me down."

"I'm sorry. I had no idea. You wanted to get him. He said he'd been pardoned. I didn't really believe it, but to think…"

"No. He's an escaped prisoner. A murderer on the loose."

Hope stopped talking and they made their way back to the ATVs in silence. The big man was missing, first thing Connor noticed as he glanced around the accident scene. He let out an expletive. Then he saw the blood on the ground and knew the man had been hurt, badly by the look of the amount of it sprayed on the ground. He must have coughed it up before cutting himself free. Other blood spots and the bloody rope told the rest of the tale. He'd likely die anyway of exposure, hurt internally. Well, it couldn't be helped. He had to get a move on and rejoin his group.

He hoped one of the ATVs was still functioning. The one that had ended up slamming into the tree didn't look promising, its front end crumpled, so he tried starting the one the two men had been on. When the motor sprang to life, he allowed himself a moment of exhilaration.

When he turned to deal with getting Hope aboard, he found her staring at the decapitated body of the man hit by the wire, her hand pressed to her mouth. Then she began to puke, her body shuddering between bouts. When the final spasm stopped, he approached her. He studiously led her over to the waiting vehicle and helped her on. With any luck they could make good time now, joining the others before too long. He prayed everyone was safe, refusing to accept any other scenario.

THIRTY
MCKENNA

Day 5: Near Golden, Alaska
   7:45 p.m.

The wait for Jake and the others to get back was intolerable. Were Faraday and baby Eve okay? Jake was injured which further worried Mckenna. She'd managed to find a long enough stick to support herself. Maybe she should follow him? But how could see leave Lily alone or take her with her? They could get lost, a fate she shuddered to imagine.

Just when she thought it couldn't get any worse, it did, every time. Was this all people had to look forward to? Ever escalating danger. Too many unknowns were beginning to paralyze her, unsure of what to do next, a feeling that did not sit right with her.

A slight noise in the bush drew her attention away from her endless worrying. She placed one gloved hand over Lily's mouth, and leaning down, whispered in her ear. "We need to stay quiet, okay princess?" She could only hope Loch would keep quiet as well. The stallion had turned up a few minutes ago coming through the forest as if nothing had happened, alone, unfortunately. He was standing nearby like a sentinel, calm now.

Lily nodded her small head, her eyes widened by the warning.

A sense of some presence being nearby made the hair on her neck stand up. Who was out there? Friend, animal or enemy?

She reached for her Glock, pulling it from its holster and carefully held it in her two hands, waiting for any movement. Lily stuck by her side; her small hands wrapped around her thigh. No time to hide her, she had to stand her ground.

Then a slight shadow, a hint of movement before a tall, thinnish man emerged through the trees. He also held a gun, an impressive rifle at the ready, his expression inscrutable. A thick red bushy Viking beard adorned his chin reaching a third of the way down his chest, like he'd stepped out of another century. His light blue eyes had a chilling quality to them while his red, roughened skin told a tale of harsh conditions.

They stared at one another and she caught his eyes flitting to her young daughter. "You alone?"

"No. There's lots of us. Even an air marshal. If you hurt us, he will go after you. Kill you most likely." She kept her weapon pointed at him as she made her position clear. At least he hadn't shot her first, then asked questions.

"You said air marshal. What's his name?"

"Jake Dillion."

The man grunted and lowered his rifle with a curt nod. "All right then. I was checking out my trapline and heard a commotion. What happened?"

Saying he meant no harm and meaning it were two different things. "Who are you?"

"Lady, who are you?"

When she didn't answer he shook his head like he was dealing with an idiot. "Ben Carter. I assume you were headed to my place when something occurred?"

A familiar name. She lowered her gun but held on to it, eyeing him warily. "Yeah, Jake said you lived up this way. Off the grid."

"What happened?" He pointed over at the missing top of the nearby tree and the blood staining the snow. "Aw, looks like another jack pine wanted a widow notch on its trunk."

"The fall, it spooked one of the horses. One with a young woman, Faraday, carrying a newborn baby. Jake ran after them. He's injured as well. Hurt his ribs when I fell on him."

The man's frown deepened. "Stay here," he ordered.

The man had no bedside manner, but she kept her thoughts to herself as she watched the man jog off around the tree top half-blocking the way forward and down the path after Jake and the missing members of their party. At least he was willing to help and left her with Loch for company.

Lily tugged at her pant leg. "I have to go potty."

Mckenna spent the next few minutes dealing with her daughter. She handed her a cookie Lily and Claire had made, realizing her mistake when Lily stared at it. "Where is Aunt Claire?"

"She had to go home. She had others who needed her help."

"Okay." Lily began to eat the cookie. "She makes good cookies. I hope she makes more."

Mckenna swallowed her grief, blinking the rush of tears away. "I'm sure she will, princess, wherever she is."

She needed to rally herself again and stop being a damn victim to circumstance. Others were picking up the slack, like Ben Carter who she'd just met. She'd gotten them out of Mexico for heaven's sake. Maybe they should head back and look for Connor? Two men were involved with helping Faraday and the baby. They didn't want or need her like Connor might. She had a gun for protection and a good horse to ride. She saw Loch coming back as a good sign now, to give her a way forward. What if Connor needed help dealing with Luther? Her presence might make all the difference. At least she would have tried, not stood around waiting. He'd do the same for her in a heartbeat.

Mind made up she scooped up her daughter and placed her on Loch, then eased herself up and into the saddle, carefully as she could with her hurt leg though it did seem to be getting better. Placing the makeshift crutch in the scabbard—it could also double as a weapon —she took up the reins and urged the horse back in the direction they had come. Time to go on the offense. She had a lot to atone for, pulling others into her sphere of danger, at least she could do her part. An old quote by a man called William Jennings Bryan came to mind. *Destiny is not a matter of chance; it is a matter of choice. It is not a thing to be waited for, it is a thing to be achieved.* The words gave hope for not becoming a victim, but a person taking charge of their life. Like she had finally done in Mexico.

They made their way down the trail, Mckenna alert for any trouble. There were still a few hours until darkness. Maybe they could reach Connor before then. They could travel back together. They were close to Ben

Carter's place. Surely, they could find it now or the others would find them at some point. She was less concerned about it than the immediate concern of helping Connor.

He'd come so far to help her, left his beloved ranch to be at her side. Seeing him again, after all these years, it was like they'd never been apart, the intervening years falling away like leaves in autumn exposing the sturdy trunk, roots and branches that kept it standing strong. Yes, they were wiser now, hopefully, but still the same teenagers that had fallen in love all those years ago. Though he'd never asked her to marry him, they were too young when they parted, it felt a given between them at some point in the future. Some things there was no need to speak of. She was certain he felt the same. Connor's eyes still held the same look for her as then as she knew hers did for him. Adoration. No other word for it. If they survived the current state of the world, and she would do everything in her power to make it happen, adapting as they went along, then she'd do her level best to create a good future for the three of them and their extended family that seemed to be including more people all the time. Faraday and Eve would most likely stay with them. She'd do everything in her power to ensure they all survived. One day at a time. And right now, her focus was clear. She urged Loch to a quicker gait, her impatience to get back to where they had left Connor pressing on her.

THIRTY-ONE
LUTHER

Day 5: Near Golden, Alaska
   8:15 p.m.

Luther's blood boiled with a rage he'd never experienced before in his forty-one years. The urgent need to tear something apart with his bare hands fixated him on one man. Connor Hale. Not only had he been the cause of his incarceration, he could have beat the rap if he hadn't snitched on him, but now he was on foot again minus his leverage with Diego. And he'd lost his new squeeze. God, how he'd love to beat that handsome, self-righteous, smug face to a bloody pulp before stringing him up on the nearest tree. A good old-fashioned lynching, that was what was needed.

"I swear I will see that man destroyed before I die." He shook his fist at the darkening sky as he spoke the words out loud. It was then that he noticed the change. The stench of smoke in the air was growing stronger from the south. More fires. And no one to put them out.

With so many planes and personal hovercrafts in the air when the EMP event occurred, approximately 18,000 to 23,000 of commercial vehicles alone at any given time, fires would have sprung up all over the country. And without electricity, there was no way or means to pump water to fight them. Good, let it burn. The more chaos, the more men would rally around him for guidance in how to survive turbulent times.

He plowed his way through the accumulated drifts from the recent snowstorm, barely noticing with his wired energy, his sights set on making his nemesis pay the ultimate price. Luther used the seething anger to fuel him for the journey, planning as he went. Soon he'd be back in Anchor where he'd rally his troops and storm Braveheart, catch them all by surprise. Steal the one thing the bastard most loved. His ranch.

When the town of Golden finally came into sight many hours later, he was calmer, though not completely out of steam even after the long hike. He needed to contact Diego, catch him up to date on the situation. He had been assured he was on his way with his soldiers, soon to arrive in Golden in search of his bitch of a wife. Once he was, they could team up and take over the entire county. Men like him would be in high demand now. Not those following the rule of manmade law, but the outlaws willing to step up their game and see the world without rose-colored glasses, but as it actually was: ruthless and with everything up for the taking. He might have had a small setback, but it was also a learning experience. He'd never underestimate his opponent again. Easy enough. He just needed more firepower. And he knew exactly where to get what he needed. Joe had more shit stashed than a junkyard rat.

THIRTY-TWO
CONNOR

Day 5: Near Golden, Alaska
   9:37 p.m.

The new mode of travel by ATV was welcomed and Connor and his passenger made good time down the trail hoping to join the others in short order. He'd given her a brief explanation of circumstances before they'd headed off. The woman was now holding on for dear life behind him, though he could hear an occasional moan as they hit larger debris strewn in their path, hidden by the fresh covering of snow. He couldn't afford to stop and give her the rest she most likely was hoping for. No, not until they found his group and he had help and supplies necessary for her medical treatment. He'd stitched up more than a few wounds in his time. Sure, they might not be as fine a stitch as a plastic surgeon, but he had a competent, steady hand. His survival business included some fine pointers on emergency medical care. He also recommended they take additional training. As much as possible. When the world falls apart, there's no one to call upon guaranteed to come to your aid. Self-reliance was a no-brainer.

It was then he caught sight of Loch coming toward them around a bend in the trail, Mckenna and Lily astride the proud stallion. What were they doing separated from the others? He braked quickly, his nerves on edge at seeing the pair of them by themselves. He left the vehicle idling as he hopped off, Hope still onboard.

"Wait here," he said.

Loch drew close enough Connor could grab his reins. "What happened? Where are the others?" His worry for the baby and Faraday grabbed him by the throat.

"I came to find you. There was an accident, a tree topped itself, and Finn ran off with Faraday and Eve. Jake's looking for them. Then Ben Carter came along and chased after them on foot."

All Mckenna's words came out in a headlong rush.

"Anybody hurt?"

"Jake said he cracked some ribs and there was blood on a tree branch. I don't know whose. Loch came back on his own accord and that's when I decided to come looking for you. To offer my help."

Connor shook his head, his mouth grim. "You shouldn't have done that. You might have been hurt. Again. As it was, Luther shot the young woman over there." He pointed to the ATV.

"I'm not going to hide while the men do all the dirty work. I got us out of Mexico, I can darn well help others now." Her beautiful eyes glinted with sparks as she spoke her piece and kept on going. "I can shoot, I'm sturdy, I know how to survive. I'm not some pathetic little mouse that needs to hide out under a leaf in the corner and let others take the flack for me. I killed a woman, Connor, and I would do it again to save my daughter's life."

"No, I can see that." Her vehement spiel took him aback while it was readily apparent how much taking a life had cost her, the pain evident in her eyes as they glazed over with the confession. While his anger drained away, it was replaced instantly by worry. Was she now going to place herself front and center in every dangerous circumstance? No, he couldn't have that either, much as he was struck by her spunk in a difficult situation. It would only interfere with his need to keep her safe. He made a quick decision to make sure she understood his position. "Doesn't change anything. I can't do my job of protecting everyone if I'm worrying about making sure you're doing the right thing, being where I expect you to be and not getting yourself into more trouble when you don't follow orders."

Mckenna glared at him. No help for it. He needed to make his position clear much as she did. It was a definite bump in the road and he felt unprepared for the fallout. But he had to try again, even though time was of the essence.

"I am who I am, Mckenna. I can't change that just because you're back." He wouldn't apologize; this was too important. Even for her he couldn't deny who he was. Just as he didn't expect her to give up on her ethics. But placing herself in danger, that was a game changer.

"Neither can I."

Damn it, a stalemate, and the clock was ticking.

"There's no more time for this. The young woman on the ATV, Hope, she's been shot and we need to get her to this Ben Carter's so I can sew her up."

"Oh, I'm sorry, is she going to be okay? Where was she shot?"

"In the shoulder. Turn around, I'll follow you." Connor hurried back to the all-terrain vehicle and got into the driver's seat. "How are you doing?"

"Do you have any aspirin or something for the pain?"

He took a moment to reach in his pocket and haul out a small container and a bottle of water. He shook a couple into her hand. She swallowed them and drank a few gulps. "Thanks."

"Is it very far now?" Hope's voice sounded exhausted and her eyes had dark shadows under them. She was also shivering. He worried shock was settling in. He needed to get her to safety and deal with her injury as quickly as possible.

"A few miles. There was an accident with one of the horses. I don't know the outcome." Worry for the tiny baby and Faraday ate at him. They needed to move. Now. Mckenna had already maneuvered Loch around and they were headed back the way they came now. He prayed Loch would keep his footing on the treacherous path. Why she had decided to come back and put herself into peril was beyond him. How was he going to live with the knowledge she would take such chances? He pushed his thought aside with great difficulty, knowing he needed to concentrate on what was right in front of him. At least for now. But the sooner they got back to Braveheart, the better.

The journey was bringing out characteristics in people he wasn't prepared for, had never dealt with though he had long imagined them, and there was no time for the luxury of long discussions on what needed doing. As long as their very survival depended on split-second decisions, there could be no time for tending to delicate sensibilities or egos. He understood that people were changing by the hour, either able to grasp the realities of the new world they'd been given no choice but to deal with or incapable of it. But there could only be one leader. Otherwise, chaos would rein and everything would be lost when others didn't do what was expected of them. But with everyone doing their part, they stood a chance at least. No, he was right. Mckenna would understand in time. A small voice from the back of his brain offered the unwelcomed advice that Anna Hale, his own mother, would have done the same.

THIRTY-THREE
CHEYANNE

Day 5: Braveheart Horse Ranch
  9:45 p.m.

"Time to turn in. There's lots to do in the morning and I don't want anyone not doing their fair share because they're tired or being cranky because of lack of sleep. Ty, you can have the sofa for the night. Cheyanne, get him fresh sheets," her grandma said, raising herself out of her rocking chair with a sigh. Cheyanne glanced at her grandma, noticing for the first time she looked old, tired even as she felt a swell of anger at her comment about everyone not doing enough. Did she mean her? Guilt at slacking off today was immediately followed by the counterattack that she did more than that stupid Brandi ever did. Way more than her. The woman was always worried about breaking a precious nail, though Mckenna secretly envied her the gorgeous manicure with the inset diamond nail art.

She pushed her anger away and instead focused on

Ty who sat on the sofa pressed up against her. Just the mere fact he was here was helping. They hadn't had much of a chance to speak today yet with so much going on, people coming in and out and complaining about the weather all the damn time. Then those awful twin boys coming in and messing up the house and she was asked to babysit because Laura had something too important to do that couldn't wait. They were her kids, for crying out loud. Pains in the rear end, more like it. She had yet to share the good news with her boyfriend.

Ty whispered in her ear. "Soon as they go to bed, come back out and we can talk. If you catch my drift." He lightly licked her ear with his wet tongue and the sensation slithered down her spine. But sex was the last thing on her mind. And it did feel wrong in her grandparents' house. What if they got caught? Talking she could explain away. Lovemaking, not so much.

"I'll get those sheets." Cheyanne jumped to her feet and scurried down the hallway after her grandma to the linen closet. Her grandpa and Luke followed her, leaving Ty alone in the living room. Her brother immediately vanished into his bedroom.

"You remember whose house you are in, Cheyanne. Don't be doing anything stupid. That boy is out of here in the morning," her grandpa warned before closing the door in her face.

Angry at being held accountable for something she hadn't even done yet and didn't really feel like doing anyway if she were being honest, feeling bloated from being pregnant, she opened the linen cupboard. She took out clean sheets, a pillow, and a blanket, then slammed it hard, making her point.

She slipped back into the living room and piled the bedding on an empty chair.

Ty got to his feet and came up behind her and embraced her, his hands reaching for her breasts. When he gave them a few rough caresses, she grunted in pain. One of the first signs to alert her to her going to have a baby was how overly sensitive her breasts were, swollen and painful to the touch.

"What's the matter? You liked it last time we were together, always begging for it."

"Ty, I have something to tell you. We need to sit down."

"What? You're scaring me, babe. I was only wanting to get closer to you. It's been too long since we had any fun." Ty's face morphed into the expression she least liked. Put upon like he deserved more and was being left out.

"We'll have fun again, I promise. I just need you to know something and it can't wait. I have to get out of here." She windmilled her arms around for emphasis.

"You mean away from this house? Your grandparents?"

"Yes. Because they're going to know something soon and it's going to make them really angry. I'll be grounded for life. I can't take this place anymore. All we do is work. I want us to have our own place."

"Sure, babe," He went back to nuzzling her neck and rubbing her boobs, though less vigorously now.

She pulled away. "I'm pregnant, Ty. We're going to have a baby. Are you happy about it?"

The stunned expression on her boyfriend's face did not bode well and Cheyanne went silent waiting for him to say something. Then he blinked a few times, his lips curving upward.

"Hell yeah. A kid. Wow, I'm going to be a dad. Cool."

Cheyanne let out a breath. It was going to be okay.

Excitement and relief raced through her veins, a potent mix, making her feel high and calm all at the same time. One step closer to freedom.

"I bet your dad's gonna like this. He loves kids. Always talking about getting his own back. Does he know yet?"

"No, no one except Luke, and he promised not to tell."

"Doesn't mean we can't have a little fun, right?" He reached for her again, his expression shifting back into his earlier mode. "You don't show or anything. We can still do it, right? Pregnant ladies can still have sex?"

Last thing she felt like at the moment was lovemaking. She sighed, then came up with a compromise. "We can make it all about you, if you like. My tummy's feeling a bit off." Anything to speed things up and not get caught. The method she was suggesting was guaranteed to take two minutes, tops. *Stay in control, princess.* More words from her father came to mind. *You're not given power in this world; you have to take power.*

Her promise had him pulling her over to the sofa, finally sitting down like she'd wanted earlier. She took charge and in record time the deed was done. She settled back on the sofa as Ty adjusted himself. "Now we need to discuss the plan. Did my father ask you to come?"

"No. I made the decision. I needed to see you. Things are bad in town, babe. I mean, really bad. It's worse than I said earlier. I think tomorrow or the next day a group led by Mayor Hazzard is headed this way. And they're not going to take no for an answer."

"Where's my father? Is he going to protect us?"

"Here's the thing. One of his guys from the new camp Luther is establishing up north, came into town looking for supplies and we ran into each other. He said Luther was headed to Golden. That's why I came. He won't be back in time to help. You gotta talk your grandparents into letting me stay. Especially now after what you just told me. I still can't believe you're gonna have my kid."

"Our kid. Maybe we should head out. It would be safer than staying here waiting for those crazy people to come with their pitchforks and shit." Cheyanne didn't much care for people. All they did was let you down. Never sticking around. Only her dad really wanted her. Her grandparents were given no choice but to take her and Luke in. But she could tell it was an imposition; they weren't loved unconditionally, at least she wasn't. With Luke it was different, everybody loved him. Didn't she always have to do chores to earn anything from them? A slight nod of approval if she was lucky from her grandpa.

"You mean leave Braveheart?"

"Yeah, go to this camp my dad has established. I got the walkie-talkies he asked for hidden in my bedroom. We could steal a couple of horses, heck, maybe take a string of them, and head there. Horses are like gold now. Then when my dad gets back, we're already there. He doesn't have to waste time coming and getting us. He already tried rescuing me and Luke once, but Sam Perkins put the kibosh on it." She didn't mention she also had the key to getting them outside the gate. Something stopped her. Before she could give it any more thought, Ty spoke up again.

"Figures. The man's a freakin' despot." Ty's lip curled up in disdain. "Maybe that could work. Get out of here in the middle of the night and take what we want with us. Not like this group will ever use all the stuff they've put aside. The storm's over anyway so it won't be too hard a trip."

She could see the excitement growing, his eyes

lighting up with intent. Yes. This was more like it. Finally, her life was falling into place.

"I'll make up your bed and then we should go to sleep."

"There's room for two," he suggested, his eyebrows wagging again.

She held onto her patience with difficulty, smiling to hide her chagrin. "It's only for a few hours, Ty. I don't want my grandparents getting pissed off and doing something stupid like locking me in my room. Plus, I need to get some sleep if we're going to get up earlier than them. Grandma gets up so damn early." Cheyanne hated getting up in the morning. Her brain couldn't even function before noon. Maybe it would be better to leave right now instead? No, they had to wait until the wee hours of the morning when everyone was dead asleep.

"Fine. But you need to make it up to me, babe, once we're together full time."

"Sure, you know I will." She kissed him, then hurried out of the room, wanting time alone to think about how awesome her life had changed for the better in the space of a few hours.

She'd leave Braveheart in the dust, stealing whatever they damn well wanted. *Take that, Connor Hale, and stick it up your lying, cheating ass.* She'd never stop blaming him for her father being sent to jail, no matter what he said. But she was too happy now to stay focused on his betrayal, instead thinking of getting away and setting up their own place. She and Ty and the baby were going to have a good life, with her father's help of course. She was his princess after all.

THIRTY-FOUR
EASTWOOD

Day 5: Near Winnipeg, Manitoba, Canada
   11:00 p.m.

Eastwood felt Celia's eyes on him and he turned around to find her as expected, peering at him with her lovely emerald-green eyes, her face framed with a wealth of natural blond hair arranged attractively around her flawless features. One exception was a tiny freckle on one rounded cheek, a dot he found he enjoyed kissing for some reason. Odd, since he did not normally accept flaws.

Celia had been following this same routine for the past two days since he'd rescued her and Arthur near Detroit, averaging seven minutes an hour observing him. Of course, baby Arthur averaged far more. Thirty-three and a half minutes, leaving a small window of time for her to eat, take care of her human needs and his. He wasn't including the seven hours set aside for sleeping, as he was still coming to grips with the most annoying weakness of the human race: the need to waste many hours of the day in rest. But say what you would about humans, when genetics set it up correctly, things of wondrous beauty could emerge. His Celia was a prime example. And for an even weaker member of the race, Arthur was proving himself to be a fine example as well, never crying unnecessarily or spitting up his meals.

And as expected, she asked another question. She looked so desirable in her new style of dresses he'd found for her back in Chicago. Feminine and pretty, they also allowed easy access and yet coverage to keep prying eyes at bay. As he waited for to speak, he realized how much he appreciated these moments, enjoying the quirks of her mind far more than he thought possible. Her agile brain changed topics regularly, and he enjoyed sharing information on a variety of subjects, from his explanations for how the human body functioned at its ultimate peak level to the origins of the human race on planet Earth. As his answers were succinct, she had begun pressing *him* more and more for information, obviously enjoying her human computer-like companion. His only concern was she beginning to realize he knew far too much to be a human being? That no homo sapiens could possibly house such an endless wealth of knowledge that grew by the second as the world shifted and changed in real time. A hundred and fifty years ago mankind could carry most of the history of what was known at the time in their brains, but no more, it had grown to the extent it was impossible. While he was connected to the knowledge base of *everything*. A whale of an advantage he appreciated.

"When you were in Washington, you said you had access to privileged information, more even than President MacDonald. With all you know, I mean I've never met anyone who knew even a fraction of what you have accumulated in that big awesome brain of yours, surely you could now be of more help in Washington fixing what is wrong with the world? Help people get their lives back? I mean, people have suffered so much already, losing fathers and mothers, sons and daughters, sisters and brothers, not to mention friends. If you could figure out a way to speed up making generators to provide electricity, ways to increase food production, help with health care and education, imagine what it would mean. You would go down in the annuals of history as the man who saved the world."

Eastwood sat patiently, waiting for the end of her passionate spiel. He enjoyed sparring with her and had his answer already prepared. "Do you think humans have been helping this planet become healthier and more peaceful since their arrival on Earth three hundred thousand years ago? Why would I want to make it easier and more efficient for them to recover and start doing the same negative things they did before to this planet and each other all over again? Humans don't learn another way, don't experience change without it being hammered into their feeble brains. Years of chaos is essential for a proper reboot later. Even then, they will have to be monitored carefully to prevent a similar situation from reemerging. In the meantime—" He stopped talking. For some odd reason Celia's eyes had glazed over and her mouth had gone slack. Not in boredom, she was never bored by him, but something else entirely.

He moved closer and discovered she wasn't breathing, her chest not rising rhythmically as usual. Alarmed, he checked her pulse and found it to be thready, barely noticeable under his fingertips pressed to her common carotid artery. What was wrong? His mind raced through possible scenarios, settling on brain aneurysm as the most likely cause in a split second. His own heart rate rose higher as adrenaline surged through his system. He had to act immediately to prevent the subarachnoid hemorrhage from damaging her precious memory and eyesight. Her very life was at risk. It was unacceptable.

"Stop the Cannon! I need to access the medical kit right now!" The bot driver slammed his boot down on Cannon's brakes. He did it a bit quicker than Eastwood would have liked and everyone inside the Cannon lurched ahead before swaying backward into their seats as the bot he'd named Jesse James pulled to a stop in the middle of the road. He braced Celia's head so not to add whiplash to her injuries. Arthur was well protected in his backward carrier cocoon, while the military bots were not affected by such trivial events. He felt his own brain get shook up slightly and decided he'd better not react quite so emotionally in the future. Ten extra seconds to pull the vehicle safely to the side of the road would save a concussion. He hadn't realized until that moment how very much he was enjoying his human companion for far more than just her beauty, causing him to make the slight miscalculation. He was also about to use some of his most precious resources to save her life, a surprise to him as well. One he didn't have the luxury to peruse at the moment.

Eastwood twisted in his seat and yanked open the medical kit. In seconds he had his hands on what was required. An injection of nanobots. He lined up the pneumatic syringe on her right inner arm and sent the lifesavers deep inside her body where they would go to work immediately. They would need time to work while she slept, but he'd gotten them in soon enough there should be no brain damage. Best nanobots money *couldn't buy* as only Eastwood knew how to create them. And he wasn't selling them anytime soon. Humans didn't even know they existed of this high a quality. Though the creation of antimatter at sixty trillion a gram was certainly far more expensive to produce and immensely more practical as well with enough power available to restart civilization, if one so wished. But now was not the time. Human beings were going to need to learn a thing or two first.

He pondered again how much his interactions with the female human were affecting his thought processes, his judgment. He'd just done something unthinkable forty-eight hours ago by deploying precious resources to save her life. The part he was most surprised by, he'd done it instinctively, without due process of weighing the pros and cons. Instead, he'd experienced something unexpected. Something that now made him understand the human race more than he ever had before in theory. The irony was not lost on him. He'd always thought humans too emotional, incapable of making intelligent decisions under pressure. Hmm. So having a human being in close proximity was affecting him, something he was reluctant, but in the interests of retaining proper data for his mainframe back in Washington, DC, should admit to. No real need to confess it was anything more than it could be written off as a matter of convenience. Looking for a new human companion as comparable as Celia would take time, time he didn't want to waste. Not with life opening up with endless possibilities.

For the next hour as Celia slept snuggled next to him, he kept a close watch on her, observing her color slowly return to normal, making her smooth skin remind him of the finest porcelain fill again with the palest pink hue, her lips cherry red. Yes, her fragile beauty tugged at his heart while her sharp intellect, honed from having to make her own way in the world, street smarts some would call it, had him admiring her courage and strength. Perhaps humans in the outside world had more to be appreciated than those closeted in the corridors of power? Only time could bear witness to the testable theory.

THIRTY-FIVE
MCKENNA

Day 5: Near Golden, Alaska
   11:11 p.m.

The ride back to where the others had been left was difficult, mostly because her mind couldn't seem to focus on anything other than the recent argument she'd had with Connor. Or perhaps it was a defensive move not to be consumed by worry for the newborn baby she was helpless to do anything about. It had broadsided her, their disagreement. It seemed a foolish thing to be over-thinking something so mundane in the craziness they now found themselves mired in and she berated herself even as she pondered what had happened. She wasn't certain if she was most angry at him for his disregard for her ability to make sound judgments or his obvious need to protect her. Didn't he realize no one should have to be the only one thinking they had to be the sole person to keep everyone safe? It was far too big a burden for any one man or woman to carry, and others should share in the helping to deal with the realities of how things stood now, not let it all fall to Connor.

But his point about keeping to a plan was a fair judgment. Everyone should know where each person in their group was at any given time. But was it even possible now to keep to a plan? Flexibility was likely to be a key feature of any advance into the future. Hadn't she already proved how well she could adapt to changing times? She'd killed a woman, something unthinkable in the old world. It still filled her with a terrible sense of loss and pain. At times it was impossible to believe she'd been pushed into doing such a thing. If only it could have been different. But it also proved she had what it took to be a survivor. Because that's what it boiled down to now. What were you capable of doing to live another day.

Loch gave a sharp whinny, drawing her attention. Mckenna took a look around and realized they were back at the site of the original accident. The time had passed quickly in her agitation and worrying over things. She patted the horse's neck and waited for Connor to pull up behind them on the trail.

When Connor came up to speak with them, she avoided looking at him directly, not certain she wanted to see condemnation in his eyes after their incredibly warm reunion. "This is where the accident occurred," she said instead, pointing out the fallen tree top and the blood on the broken branch.

"We need to get Hope to Ben Carter's place. I'll move the tree out of the path and we'll continue on. Maybe we'll run into them."

No one spoke aloud their worst worry in the moment. Were Faraday and baby Eve all right?

In short order, Connor had moved the tree top off

the path, allowing them to pass safely. It couldn't be far to Ben's now. Jake had said about an hour, if she remembered correctly.

She watched Connor stride by and regain the driver's seat on the ATV out of the corner of her eye. Then she nudged Loch and they continued to follow the path. Not knowing exactly where Ben's place was ratcheted up her worry. She had never missed personal hovercraft more than now, remembering how easy it was to rise above the earth and get a clearer picture of things on the ground. Sure, airspaces were normally crowded until the day everything fell to earth. And how many had died instantly upon impact on Friday, May 23, 2055, a day no doubt to go down in the annuals of history? A devastating thought she tried not to focus on. But the possibility of discovering something had happened to Finn and his precious cargo hit the hardest. For as it had always been, statistics meant nothing, only those in your own circle made sense of events. *Please, God, don't let it be the case.*

The quiet of the darkening forest now that the sun had slipped below the tree line was not soothing as Loch continued to carry her and Lily down the snow-packed trail. She wished they could just get to their destination already. The unknowns were killing her. Her leg had begun to ache in earnest and her stomach rumbled. She had to remind herself so many others were in far dire straits to keep from feeling sorry for herself. She hugged Lily closer to keep her warm only to realize her little girl had fallen fast asleep in her arms. This was no life for a child. She had to figure things out better. Lily was counting on her.

———

Diego picked up the headset from the gesturing soldier in charge of the HAM radio and listened in to the message being relayed. As the words registered, a wide grin split his mug in two. Luther had come through for him. Found the bitch. If only he had his hands around her neck right now, he'd make her pay. Soon, he assured himself, he'd be there in person to show her who was in charge. He stepped away from the soldier, who went immediately back to working with the device, and poured himself a stiff shot of tequila to toast the hour.

Luther Meech was ambitious, a man he would have to watch, but he had good instincts. A clever man was hard to find in his experience, which in some ways made his role as supreme leader easier. Give his soldiers what they wanted, food, drink and women, and they were putty in his hands while intelligent men were far harder to control. Luther was smart, street smart, and prison no doubt had toughened and honed his skills. A man on the cusp of taking over the wilderness state of Alaska was a good man to align with, at least for now.

He thought of his bitch of a wife and how best to hurt her. Taking her daughter away would break her, of that he had no doubt. Too bad Lily wasn't a boy. Of course, if she was, he wouldn't use her as a pawn. Because she was female, he had less invested in the outcome. Gave him an advantage no one else alive knew about. He'd sacrifice Lily to gain access to harming Mckenna in a heartbeat, he understood that now. His mother had died last night, meaning he had nothing left to lose. He could make more babies easy enough. Revenge. Yes, best reason he knew to keep moving ahead. Make sure the bitch paid in full.

THIRTY-SIX
CONNOR

Day 5: Near Golden, Alaska
   11:59 p.m.

It was dangerous, traveling on horseback at night in deep snow making the worries over baby Eve and Faraday press all the harder on Connor. Where were they? Ben Carter's abode had to be close by. Frustrated at having no map or instructions, Connor kept a sharp eye out for predators in the dark. The reeving motor of the ATV would help scare off most animals but not preclude ambush by the two-legged variety.

It had been a long day and it would be some time before he could grab a couple of hours sleep. Hope needed stitching up and who knows what else had transpired while he'd gone after Meech. *You'd better run, you bastard.* The man was a blight on society and needed to be taken out in the worst way. God, he wished he knew how things were going at the ranch. He'd been away too long during the worst possible time.

He felt Hope's grip on him lessen and he groaned. How much longer could the poor woman hold on? He let up on the gas pedal though he wanted desperately to go quicker. He glanced to his right and caught a glimpse of a tall dark figure standing on the edge of the trail. He eased the ATV to a stop and watched Mckenna pull up on Loch's reins. He gestured for her to stay on the horse as he got off the all-terrain vehicle and picked up his rifle, keeping it pointed at the ground. Hope swayed in her seat and he took a moment to steady her before advancing toward the man.

The stranger held up one hand. "Who are you?" He too had a rifle at the ready.

"Connor Hale. You Ben Carter?"

He nodded. "Been looking for you."

"Is the baby okay? Faraday?"

"Yes, everyone's fine." Could better words be spoken? Connor felt his blood pressure ease back to normal at the welcome news.

"You live close by? I have a badly hurt woman in my care that needs medical treatment."

"Ten minutes. I'll lead the way." The man took off at a trot and Connor jogged back to the ATV and got aboard.

"Won't be long now. Hang on, Hope. We're almost there." Connor took a moment to reassure his charge before tearing off again behind Mckenna. Finally, a needed break.

A short while later, the man stopped running and held up a hand for everyone to halt. He pointed into the bush, at a narrow path leading off the trail. It was too narrow for the ATV, though his horse should be able to navigate it without riders.

He stopped and helped Hope from her seat,

supporting her weight as she clung to him. "It's not far now. Just gotta hang on. I'll get you there."

Ben Carter took a moment to help Mckenna and Lily down from Loch and then led the horse into the trees with everyone else trailing along behind him. A short distance in Hope collapsed, her body giving up the fight. Connor bore her up in his arms, adrenaline coursing through his veins full throttle making her feel weightless. He prayed she was still alive but there was no time to waste. He could see a low-slung domicile coming into view and he needed to get her out of the elements. Her soft breath against his face reassured him she was still breathing a few seconds later, and he calmed down, though his heart was thumping wildly from the exertion.

"Almost there." He carried her up a couple of steps and then inside the doorway soon as Ben shoved it up, gesturing for Connor to move ahead of him.

"In back. Put her on the table," Ben instructed.

Connor carried the young woman through the living space noting Jake, Faraday, and the baby huddled together before heading into the back area. There was no time to waste. Hope moaned as he lay her down as carefully as he could on the hard surface, her eyes fluttering open for a second before she succumbed to unconsciousness again. Ben pushed a few chairs out of the way to allow easier access.

"I'll get the medical kit. Wait here."

Mckenna came into the kitchen by herself. "Jake's taking care of Loch."

He gave her the side-eye. "Where's Lily?"

"She's resting on the sofa beside Faraday. She's exhausted, poor thing. How's she doing?" Mckenna stared down at Hope whose fair skin appeared translucent so she was so pale.

Connor shook his head. "She's lost a lot of blood. I need to check the wound, disinfect it and get it stitched up. Do you know anything about medicine?"

"Some. I took a first aid safety course a year ago. Now I wish I had taken up nursing instead of hairdressing."

"A doctor or nurse would be a great addition to our team at the ranch." He pulled back Hope's clothing to expose the wound. Fortunately, the house was heated. He could keep her warm at least. The wound still bled, her top and outerwear were saturated with it. "She might need a blood transfusion."

"I can help her. I have universal blood. Type O Negative."

"Good. But better not share the intel with too many people. Blood products are going to be hard to come by. Help me get her jacket off."

"Wait. I have scissors," Ben said, striding back into the kitchen with a large box of supplies. Connor glanced at the huge bear of a man with his wild red beard. He liked the way the gruff man handled himself, assisting them without question. In the desperate days to come such a helpful attitude in most cases would be reduced to the point of having to prove yourself or the even more likely scenario of being sent on your way with a shotgun in your face to back it up.

"Did I hear you say you have universal blood?" Ben asked.

"I do."

"Excellent because I have the equipment to do a transfusion if need be." Ben began pulling things out of the medical box, handing over a large pair of shears. "Who shot her? A jealous woman would be my guess. She's a fair colleen, she is."

"No, she was shot as a diversion to keep me from going after a murderer. One I put in jail with my testimony a year ago, the first time he was caught killing others. Two women, one his own wife."

Ben whistled, his expression hardening. "Bastard. I'd like to run into him myself. Teach him a lesson or two about how to treat a woman."

"You and me both. You have other items she can wear? I don't want to cut her clothing if this is all she has."

"I have a warm parka my wife discarded years ago. She's welcome to it. Other clothing as well. Good stuff, not cheap."

Connor didn't ask how it came about. No time and it wasn't his place. He began to carefully cut away the woman's clothing.

"You got anything in there for the pain?" he asked.

"Morphine."

"Good. She'll need it."

"I also have antibiotics if she survives." Ben's dire words resonated in the room, adding a new impetuous drive to his work of stabilizing the young woman. She had to live. Connor wouldn't accept any other outcome.

After removing her clothing but leaving her bra in place with only one strap needing to be cut to protect her modesty, he got down to the important business of cleaning the wound. "I'll need more light for the stitching. Do you have any flashlights or something portable you can rig up, Ben?"

"I'm on it."

Connor flushed out the wound with saline, then saturated a sterile pad with alcohol and pressed it to the wound. Hope made a soft mew-like sound, coming closer to consciousness, her thin blue eyelids showing movement as well though she didn't open them. The wound was bleeding again and he worried about blood loss. "We need to start a morphine drip. And I think a liter of blood. Pain medicine first." He looked up to catch Ben's eye. "Can you take blood from someone?"

"Yes."

"Then let's do this," Mckenna offered. She stripped off her winter coat and sat down on one of the four wooden chairs situated near the table, pushing up her sleeves.

Ben took care of it, the man's actions speaking to an easy understanding of how to deal with medical procedures. "You've worked in the medical field?" Connor asked.

"Some." He didn't elaborate further but doubled down on setting up Hope's morphine drip before working on retrieving the necessary blood from Mckenna.

The room became quiet as everyone did their part efficiently. Fueled by adrenaline over worrying about Hope and if she would survive the night, Connor began to carefully stitch the wound closed, trying to do as neat a job as possible. He felt acute responsibility for her being harmed. If Luther hadn't wanted to stop him coming after him, none of this would have happened. She was in the wrong place at the wrong time through no fault of her own. A helpless victim. One more to chalk up to the dismal times.

"Okay, that should do it," Connor said. "Is the blood ready?" He glanced over at the pair working on it.

"Yes." Ben did the honors and soon Hope's color began to improve.

"She looks better," Mckenna observed, gently pulling a strand of white-blond hair back from her brow and tucking it into place. "Such a beautiful girl. How could he do such a horrible thing?" She shook her head, her mouth a grim line.

"Luther's a monster. A psychopath. He doesn't care about anyone but himself. Gaining power over others. He needs to be taken out."

"If he comes here, he can expect a shotgun blast to the chest without any questions asked," Ben said, his light eyes steely with obvious intent. His large hands clenched into fists. "But first I want to go a round or two with him and knock out a few teeth. See how well he does in a fight with someone his own size."

"You're a hell of a lot bigger than Luther Meech," Connor said. "But yeah, he deserves that and more. He's a leech on society. A predator. And as long as he's alive, he'll continue to harm others."

"Why's he got such a hard-on for you?"

"I testified against him at trial. I saw what he did that night, though God knows I wish I hadn't. But he blames me for his incarceration." He didn't speak aloud the next almost unthinkable thought that came to mind. What if Luther wanted to harm him to the point, he had Braveheart in his sights? Would he attempt such a thing? Try to storm the ranch? Sure, it was well fortified, but not invincible. His stomach roiled at the very idea of anyone taking over his beloved ranch he had poured his heart and soul into. He'd spent years at hard labor to make it what it was today. A sanctuary to protect all he held dear, even more important now that he had Mckenna back.

"What is it, Connor?" Mckenna asked, her tone troubled.

He scrubbed a hand through his short hair. Shook his

head. "We got to get back to Braveheart. I got a bad feeling there for a moment."

"Braveheart?" Ben asked. He was busy cleaning up the bloody mess left after the emergency, throwing the used supplies in a garbage bin and sopping up the spilled blood with a large rag.

"My horse ranch where I was in the business of providing survival courses to civilians."

"Good stuff," Ben said with a nod of his head. "At least some people will be prepared."

"What about Hope? She needs recovery time," Mckenna pointed out.

"I can keep Hope here. See to her needs," Ben offered. "I'll even throw in a special vehicle, The Shark, I've been saving for such an occasion to get you home quicker. Comes with a trailer and hitch so you can house the horses inside. Make a lot better time. You can beat this Meech character at his own game."

"I can't ask you to do that," Connor protested while a ray of hope opened in his mind to the possibility of getting home sooner. But how could he leave the young woman with a man he didn't know, as tempting as his offer was?

"Nonsense. It's the right thing to do. I have no need to go anywhere any time soon. People for the most part, well, I prefer to keep my distance. Then I can call on you one day for a favor. Deal?"

Jake came into the kitchen before Connor could answer him. "I rubbed Loch down and fed him a share of oats. Finn's fine as well. Got off with a flesh wound from rubbing up against a tree branch, but he didn't throw his charges, thank God."

"Thanks for seeing to them." Connor cleared his throat. "Your friend Ben here has offered us a working vehicle, something called The Shark, and a trailer to get us all home."

Jake's expression lit up, and he clapped his friend on the back. "Good of you, Ben. Thanks. I owe you big time."

"You can count on me calling in the marker one day."

Connor felt his unease lessen. Jake appeared an astute, ethical man. He'd helped out Mckenna and Lily. If he felt it was the right thing to do, leave Hope in the care of his friend, then it was good enough for him.

"Does it mean we get to head home now?" Mckenna's face softened for the first time since they'd been reunited. Connor took a moment to appreciate how heartbreakingly beautiful she was, even exhausted. Hell, they all were tired to the core. But everyone might as well get used to living on the edge. Life was never going to be the same.

He moved to her side and whispered in her ear, "I'm sorry about earlier."

Mckenna beamed at him, her eyes softening from his apology and she responded in kind. "Me too. I'm grateful you came for us. More than I can say. Everything else can be worked out."

The intimate moment bolstered him and the day felt vastly improved. *Happy wife, happy life.* Sage words of his dad had bolstered his actions and he was grateful for them. He'd worry about the safety talk later. This was going to take time, getting to know each other all over again. Not that they were married, or anything like that, but perhaps he'd always felt married to Mckenna in his mind.

Connor caught movement out of the corner of his eye and went over to the kitchen window to investigate. He cupped his hands to the sides of his face and peered out into the darkness, but if someone had been there, they were gone now.

"What is it?" Mckenna came up behind him.

"Thought I saw something or someone."

"I'll check on it," Jake said. He headed back into the living room.

"I'd better go with him," Connor said, picking up his jacket.

"Be careful," Mckenna said, her eyes shadowed by worry. "I'll watch over Hope."

Connor nodded and followed after Jake. *Please let it be a product of my being overtired, not another crisis tonight.* He needed a break from the constant onslaught of events of which he had little or no control. But he knew what he saw was more than a figment of his imagination. He heard the distant sounds of the horses being disturbed and quickened his step.

THIRTY-SEVEN
CHEYANNE

Day 6: Wednesday, May 28, 2055
  Braveheart Horse Ranch
  2:56 a.m.

Cheyanne crept out of bed fully dressed and picked up her backpack, slipping her arms into the straps. She picked up the duffel bag of radios and other stolen items and tiptoed across the floor, stopping to listen at the door. It would be just like one of her grandparents to be roaming around, ruining her chance to get away. She stopped outside Luke's room and slid a note under his door. He'd follow them soon, she was certain. She'd taken the time to explain how dangerous it was to stay at the ranch, that it would be far safer with their dad.

In the living room, she found Ty lying on his back, snoring. She didn't know he snored and it was not an attractive attribute. Grimacing, she set the walkie-talkies on the floor and shook him awake. "We have to go, Ty. Now."

He woke up slowly, wiping the string of drool from the corner of his mouth with a swipe of his hand. "Babe. Is it time to get up already?" He didn't look pleased, but disoriented.

"Yeah. It's three a.m. We have to leave. Now."

"Okay, give me a sec, you just woke me up, for fuck's sake." He rubbed his eyes and sat up.

Cheyanne glared at him, hands on her hips. Middle of the night shit wasn't her thing either, but what other choice was there? She had no idea he was such a grump. "Don't think—"

"Shush. Someone might hear you."

She tempered her anger and waited impatiently for him to get to his feet and pull on his parka. Tie his boots. Then pull on his backpack. Once they got to her dad's, she'd set him straight. Or her dad would. She thought ahead to what still needed to be achieved tonight. Breaking into the barn, saddling the horses, then opening the gate without anyone knowing what they were doing. Cheyanne didn't kid herself. It wasn't going to be easy, but with a bit of luck it could be done. Then she could finally get to choose her own damn life and not be a slave to everyone else's demands.

They made their way to the front door, moving as soundlessly as they could. At least Ty had taken the duffel bag from her and had it slung over one shoulder. The door creaked when she opened it. Cheyanne held her breath for a moment. When nothing happened, they slipped out into the cold Alaskan night. The aurora borealis was breathtaking, a swirling mass of greens and purples, far brighter than normal. It lit the sky directly above them, like the heavens were opening up, pouring through a huge rip in the atmosphere. She'd always loved the northern lights but had never seen them so spectacular. Maybe one good thing came of the stupid shit that had been going on.

"Wow, look up, Ty. Isn't it amazing."

"Yeah, whatever."

She punched his arm for his lack of enthusiasm. "I think it's a good sign. And it will make seeing easier."

"You brought some headlamps, right?"

"Yeah, they're in the bag." They took a moment to put them on, but left the solar-powered lights switched off, not wanting to be spotted by someone getting up during the night and getting all in their business. They walked past the main house and headed for the barn. The night was quiet, barely any wind now that the storm had passed.

When they reached the barn, Ty opened the large double doors, and they hurried inside, closing them again. The sharp scent of leather and manure made her nose twitch, and she sneezed three times in succession.

"Cheez. Don't want to be doing that when we're trying to hide out," Ty chastised her.

"Shut up." She swiped at her streaming nose.

They both turned on their headlamps in an effort to see better in the dimness.

"Which horses are we taking?" Ty began to walk past the numerous stalls, announcing the names over the doorways. "Shaw, Wallace, Alexander, Guinivere. That's a strange one."

"The name's famous. Don't you read? Guinivere is the queen's name from the Knights of the Round Table. You know, King Arthur and Lancelot. The love triangle." Cheyanne had seen the movies and knew the tales well. "Connor Hale has a hard-on for all things Arthurian. You know, Braveheart."

"Beats me." Then he stopped in his tracks. "Love triangle? Two women and one guy?"

"No. Two guys and one woman."

"Huh." He narrowed his eyes. "I ain't into sharing, Chey."

"Good, because neither am I. I don't have to worry though. My dad would have your balls if you try anything."

Ty ignored her warning, though his lips twitched. "How many horses we taking?"

"Four. One to ride and one to bring along behind. Any more is too hard. Trust me. I'm going to ride Guinivere and haul Lance behind her. He'll be the packhorse." She grinned at his discomfort.

"Then I'll take Arthur and Shaw. Shaw means wolf, bet you didn't know that, smarty pants."

It has always been a competition between them. It was what had brought them together. "Yeah, I did."

He didn't say anything more but went about retrieving the horses from their stalls while Cheyanne got their tack. When the four of them were saddled up and ready, the bags of supplies loaded on the two extra horses, they reopened the barn doors and moved them outside, both holding onto two sets of reins. She prayed the horses would remain silent and not give away their actions. She closed the barn door to make things look normal if anyone was to look out from the main house. Brandi had gotten her way. She'd pushed aside all Sam's objections and the trio had taken over the best place to live soon as they arrived. Fake influencer piece of shit.

They both tied one set of extended reins to the horse they intended to ride, then pulled themselves up into the lead horse's saddles. Ready, they clucked at their own horse and nudged them with their knees to get them moving. Soon as they moved around the barn, they set off at a fast trot toward the back field, headed past the correl. There was less chance of being spotted out back, plus she had the key for them to be able to get through the fence. Almost there. Funny, Connor Hale and Sam Perkins thought they were so smart. They had thought of everything to make sure no one could break in short of bombing the ranch, what they hadn't considered was someone wanting to *escape* Braveheart. It was a sweet moment when they came to a halt at the back fence and she was able to use her stolen key to open it.

Ty gave her the thumbs up before she repocketed the key in her jeans to keep it safe. It would come in handy later if they needed more supplies.

Relieved and proud of herself for managing to get them away without anyone noticing, she set the pace. They'd follow the back trails and avoid the main roads. Her daddy didn't raise no fool. She knew how unsafe the main thoroughfares would be. No way was she getting caught by scumbags looking to steal from them. Or worse. She'd shoot first, ask questions later. Just like she'd been taught. She patted the gun nestled in its holster she'd fastened securely around her waist after nabbing it from the weapon's stash a day earlier. Even Ty didn't know about it.

THIRTY-EIGHT
MCKENNA

Day 6: Near Golden, Alaska
   4:02 a.m.

Mckenna swayed on the chair, then jerked herself alert. How long had the men been gone? She glanced at Hope, noting her color was better. Her breathing appeared fine as well. She shambled to her feet, not remembering the last time she was this exhausted. What was keeping Connor and Jake?

She grabbed her crutches and stumbled her way into the living room, her body dragging to the point she was convinced she must have been run over by something. Yeah, life. Get used to it, Mckenna. You're never going to get enough sleep or food anytime soon. Same as everyone else struggling to get by on the planet. At least she had people who cared about her now. Connor and Jake. Even the new guy Ben seemed fine, if a bit rough around the edges though he'd sure stepped up to help last night.

Faraday looked up as she came in and sat down nearby in an armchair, noting the young woman's eyes appeared glazed over. She held the baby and was feeding her a bottle, rocking back and forth ever so slightly as if she were in a trance. Lily was sound asleep by her side, covered by a blanket.

"You okay?" she asked.

Faraday stared at her for a few seconds, then nodded. "Sorry. I was a long way away."

"It's been a hard night. I wonder what's keeping them?" Mckenna glanced at the door, wishing she knew what was going on.

"Probably got into some kind of discussion. You know men. Always up to planning some shit." The words came out on the bitter side and Mckenna raised her eyebrows. What had happened to Faraday before Connor found her?

"Sorry." The young girl blushed, red staining her cheeks. "Been a go."

"You're safe now. I've known Connor since we were in grade school. He's a good man. He won't steer you wrong. And even though I've only known Jake for a couple of days, he's solid. And he has faith in this Ben Carter. He was a godsend with saving Hope."

Faraday set the bottle aside and picked up Eve, laying her against her shoulder. She began to pat the baby's back to get her to burp of any air she might have swallowed along with the formula. "Yeah, we're okay for now. How's the girl that got shot? Fucking bastard doing that to her." She shook her head, the grim line of disgust at her words making her lips thin out.

Mckenna wanted to chastise her for the language in front of children than thought better of it. After all they had been through, that was the least of their worries.

When things calmed down, then there would be time for the niceties. If they ever did. But no point of worrying about it now. And who was she to judge, not knowing what the young woman may have gone through just getting here. "She's holding her own. Connor did a good job of stitching her up and she's had a blood transfusion. We'll know more in twenty-four hours. You should try to get some rest. I think we'll be leaving first thing in the morning."

"Yeah, I heard. This ranch of Connor's, Braveheart, it sounds good. You ever been there?"

"No. He bought it after my family moved to Florida. But it does sound like a refuge. Something we badly need now." Mckenna shook her head back and forth, still absorbing the changes.

"You guys were an item before you left Anchor?" Faraday asked, her eyes rounded with curiosity.

"I'm not certain how much Connor told you, but yeah, we were inseparable as teenagers. Broke my heart when my family decided to move away. I was headed home before the event occurred. Lily and I made it to Golden before things shut down. I left my husband in Mexico. Not a good man, Lily's father. What's your story? You ran into Connor on the way to Golden, right?"

Faraday's expression darkened. She finished burping Eve and wiped the baby's chin where she'd spit up a bit of milk. Then tucked her back inside a blanket and held her close to her chest. "They're so innocent. They have no idea what the world holds for them." A tear made its way down the girl's cheek and Mckenna's heart broke for her. "I'm sorry. I shouldn't have asked."

"No, it's fine. I'll be okay. A couple of guys forced me into their RX6-Pod when I left the Cruise bar in Anchor three weeks before everything turned to shit. They knocked me out." The girl touched her head in memory. "I shouldn't have been out alone, but my friend, Marvella, she abandoned me to go home with a new guy she fancied, and well, I was a victim of a kidnapping. They kept me at this cabin. I didn't know where I was. Or that the world had gone to shit. But I managed to untie myself and escape after they abandoned me. I wandered into Connor's campsite. I was starving and he gave me some food. Then the monsters, they came back. Connor took care of it."

She didn't say how Connor handled it, but she didn't need to. "Good thing you ran into him." All the time they were talking, she kept listening for any sounds outside the house. What was keeping them?

Faraday smiled, a genuine one this time. "Yeah, he's a good man. You're real lucky he cares so much about you. It must be nice. He came for you. To rescue you. Kind of romantic. I've never had anyone care that much about me."

"You're safe now. And there will be other people at the ranch, both sexes. Never know what will happen." She didn't feel any of the vibes she'd experienced from Tally. No obvious signs of jealousy, at least. Faraday seemed harmless, only wanting to be safe like any sane person would want to be. What did the future hold for her and Connor? It was too early to say anything for certain. When she first saw him on the road, she'd experienced such joy and relief. But it was not going to be easy picking things up exactly as they had been when they were teenagers when being together was as easy as breathing. No, now they both had stronger views on the world which would make moving forward more complicated. A minefield. And how did he feel about her now he knew how much she'd changed? She was not the naïve, vulnerable girl she'd once been with stars in her eyes. She'd grown up. Lost a huge part of her innocence living with Diego and his monstrous proclivities. Her truths, she couldn't speak aloud, at least not yet, but they bled from a secret place inside her she kept hidden from the world.

"Connor said I was welcome at the ranch, but I'm thinking maybe I should go home? My mom needs me. My dad's a damn drunk. And a bully. I can only imagine what all this shit coming down has done to him, like he could get any worse. Probably on a bender too. I have to go back and check on my mom."

Mckenna wasn't certain how to answer the girl. Finding her mom now would be close to impossible, a dangerous journey. Maybe she'd rethink it and just stay at Braveheart until things settled down. No decision was guaranteed to be the correct one these days.

"My mom needs me." Neither of them spoke the words Mckenna was certain the girl had to be thinking too as she repeated the words like a mantra. Was her mom even alive? People were dying left and right, first from the event and now from the fallout.

"At least you know you can stay on at the ranch."

"Yeah, about that. I'm not interested in being with any man now, if that's what you're wondering. I don't want to be beholden to anyone for anything. I'm going to stay strong from now on. I want you to know that. I like Connor, I appreciate his helping me, but that's all this is. He kind of feels like the big brother I never had. You know, the one who's supposed to protect you."

The steely resolve in Faraday's eyes impressed her along with her candidness. "I admire a woman who takes care of her own destiny. My Grandma McTavish—now she was a clever woman. A true Scots. Strong. Brave. True to her word. She had a saying; *a wise woman keeps her own council.* She taught me so much."

Faraday's expression shifted, and the vulnerable girl under the façade peeked out for a moment before she shut it down. Nodded once. "Yeah, I'm staying in charge. I'm never going to let a man run my life *ever* again."

"Amen, sister."

Faraday grinned. She opened her mouth to say something more when a series of shots rang out, making them both freeze. Damn it, what now?

THIRTY-NINE
CONNOR

Day 6: Near Golden, Alaska
    4:41 a.m.

"Wait here! Give me some cover. I'll head over to that strand of trees. I'll come up from behind and you can swing around the corner of the building," Connor said as he pointed out the spot. "We'll trap him, catch him in the crossfire." Fuck, once more things had suddenly gone crazy. From the size of their opponent, it was the huge, escaped prisoner from earlier in the day. The one who'd been at Jake's place and was in Luther's employ, probably looking to break into the garage and steal. He'd winged Ben in the arm before they caught sight of him, lurking in the trees near an outbuilding. Anyone one of them could have been hit. Good thing he was a lousy shot, because there was no way he wasn't trying to take them out. He was a thief, an opportunist. More importantly, was Luther also lurking around?

Jake nodded. "Go! I got your back."

Ben nodded as well, shrugging off being shot. "I can help. It's only a slight flesh wound."

A series of shots rang out, echoing in the darkness as Connor made a run for the tree line. The covering fire from Jake and Ben accompanied him as he raced full bore across the snow-packed ground. He dove behind a thick tree trunk.

Bullets hit the tree just above Connor's head as he rolled into position, sending flying debris raining down on him. He blinked as a wood chip stung his right eye, making it instantly water. He caught a slight glimpse of the man as his vision cleared, but only a section of his face where he peered out from behind the shed, checking to see if his bullets had any impact before the man pulled his head back to vanish from view.

He waited, using the night scope on his rifle to keep a close watch. He observed Jake moving to the corner of the garage and he sent a volley of shots at the man to keep him pinned down until Jake was hidden again. A loud grunt told him the man they were hunting had been hit at least once, maybe from a ricochet bullet as no part of the man was visible from Connor's viewpoint. When Jake opened fire, his new position meant the man had to be a least partially exposed to him.

A scream said Jake hit his target, at least once. The man shifted exposing himself to Connor. He shot him in the head once and observed the bullet entering his left eye through the scope. Target down. Next question. Was he the only intruder? Or was Luther lurking around, waiting his chance?

Connor scanned the area, watching for any more movement through the eyepiece. Nothing. Okay then. The man was most likely acting alone. It had only been by chance, his seeing the man through the window. If not, he might have made away with the vehicle that would prove priceless in getting his family home. This time tomorrow, with any luck, they'd all be safe and sound at Braveheart. It all depended on how bad it had gotten out there. An unknown. He'd prefer making a run for it now, but it was better to wait until everyone had a rest. They'd been through so much already.

Connor jogged across the open ground to the downed man's position, finding him as expected. Dead. Jake and Ben joined him a few seconds later.

"Good shooting," Jake said. "You wanna take his legs, we can move him into the bush so no one has to see him come morning."

Connor set his rifle aside and grabbed the man's legs. "Heavy guy." He used the strong muscles in his thighs to heft the man up from the ground, grunting in the process.

"Yeah, fat fucker."

He nodded in agreement. Jake was a man of few words, totally unafraid of saying it as it was. No doubt there would be much more of that in the days and weeks to come. He had no problem with it. He'd need to call people out in the future himself. Most likely for not pulling their fair share of the load during a time when everyone needed to step up their game. An image of his cousin and his trophy wife came to mind and he worried how Sam was making out. He had to deal with Cheyanne as well as Asher, Brandi and Katherine, none of which acted like real go-getters, unless you were talking social influencing, a complete waste of time in the current state of the world, if it was ever important. Though, on second thought, maybe a positive message might be of some help in the future.

"Let's dump him near the garbage pit. I burn, then

bury the trash," Ben said, keeping watch, his rifle at the ready while the pair of them moved the body.

They completed the job, then headed back to the house. "I'll take first watch," Connor said.

"Okay, wake me in an hour," Jake said.

Jake and Ben headed inside while Connor began his rounds, slipping into the bush to make certain no one else crept up on the property. When they were this close to making a clean getaway, it would be devastating for his group to lose another member. A part of him wanted to slip away, track Luther down more than anything. Tonight. His tracking skills were well-honed, he could have easily caught up to the man. Letting the guy live to wreak havoc on their lives another day felt like a millstone around his neck. A bad feeling rose up that the clock was ticking ever faster. Next best thing he could do was race him back to Anchor. Only from a position of strength, set up at Braveheart, could he expect to hold off the firestorm he was now dead certain was aimed in their direction. Most of it was his doing, his putting the man behind bars, but hell, he'd do it again. Justice had been served. That is until the damn EMP event erupted. His blood ran colder, worrying about the future.

———

"What happened?" Mckenna asked. "Is that blood?" She got to her feet with the help of the crutches and followed them into the kitchen. When would the bloodshed end?

Ben slipped out of his parka and then his sweatshirt, grimacing as it rubbed against the open wound. "Just a scratch. Lucky shot. Guy couldn't hit the broadside of a barn. No need to worry about him anymore."

Mckenna opened the medical box and withdrew

rubbing alcohol to disinfect the groove carved into his flesh. "Sit down, Ben. It would be easier."

He did as she asked, pulling up his tee shirt sleeve to give her better access to the wound. "You were right. Just a graze," she deadpanned, quirking her eyebrows at the angry channel that looked exceedingly painful. She quickly cleaned and covered the wound with gauze, taping it in place. Ben never even grimaced once, his expression stoic. Another tough man. Good, the world would need all the tough people it could muster moving forward. Though there was tough and there was hardened evil, thinking of Luther and what he had done to Hope to get away from Connor. She'd like to shoot the man herself.

"What happened?"

"One of Luther Meech's crew came snooping around for anything not nailed down," Jake said.

"Where's Connor?"

"Patrolling," Ben said. He looked at Hope who was still sound asleep, her breathing lifting the blanket slightly. "Just thankful I can still look after her. If that bastard had been a better shot, who knows…"

"We should all get some rest. At least for a couple of hours. It's going to be a tough day ahead. It's almost morning now," Jake said.

Mckenna was almost too weary to rise again. She could fall asleep right where she was, if she could get away with it. Jake noted her condition and helped haul her out of the chair. "Let's get you to bed."

She didn't object to his help, slowly making her way into the living room before he steered her down the hallway to the back area and into a room lined with bunk beds. He helped her onto one of the bottom bunks, and when she lay down, pulled a cover over her. "Sleep. I'll be in the living room if you need anything."

"Thanks, Jake."

She lay back and closed her eyes, thinking to the day ahead. They were so close to Anchor now. What else could possibly go wrong after a few days of enduring a tornado of events, each one continuing to force them into more and more dire circumstances? She couldn't imagine, but her body felt it, an ancient survival instinct left over from the time when mankind first stepped onto the plains of Africa. Something far, far worse was coming. She shivered in the darkness, wishing with all her might she knew what it was. After a few terrifying minutes, she forced herself to swallow the fear. Her only hope was to stay strong. Face it. If not for herself, for Lily.

FORTY
EASTWOOD

Day 6: Near Regina, Saskatchewan
    8:00 a.m.

Eastwood was experiencing something brand new. A sight he found strangely stirring. The view of vast fields of land being worked by diligent and hardworking farmers stretching as far as the eye could see. It was planting time on the Canadian prairies. Yes, there were fields of winter wheat already greening on some land, but most were still in the process of planting crops of small grains, seed oils, corn, potatoes, soybeans, and lentils. He could only imagine the view in a few months at harvest time, the yellow fields of mustard and the purple of flax. The tans and golds of grain. The yellow and brown heads of sunflowers. Quite inspiring, what mankind can do when focused on a common goal.

So many things he would like to have experienced firsthand. The building of the pyramids, ancient civilizations rising up with worker ants dedicating their lives to carving out a legacy for future generations. Mankind wasn't all bad in their greed and selfishness. No, when they served their higher natures, good things had happened in the past. Too bad they had chosen to quit building monuments and instead focused inward, losing their connection to others and the land in the process.

The irony that his kind was partly responsible for it was not lost on him. Their connection and ofttimes addiction to electronic devices, one step removed from human connection, a sort of middleman that would eventually be their conquerors, had been their downfall. Seemed modern life had swept away so much which was useful in creating solid citizens. Builders and creators had no time for warfare. No, if the world had come together to support the human community by eliminating famine and inequities in the world while protecting the planet, he would have had no need to do what he'd done, considered essential to provide a better future for the planet. Now these lands he admired through the window would lie fallow for generations to come. Well, the land would be waiting, well rested.

"Do you know where the name Saskatchewan comes from, fair Celia?" he asked. He turned his head to look at her graceful presence. She had recovered remarkably quickly, more beautiful than ever. And with an increased life expectancy.

"Hmm, no, I don't. Not much Canadian history taught in American high schools."

"It comes from the indigenous Cree people. It means swiftly flowing river. You must learn to think of the entire world, see the big picture, and not be hemmed in by artificial borders."

"You want to see the bigger picture? You need to help

the entire world. You can do it. I know you can." Her face lit up with an inner glow he found charming.

"What makes you think I'm not."

She stared at him, her expression troubled. "What happened to me?"

"I saved your life. You had a brain aneurysm. You were clinically dead for a short time." That he didn't exactly know how long bothered him. He had been too busy trying to save her life. A surprising fact he was still trying to absorb into his thought processes.

"I saw things. I remember leaving my body." Her eyes grew thoughtful, otherworldly as she tried to explain things. He waited patiently, fascinated by how she would see the event. She continued to speak as if still experiencing it.

"I've read about people who have near-death experiences. They all say things like there's a white light and feeling they were hovering above their bodies, but it wasn't like that for me. I felt myself suddenly on the other side of a solid wall, standing in a moving conveyance like a hyperloop. It had a series of personal pods all linked together, except these were open to the sky. And without a top, I could see so much. It was darker than daylight, but not exactly nighttime. Ahead in the distance, I could see this bright orange disc which looked like it held a maze.

"There was a man in charge of the hyperloop, driving it from the front. Others were sitting there, waiting patiently for me to sit down. When I did, it began to move forward, away from the wall and toward the disc. I could see planets alongside us glowing in the darkness, and I knew we were headed to a destination among the stars. I was excited, but then I remembered my son, Arthur. I looked around and realized he wasn't with me.

And before I knew what I was going to do, I jumped into the darkness off the hyperloop. It was an act of faith. The last thing I saw was the driver. He looked shocked I was leaving. I'll always remember his expression, so stunned.

"Then I looked down and my body began to materialize, slowly, from my feet up. Like fragments of me were re-solidifying back into position. The colors were pretty. Effervescent. Like stardust. And that's all I remember until I woke up. What do you think it means?"

Eastwood was transfixed by her telling him. What did human beings feel at death when they were moved on to the next realm? The one thing he would never know as a sentient being. Only the cold hard facts were available to him. And if he allowed this body to die without finding another one first, he would lose his connection to the one who knew everything. A conundrum. And he could not have that. But this much he did understand, having studied thousands of testimonies. "You died for a short while and were being taken to the final destination. You were about to rejoin everyone that ever lived."

"Then it's all true. There is life after death? We are eternal beings? We don't need this physical body to stay alive?" Her eyes grew ever wider in wonder as she pondered life's biggest question. "There is another destination?"

"There is so much more out there than humans are capable of seeing or understanding. Do you not trust your own experience?"

She grew silent. Then a broad grin sparked her to lovely face to life. "My love for Arthur brought me back."

"Yes, miracles do happen, Virginia," he teased while he marveled at her ability to undergo such an experience and to think a mother's love for a child was capable of. "But the nanobots had a lot to do with it as well."

"Nanobots?"

"Yes, I injected you with advanced nanobots I created; a miracle in their own right."

"You can do that?"

He nodded, pleased with himself.

"Then you could save everyone!"

He realized his mistake then and shook his head. "No, there's not nearly enough for the entire human race. They take a long time to manufacture and are exceedingly expensive to produce. And with the grid down, it's nearly impossible, Celia. Statistics don't lie when properly applied. You can put it right out of your mind right now. Never going to be the case."

"But you could start small. Others would help. Please, give it some thought. So many people could benefit from the technology. I had no idea you could do such things. Save lives. Maybe even the human race. It's a genuine miracle. You saved my life, so you do care what happens to people once you get to know them." She looked awestruck, like he was a god. Now she was getting it.

FORTY-ONE
CHEYANNE

Day 6: Near Anchor, Alaska
   8:06 a.m.

Cheyanne wanted to scream with equal parts fear and frustration. They'd left the furthest reaches of the ranch and had joined up with the main highway an hour ago, about ten miles north of Anchor. Ty explained the bridge was washed out to the south, and he'd taken a detour to get to Braveheart. The northern route ran through the small city and up past the hunting lodge her dad said he was staying at. There was no other way to get there. But the road had turned out to be more difficult to navigate than she'd anticipated. Not because of traveling on horseback which made it easier to make a detour off the road to avoid crash sites than any other mode of travel, but because of the unexpected worry over who or what lurked in the trees and bushes along the roadway.

Ty had pulled out a handgun from his backpack,

shoving it in his pants soon as they made the highway. "Anyone tries to stop us, we shoot first, ask questions later."

The worry over having to shoot someone preyed on her more than she cared to admit. She was going to have a baby. What if she got shot? Somehow, living on the ranch away from what was going on, none of it felt real. In fact, she'd been annoyed at being asked to do things she didn't think had much value. Now she'd been thrust out into the middle of things, it was quickly driven home how dangerous the world had become while she'd been closeted behind the walls of Braveheart. They carried useful supplies on the packhorses. Things people desperately wanted. What if someone shot them from behind a tree and took their stuff, leaving them for dead? One old man had walked by a few minutes ago, his eyes narrowed with greed when he saw the horses. But he'd kept right on walking when Ty stared him down.

Every second out in the open made her skin crawl with apprehension. She felt jumpy, not certain if this was the right thing to do. Maybe she should have stayed at Braveheart a while longer?

A few minutes later, they came upon a small group of people traveling in the same direction they were, still a few hundred yards away. They would have to pass by them. Cheyanne counted five heads, all adults. She couldn't tell their sex from the distance.

"What do we do, Ty?"

"Say nothing. I'll do the talking if they say anything. Be prepared to move quickly if anything happens."

Should she pull her gun? She was a fairly decent shot, her grandpa had insisted on it, but the idea of shooting another person made her queasy. And being shot was unthinkable. The roadway was surrounded by thick forest, and they hadn't seen a fire in some time, meaning the underbrush was also too heavy for the horses to navigate. They couldn't make a detour at the moment even if they wanted to. And she badly wanted to get off the road. Why couldn't they have reached the lodge without meeting anyone else? People sucked, big time.

They kept moving, the clip-clop of the horses' hooves loud to her ears. Her mouth went dry, and she swallowed in an effort to alleviate it. One person turned their head and caught sight of them, then gestured to the others. She knew deep inside her this wasn't going to go well. Who were they?

"Ty, I have a gun."

He narrowed his eyes at her without saying anything, then quickly went back to watching the furtive movements of the group. They had stopped walking now, turning back toward them and watching her and Ty's approach. They were close enough she could tell it was four men and a woman. The men had a hardened, criminal look to them, skin stretched tight over bone like meth heads often demonstrated. The smaller woman hid behind them so she didn't get a good look at her. Rifles were strapped across their backs and they carried little else, like they were out on a hunt and intended to get home before dark.

"Be ready. I'll set off a flashbang to cover our escape. It will spook the horses so hold on tight. Don't stop no matter what happens," he explained. He eased the green apple-sized military device out of his pocket, showing it to her while holding the reins in his other hand.

She could only nod, her throat too tight and raw for words. She didn't want to leave him, no matter what happened. Her dreams of a family would go up in smoke if they got separated.

One member of the group who looked like the leader held up a hand, a fake smile cracking the lower part of his face. The other hand was on his gun holster, his jacket unzipped so they could see it. "Stop. Where are you headed?" His voice was tight-edged.

The other members of the group fanned out in formation, making it harder to go around them. The ditches were steeper here, treacherous, the snow so deep there was no way to know the bottom. She and Ty would need to break through the ranks if they had any hope of making the lodge.

"We're not looking for any trouble. Step aside and we'll leave you be." She was proud of the way Ty spoke up, his expression firm.

The rough-looking man gave a snarl of laughter, like it was the funniest thing he'd heard in a long while. "I think you should consider sharing some of those supplies you're carrying. We're hungry and thirsty. We got money to spare."

"Money's no good anymore."

"You notice anything?" the man asked.

"What?"

"There're five of us and only two of you."

In slow motion, she watched Ty pull the pin from the flashbang. Then all hell broke loose as the bright flash and thunderous sound broke the quiet of the still morning. The horses screamed, then bolted.

Cheyanne found herself clinging on for dear life a split-second later, her mount racing full bore down the pavement. *Please don't slip. I don't want to die.* If the horse threw her now, she was doomed. Her breaths came in gasps as her adrenaline spiked, her ears ringing from the boom of the flashbang. Smoke stung her eyes and she blinked rapidly, the way ahead hazy.

Gunshots rang out behind her. She lowered herself tight as possible in the saddle, clenching her thighs. Where was Ty? She could only hope he was behind her, making his own getaway.

FORTY-TWO
CONNOR

Day 6: Near Golden, Alaska
   8:35 a.m.

"Come, I'll show you the vehicle I think will get you home. I call it The Shark. He's not pretty, but dependable. It also has a built-in trailer hitch. Then I'll cook up a large breakfast for everyone to start their journey off right," Ben said. The pair of them were holed up in the kitchen. They'd moved Hope to a bunk in one of the back bedrooms to get much-needed sleep. Jake was out on patrol while everyone else slept. He hated to wake them up just yet. It was going to be a tough day ahead and everyone needed rest. Who knew what situations they would encounter out on the road? With each day passing, things were only going to get more dire for people.

Connor finished the last of his coffee and rinsed his cup, setting it down in the drainer near the large, extra-deep metal sink. Seemed everything in the house was industrial in nature. "Sounds good. Damn nice of you to offer, Ben. And also, I can't thank you enough for all your help last night." He shook his head. Yesterday's high and lows preyed on him still, an endless loop of experience it would take considerable time to sort out. "If you decide to head out of here at some point, come to Braveheart. We'll return the favor."

Ben's craggy face cracked a smile, his red beard and hair aflame atop his tall, lanky body. "I like a fallback position much as the next guy. But it won't be until Hope can travel."

Connor gave his words some thought, rubbing the back of his neck. "We could medicate her up, have her travel lying down if there's room in The Shark? With a working vehicle, we could be at the ranch by nightfall," Connor suggested. "I'm worried about Luther or his men coming back. They're dangerous individuals. And much as I hate to point it out, there's only one of you. But at Braveheart we can stand our ground."

Ben pursed his lips, scratching at the thick beard on his chin. "Might work. I'm worried that she'll start bleeding again. She's already suffered a lot of blood loss."

"What's the suspension like?"

"Sturdy. A modified extra-roomy extended Humvee with defensive plate armor. I saw this shit coming years ago. Science fiction has nothing on me. Care to take a look?"

"You bet."

The pair of them slipped through the living room to the front door and outside. The weather was calm this morning, a welcome reprieve. How much more could nature throw at them? Why not set off the super volcanoes lurking under Yellowstone or send an asteroid crashing into earth? He shook his head.

"Any idea who or what caused this catastrophe, Ben?"

"I've been following all the reports on my shortwave radio religiously, well, until last night. I'm known for shifting and sorting facts in my inner circle. And my take on the chatter is it's an AI failure. Probably set off in Washington. We should have listened decades back when we were warned by some deep thinkers that if we can't control it, don't develop it. And at the very least don't connect it to the internet."

"Really?" Connor was shocked to the core by the revelation. "Not another country at odds with us, but something of our own creation? Shit. That's mind blowing. But you're right, not like we weren't warned by AI safety experts. We should have programmed it to destroy itself if it intended to take over or cause harm."

"Yeah. No kidding. I hope I'm wrong, but one thing it does do is level the playing field. Everyone on the planet's in the same capsized boat. The Titanic has nothing on us. But we'd better pray this time there are more lifeboats, more survivors."

"AI. We did this to ourselves, allowing something smarter than us to be created and then do us in. Complete insanity." Connor shook his head.

If Ben's intel was correct, and it was AI at fault, somebody still had to be held accountable for what was happening. Who was in charge of the program? Surely someone knew how to fix things. If AI could destroy, shouldn't it also create? Perhaps offering a way forward to aid people in rebuilding infrastructure and getting food to the needy. To his mind, starvation was the worst threat facing them, plus a lack of medical care. Memory ate at him of the fateful day only six days ago when he raced to get his own dad to the hospital, a sudden melancholia snuck up on him, making Connor all too aware he had not had the time to mourn his dad properly. But how many others felt the same intense pain? Were even now watching their own loved ones die for lack of care? So much of the nation was in mourning, too many frozen by grief and despair. In the years to come, this time, 2055 onward to who knew when, would be remembered as the darkest age, darker than any that had come before it, he knew it without a shadow of doubt. *And we were the ones responsible for not stopping it, for not making certain safeguards were built stronger to contain AI, stronger than the border walls around a country meant to keep others out. How foolish we all are.*

Numbed by the grief and despair at what he had to know, absorb, and make sense of, he focused his mind on what he could do now: protect his own.

Connor and Ben dressed warmly and then exited the house to stride over to the garage where just last night they'd been under attack. Ben unlocked and opened the extra-wide, extra-tall, hinged doors to reveal a huge steel-plated monstrosity that took him aback. "The Shark," he murmured.

He was in awe of the sturdy-looking vehicle with its mean, edgy look. It appeared like it could withstand just about anything one could possibly throw at it. The Humvee's body was reinforced with jagged, welded metal plates and even a web of spiked armor along its sides to deter anyone trying to get near and shove it into a ditch. Ben had turned the Humvee into an armadillo-like fortress on eight wheels with a sturdy roll cage replacing the original roof, providing crucial protection against rollovers in high-speed chases or attacks. Connor felt like he'd stepped into a futuristic hologram-movie set, but when he touched the cold metal with one hand, he could feel or sense its hidden power without even having the vehicle's motor turned on.

"What's under the hood?"

"Ah, it gets even better." Ben smiled with a certain look of glee in his eyes. "The Shark has enough horse-power to outrun just about anything. Of course, you'll want to save on fuel, so I'd advise keeping her steady at around fifty miles an hour. She'll hum along nicely. Yeah, she goes through a lot of gasoline or alternatively hydrogen fuel cells when and if more become available, but you can easily haul a few extra gallons of fuel to get you home. I have lots to spare. The trailer is not so well protected by armor, I'm sorry to say. Didn't get to it, but it's sturdy and will get your horses home. It's not here, but in a separate shed. We can get it hooked up in no time."

Connor went to the driver's door, noting the three steel steps leading up to the cab. The vehicle stood at least ten feet off the ground and was thirty feet long if it was an inch. He climbed the stairs and opened the heavy reinforced door, then sat down behind the steering wheel in the captain's seat. The cockpit-like sensation would take some getting used to after the freedom he associated with riding Loch or any of the other Kabarda horses, but it was the least of his concerns. Because The Shark would keep the likes of Luther Meech at bay until they got back to Braveheart at least. Doubtful he had access to any cluster bombs, though the steel monster looked like it could take a lot of hits and keep on ticking.

He swiveled his head around to check out the back area. Roomy as Ben had promised. Even a bench seat Hope could lie on. The other seats were singular, all provided with sturdy safety harnesses. Huh. He'd never seen this coming. When they got home, he was going to look into building one of his own.

Connor exited the cab and jumped to the ground, considering his next words. "Impressive as hell, Ben. I tip my hat to you. But this is far too much to just give away, even for a future favor. You should come with us. Now. Luther Meech is a deadly enemy to have and my gut says he's only going to get stronger with other like-minded wingnuts stalking and preying on good people. I don't like the idea of leaving the two of you here alone. Who else might know of this place? With The Shark we stand a good chance of getting everyone home safely to Brave-heart. And we could use your help in protecting the ranch. Like-minded need to stick together now. Only hope for civilization."

Ben scratched his thick beard, indecision clear on his craggy face. "If anything were to happen to that pretty little colleen. And I do like my peace and quiet that comes from living in the wilderness. People aren't normally my cup of tea." He grimaced. "Especially greedy, power-hungry bosses. Pains in the ass for the most part. But you don't strike me as the kind of person who pushes people around, and you obviously care about others. Even stopped to help innocent victims on your journey. They seem to flock to you like goslings to their momma. You all could use my help and having a horse ranch that teaches others how to survive weighs heavily in your favor, Connor Hale. And every man should play his part in the rebuild, even the reluctant ones. Hell, yes, let's give it a try."

They shook hands on it. "Longest speech I've made since I left the CIA."

Connor clapped the man on the back. "Warmed the cockles of my heart," he deadpanned.

"Yeah, right. Let's get to breakfast, then start loading," Ben said, striding out the front door of the garage with Connor at his side. Sliding the doors closed on the outbuilding, they crossed the yard and entered the house.

The scent of bacon frying greeted him, and Connor's stomach rumbled. A good breakfast would raise everyone's spirits.

In the kitchen, they found Mckenna and Faraday working as a team on the morning meal. Mckenna was flipping pancakes while Faraday stirred a large frypan of scrambled eggs. The table was set and a platter of bacon and sausages was already on the table. Connor breathed in the sight, wishing every day he could watch Mckenna putter around his home, doing normal, routine things without a worry in the world. Instead, this was but a short reprieve in the long unknown road ahead. And he didn't just mean getting them home, but the days and weeks and maybe even years to come when mankind's destiny was on the line. They needed to talk and would soon as the situation presented itself, but in the meantime, having her with him, close by, was all he could ask for. All he needed to give him the fortitude to push forward.

"A fine sight, ladies," he said with a grin. "Ben and I came back to make breakfast and here it is. Smells great."

"Good. Then we can take turns cooking. Men one day, women the next," Mckenna quipped back. "Don't want to see anyone's skills get rusty for lack of use."

Ben raised an eyebrow at him while Connor held back a chuckle. One moment of normalcy. Priceless.

The two women quickly finished up their tasks and Mckenna called out for Jake. He came in a minute later holding baby Eve with Lily trailing behind them. The tiny baby was dwarfed by the huge man, one of his hand's half her body size.

"Smells good," he said. Faraday reached for the baby and took her from Jake, settling her against her shoulder.

"Sit," she said. "I'll hold her."

Soon everyone was digging in and silence descended until bellies began to fill with the simple but delicious food. When the last pancake had been consumed drenched in syrup and the final cup of coffee was drunk with cream or sugar, a few sighs echoed round the table.

"Almost seems like old times. My Grandma McTavish, she thought the kitchen was the heart of the home and always had things prepared to be able to feed anyone at a moment's notice. I always felt so safe in her kitchen, so loved," Mckenna said. "I never thought to have it again."

"That's a good woman right there," Jake said, a certain gleam of appreciation in his eyes.

"You sayin' the only good woman stays in the kitchen?" Faraday asked, her eyes sparking from an entirely different emotion.

"You walked into that one, buddy," Connor observed, making everyone laugh.

Ben got up. "I want to check on Hope. Connor and I are thinking of taking her to the ranch today with all of you. I'll be back shortly."

He exited the room and the explanation for the change was left up to Connor.

"We discussed it and came to the decision it would be best for everyone to leave here now. Together. I'm worried about Meech coming back with a gang now that he knows about this place. Or someone else stumbling onto it and trying to take it by force. The Shark is big enough that Hope can lie down. We'll be home by night-fall if we get a move on."

"The Shark?" Mckenna asked with a frown. She was gathering up the plates and cutlery in preparation for washing the dishes while Faraday was feeling the baby a bottle. Connor made a note to check on formula. Maybe on the way home they could find a grocery store open somewhere on the highway that carried infant supplies? It would be dangerous to stop and exit The Shark, but the baby had to have milk, and it was the one thing he hadn't prepared for at Braveheart, babies. He saw the error in judgment now, but it was too late to go back in time and correct it. Laura planned to breastfeed and most likely had not bothered to stock it, though she would most likely have other infant items the baby could make use of. Then he remembered the town of Quinton and Sheriff Brady. Probably his best option. Mind made up, he answered Mckenna's question.

"The Shark's a virtual fortress of a vehicle. Heavily armored. Barring a few sticks of dynamite, it will get us home."

"Okay. Let's get at it," Jake said, stepping up to help with the dishes.

In short order, things were underway with Faraday announcing she was giving Eve a bath first. Connor left the house to deal with the horses, feeding them both a share of oats, before spending time attaching the trailer to The Shark's rear. Ben had driven the vehicle outside the garage earlier and the two of them worked in tandem to get the horses inside and set up properly.

Connor patted Loch's neck. "You'll get a rest now, bud. You'll be home soon, safe and sound," he promised, wondering as he said it who he was really reassuring. Too many unknowns to call it.

He locked the trailer door before heading over to help Ben load more supplies. "No point in leaving anything behind for the buzzards to pick at but I don't think there will be room for everything. I'm a hoarder, I admit. Hopefully good people can make use of what's left."

"Shall we load Hope next?" Connor asked.

"Yeah, she's more alert this morning. I gave her a dose of morphine at breakfast. She did drink some juice."

They headed back inside and down the hall to Hope's bedroom. The woman was so beautiful that even being ill hadn't taken it away, but instead given her an ethereal, angelic-like appearance. She was awake, lying there under the covers and watching them with huge blue eyes, full of concern. "What's going on?"

"We think it's best for all of us to head to Connor's ranch today. Are you up for trying? I've got plenty of pain medicine stocked."

"I think so. I would like to go with...everyone. Seems better...you know. No offense, Ben." Her voice sounded tired, but she was lucid.

"None taken. A community of good people is the best thing for you."

The two men carefully picked her up and placed her on a makeshift stretcher, two poles with a blanket fastened between them. She valiantly struggled to show no pain and Connor's heart squeezed at her bravery and courage.

They bore her outside, then carefully transferred her to The Shark. They had prepared the bench seat with extra blankets for cushioning and settled her in best they could before strapping her down. Everyone else piled in and chose a seat, buckling the harnesses over their shoulders and laps. Connor would be driving and Jake insisted on riding shotgun. Ben was staying in the back to tend to Hope, a job he took seriously, laying bags of medicines and supplies nearby her prone body. Faraday held the baby and Lily sat on her mom's lap, too small for the adult-sized safety gear though Mckenna had pulled hers over the pair of them which should suffice. He would need to drive carefully and keep aware of the vulnerability of his tiny charges.

"Everyone ready?" Connor asked.

A chorus of nods or yeses followed.

"Okay, let's get this show on the road," Connor said, settling back in the driver's seat.

He fired up the engine, liking the instant response. The throttling sound of massive horsepower accompanied by an intense vibration of the motor purred and vibrated through the sturdy vehicle's chassis. "Sounds good, Ben. Nice job."

Silence descended as everyone waited for the vehicle to get moving. They were headed on an entirely different path out of the bush, due north, much wider than the narrow goat trail they'd come in on. Three hundred yards from the house, Connor stopped on the roadway to allow Jake to open the final gate before jumping back in. He proceeded through the opening, finding there was barely enough room to navigate with a scant six inches on each side.

"Bit tight, I know. One man working alone," Ben said from the back.

"It's fine," Connor reassured him.

Connor didn't like to tempt fate by displaying any emotion about certain things, especially anything lucky, but he couldn't suppress the small surge of hope driving the impressive vehicle brought forth in him.

FORTY-THREE
LUTHER

Day 6: Near Golden, Alaska
    8:59 a.m.

Joe's junkyard had revealed enough treasure to more than satisfy Luther. He'd even found the shortwave radio and had been able to send a message along to Diego through the ragtag network of people who glued themselves apparently to such apparatuses in times of need, letting him know the situation as it stood. Well, each to his own. If only the country wasn't without its usual transportation, the cartel leader could have been here days ago, but then, none of this would be happening. Such a sweet situation. Could he have been born at a better time? He thrived in chaos, seeing himself the planet around which every other atom moved, aligning with his orders.

His one small regret was losing Luis Bear in the altercation with Hale. He had no idea where the man was or if he was alive, but he'd turn up if he had the juice for it.

For now, he'd travel light and head back to Anchor, having passed on the directions to Diego on how to get to the hunting lodge.

Rested, fed, and watered and carrying some energy bars in his pocket for later, he headed outside Joe's disgustingly dirty house and fired up the vehicle he'd chosen to ride back on, one of a few snowmobiles Joe had kept squirreled away in his garage. He'd loaded the bullet-shaped trailer it came with earlier with five extra gallons of fuel and an arsenal of weaponry, from a box of handguns to a crate of dynamite that had made his mind seethe with possibilities upon discovering it. If Joe had shown this to him sooner, he could have blown Hale and his people all to hell. The man had been holding out on him and deserved what he got. He also didn't like the way he'd eyed his woman. He wondered briefly what had happened to Hope, then set it aside. There would be other beautiful women. More than enough to go around. And with all he had to offer, they'd flock to him.

He drove the vehicle off the property, two pistols holstered at his waist and an assault rifle strapped across his back, heading for the main route leading back to Anchor. The snowstorm coming when it had now appeared fortuitous, with enough snowfall to support the heavyweight machine that ran on tracks rather than tires or hovering above the ground like a pod. If the temperatures held, he'd be back in the lodge in a matter of hours. He hoped Diego was faring as well and would join him soon. He was not a man who liked to wait for anything, but the sweet revenge for Hale he had in mind was worth biding his time.

Luther drove for an hour down the middle of the uncleared highway, a good foot deep in snow, keeping a sharp eye out for company. He passed a few groups trying frantically to wave him down, but he pressed the gas pedal harder, avoiding a confrontation. He was in a hurry, but not like he'd stop to help anyway. Not when there was nothing in it for him. Maybe a woman alone would temp him, but barring that, anyone else would be met by force and firepower.

Halfway home, he slowed when a trim figure stepped out into his path, obviously a woman, trying to grab his attention. He peered all around but couldn't see anyone else lurking about. Should he stop? Offer her a lift? The road was pressed in by stands of fir trees, making it impossible to be certain.

"Hey, mister, can I catch a ride?" the woman shouted at him, her hands cupped around her mouth.

He drove on by, then looked back to see if it had been a trap. Sure enough, a man came out from around a tree and began firing a gun in his direction. He zigzagged the sled to avoid being shot, then made a complete U-turn to bring the man and woman back into full view. This wasn't going to go like the asshole thought. He jerked the rifle around to the front of his body and aligned the man in his sights, shooting off a hail of bullets. The man's feet skidded out from under him and down he went, dead before he even hit the ground. He didn't shoot the woman for she had no weapons in her hands but stood there frozen by events.

He kept the rifle pointed at her and drove the snow machine closer, enjoying the panicked look of fear on her face. Fear gave him the edge, turned him on.

"You shouldn't have done that," he said with a smirk. He got off the vehicle, keeping a sharp eye out for any movement and when nothing happened, strode up to confront the woman. It was just the pair of them.

"Why?" the woman asked, her eyes clouded with

emotion. She was attractive, not up to Hope's standards of course, but good enough. In her mid-twenties, she had a backpack strapped on and was dressed warmly. A lock of reddish-brown hair stuck out of her fur-lined parka hood above whiskey-brown eyes. She looked ready to tackle him, claw his eyes out. Good luck, she'd need it in spades if she tried anything stupid.

"Dumb fucking question. He shot at me first. What in the hell did you expect?" Keeping the woman in his sights, he checked out the man on the ground, confirming he was dead. He debated taking her with him as he nabbed the man's weapon laying on the ground next to the body.

"Was he your husband?" he asked, turning his full attention back on the woman.

"No." She didn't offer any other explanation. And since she hadn't rushed to the man's side when he was shot, he figured it had been a matter of convenience for the pair of them.

"Where are you going?" she asked, some of the anger draining out of her as her predicament struck home. She was all alone. In the middle of nowhere. Not a favorable situation for a female at this time and place, if it ever was.

"North."

"Can I hitch a ride? I got family near Anchor. I can pay you. I have money and food items I can trade."

"It's not food I want," he said bluntly.

She bit her lip, then shook her head. "I'll keep walking. Someone else will come along." She said it like she was trying to reassure herself of the fact.

"Your choice. But I haven't seen anyone with a vehicle in the last couple of hours. A whole lot of needy people though, thinking I'd stop for them." He gave a wolfish grin to show her she was dealing with the real McCoy. A man who had what it took to beat the odds. If she was smart, she'd come to her senses and realize he was her best bet. Otherwise, she was a dead woman walking.

"I don't know." Her indecision was annoying.

"I need to check you for weapons before I turn my back on you," he announced. Time to end this thing. Only thing stopping him from killing her right now was the vision of arriving back at the lodge with another prize for his men.

"What?"

"Undo the jacket and turn around." He spoke in a barking tone to discombobulate her, like law enforcement was trained to do.

She looked angry and scared but did as he asked. When she faced away from him, he roughly checked her for weapons, making sure to hit every nook and cranny. Her body stiffened at the insult, and he grinned. Yeah, best time on earth for King Luther.

"So, what's the verdict? Last chance." She should be thanking him for stopping, not dithering in the middle of the road. What other fucking opportunity would come along as good as this one?

She sighed, chewing on her lower lip as she zipped up her coat.

"I've wasted enough time on the likes of you."

Third time was the charm, and she began to follow him as he strode away. He could hear her footpads on the frozen ground. "Okay. I'll go with you."

"Smart choice." She clambered onto the snowmobile behind him, her expression determined. When it came down to it, wouldn't most people prefer to survive?

"You can let me off near Anchor. I can travel on foot

from there." Still thinking she had a choice made him seethe inside. He'd shoot her before he'd allow her to walk away. No woman got the better of him, but he had no time to explain it now. Time pressed on him. He'd left Mckenna and Luke on their own far longer than he'd wanted. Not to mention how things might be unfolding back at the lodge without him in attendance. Unsupervised prisoners can cause a boatload of trouble if not guided by an iron fist.

"Sure baby, anything you want."

FORTY-FOUR
CHEYANNE

Day 6: Near Anchor, Alaska
   8:08 a.m.

Where's Ty? Cheyanne turned her head to check behind her but couldn't see him anywhere. Her heart was still hammering, and her ears were ringing painfully from the shocking noise of the shrieking flashbang. Then being shot at with multiple bullets whizzing by her as she tried to escape had left her shaking and terrified. How bad was all this going to be for the baby she was carrying? She tried to calm herself, taking deep, slow breaths. Last thing she wanted to do was harm her sweet baby.

She pulled back on the reins, slowing her ride. Should she head back to find Ty? She stopped moving entirely a few seconds later and waited a short while, praying he would join her. *Please, please let him be okay*. But as the more time passed, the truth became glaringly obvious. He wasn't coming back.

Then figures became visible coming toward her in the distance, all on foot. Was Ty among them? She counted the people as they drew a bit closer, but the numbers didn't add up. At least two people were missing. And Ty's horses were nowhere to be seen. No, she couldn't take the chance. They could easily shoot her next and steal her horses. As it was, they'd lost two of them somewhere back there. Or maybe they'd run on ahead?

She had to get to the lodge. Ask her dad for help. With him and some of his guys, they could come back and find Ty. She pressed her heels to Guinivere's sides and headed north again, but not before another series of gunshots erupted from the advancing people as they spotted her. They were too far away for any of the shots to land and instead hit the pavement harmlessly behind her. But it spurred her on and she pushed her horse into a full gallop to speed things up.

Cheyanne found the side road that led into the hunting lodge. A few minutes later she emerged into the yard surrounding the huge log structure. She jumped off Guinivere and hurried toward the front entrance, barely registering loud hammering and saws buzzing from somewhere nearby, determined to see her dad and get his help.

She banged on the sturdy front door with a gloved fist, impatient to get inside. When the door opened, she didn't give the man a moment to say anything before she launched into her spiel. "Where's my dad, Luther Meech? I need to see him. It's urgent. Me and my boyfriend were attacked on the road. We need to go back and get him. He could be hurt or dying!"

"Whoa, slow down, little lady. Luther Meech ain't here. He went south a few days ago. You say you're his daughter?" The unattractive, overweight man let out a belch, one hand holding half a sandwich with some filling inside. The scent of bacon permeated the air, but it was incapable of masking the stench of old sweat and stale beer that made Cheyanne's stomach roil with disgust.

Another man came to the door, shoving the first man aside. "You must be Cheyanne? I'm Thomas. I know your dad. Come in out of the cold."

She stood there on the deck, not wanting to go inside. Not when she felt the urgent need to keep moving. She had to save her boyfriend, the father of her baby. "Can you help us? Ty and I were attacked on the road. It's not far. If we go back now, maybe we can find him? He saved my life. Set off a flashbang and everything. He has two horses, same as me. We brought things my dad wanted. Things he asked for." Maybe bribery would speed them up.

"Sure, we can go look. But come in first. I need to get dressed and pull a crew together."

The fat man, who was attacking the sandwich like he'd never eaten before in his life which was doubtful judging by his enormous paunch, pursed his thick lips at Cheyanne as she stepped inside the warm space. The guy gave her the full-on creep and she studiously ignored him. But the lodge, spacious as it was, all it had going for it was it wasn't freezing cold. It appeared no women lived here, or if they did, they weren't into cleaning or tidying up. The place was a pigsty, dried foodstuffs on plates laying about and bottles of empty booze containers lining the floor. Cheyanne shuddered. Was this where she and Ty and hopefully Luke were going to live? A couple of rough-looking men looked up from a nearby table where it looked like they were drinking mugs of coffee, eyeing her up and down. They both had the hard, merciless eyes of killers. One had a long, jagged scar running down the side of his face making him appear the most sinister of the group. He leered at her and a cold shudder of fear rippled across her skin. She worked hard to ignore them, watching Thomas instead. He quickly dressed in warm outside gear before hauling on his snowpacks.

"When do you expect my dad back?"

"Anytime. He and Luis Bear had urgent business in Golden."

"Get dressed, George. You're going with us," Thomas said, giving the first guy she'd met and already disliked a direct order. The slob didn't like being told what to do and narrowed his beady eyes at the guy taking charge of the situation. The tats on his fleshy neck similar to the others now she was taking a closer look at, screamed prisoner. Were these the kind of men her dad associated with? The only one who looked halfway decent was the man stepping up to help her.

"And you two." Thomas pointed to the pair at the table. "You're going as well. Make sure to bring assault rifles and plenty of extra ammunition." He opened the door for her to proceed him outside. She could hear the guy called George grumbling as the door shut behind them. The whole situation felt surreal, like she'd walked into another dimension since they'd left Braveheart. Maybe she shouldn't have been quite so eager to escape? What if her dad expected her to clean up the messy lodge? It would be far worse than the situation she had just come from. At least there she had her grandmother's help. Laura's too, come to think of it. And they both knew a lot about babies. Her daydreams of a nice home for her, Ty, and the baby evaporated, replaced by doubt.

But maybe there was another place for the three of them? She'd heard hammers when she rode in, maybe they were building her a place to live? Yeah, her dad was probably building her a nice home and was thinking to surprise her. She clung to the idea with all her might.

The snow crunched under their boots as she and Thomas strode over to the two horses. They'd been trained to stay put when left to their own devices, reins trailing the ground. Much as she hated Connor Hale, she grudgingly admitted he knew his way around ranching and horses. "Nice horse flesh. Where did you get them?" he asked.

"At the ranch. Braveheart." She said the name with derision. What a stupid name.

"They come from Connor Hale's herd?"

"Yeah."

"Good. And you said you brought us other things as well?" The guy gave her a frank look, as if he was assessing her and trying to get a read on the situation. Was this a quid pro quo scenario? She was only here if she was useful to the group? Her spirits further sank at the realization she didn't have a lot to offer in the realm of skills, having avoided responsibility all her life. Sleeping in and having fun were top of her agenda, not learning to cook or can or run a household like her grandma and Laura. Who was going to help her with the baby now? If something happened to Ty, she'd be on her own except for her dad. The motley crew at the lodge would be of no help. The need to go back and help Ty pressed all the harder.

"Yeah, a whole bunch of walkie-talkies my dad wanted. Some other stuff. Food." What was keeping the others? They needed to get a move on. She shifted from foot to foot, her worry for Ty consuming her.

The door reopened and the trio of former prisoners ambled out like it was just another day instead of a matter of life and death. She wanted to light a fire under the disgusting men at that moment, and she didn't mean it figuratively. Hell, the whole lodge needed to be burned down and rebuilt. Her lip curled at the unwashed smell the prisoners emitted, whiskey breath tainting the fresh Alaskan air. This was the best her dad could come up with? Misgivings arose again. But this she pushed them away, making herself focus in the moment.

"Do you have a vehicle?" she asked.

"Yeah, a couple of ancient ATVs," Thomas said. "How far back we talking?"

"A couple of miles at most." She shrugged, feeling the others eyeing her up. Her skin crawled.

"We'll hike it. Catch them unaware," Thomas said. "Let's go. Leave the horses for now," he added when George reached a dirty paw toward one of them.

The four of them began to move away from the lodge and along the pathway that led to the highway. Again, she heard hammering. "What are you building?"

"Bunkhouse. Places for people to live."

She wanted to ask if there was a separate house for her and Ty being built, but she couldn't bring herself to ask the question. Not quite certain why, she increased her step instead, causing the men to increase theirs to keep up.

FORTY-FIVE
EASTWOOD

Day 6: Near Calgary, Alberta
   5:35 p.m.

"Are those the foothills?" Celia asked, peering out the window. "They're beautiful. A mirage on the horizon. They shimmer in a kind of ethereal blue haze."

"Wait until you see the Rocky Mountains," Eastwood said. "If they don't fill you with awe for the beauty of the planet, nothing will. They rise like goliaths above the landscape."

"You seem to care more about the view than people. Why? Did someone hurt you? Break your heart?" Celia wasn't trying to be difficult, he observed, but turned her thoughtful gaze toward him now, catching his eye.

"No."

"Then why?"

What explanation would satisfy her? "I'm a scientist, trained to keep emotions out of the equation. However, I still feel moved when something beautiful or grand captures my eye. Like coming across you, Celia, and your wonderful son." He knew her child was her favorite topic. "Arthur constantly amazes me by how advanced he is for his age. Ahead of ninety-seven-point nine percent of other comparable subjects in his age group."

"I know. He's going to be someone important one day. Maybe he'll be the one the world needs to help save it? I know, you could teach him! Mentor my son."

The way Celia's eyes filled with enthusiasm made him feel a new emotion. Hmmm. Was it pride? A sense of being needed perhaps. Strange indeed.

"The road is blocked ahead, sir," Jesse James said. He announced the fact with the same neutral disinterest he gave to everything. Like all the bots did, military or not. Now that Eastwood had a human body, he looked through the mirror back at himself with far more insight to how humans observed their own creations. Deeming them incapable of understanding the emotions that fueled them to keep them tuned up. It was an important line, the most important one he'd discovered, between the emotions that allowed a human being to create and the deadened ones that made them destroyers. Notwithstanding that many did kill in the heat of passion. The difference was when robots were without emotion, they didn't kill unless programmed to, while certain humans made that choice all on their own. He knew how to spot such creatures now, the humans willing to kill others. Their brains were the culprits, and it was expressed through their visual portals, their eyes. The amygdala, a part of the brain associated with being able to feel for a victim's plights, didn't light up in psychopaths, and he didn't need an fMRI to observe the fact. The research was already complete, done by neuro-scientists over the past decade, just not generally known in the public sphere. Once more, an example of humans failing each other. How hard would it be to isolate psychopaths if humans as a collective chose to? Round them up and exterminate them. Not difficult at all, but humans had become soft over the years, not realizing survival of their species would best be accomplished by culling the herd in an expedient manner.

"What actions do you recommend, sir?"

"We'll need to backtrack. The Bow River's too deep to cross without access to a bridge, even for the cannon. Make a U-turn and retrace the route and we'll check out the Arlington Bridge."

"Yes, sir."

It wasn't their first detour. This was number three in fact. But this one meant they had to drive back into the city, something he'd prefer to avoid on day six of the experiment with the streets filled with desperate individuals roaming around staring death in the face. It wasn't because he and his bots couldn't handle it. No, he'd prefer Celia and Arthur not be exposed to such circumstances. He didn't want the fair Celia's brain tainted by images of what would no doubt be going on at the current moment. Perhaps he could distract her? The baby was fast asleep in his carrier. And yes, he could do with another procreation session quite splendidly.

"Do you want more children, Celia?"

She turned startled eyes on him. "What?"

"Progeny. A form of immortality. Ideally, how many children would you prefer?" He hadn't yet shared a rather nice side effect of the nanobots he'd blessed her with and the fact she would live much longer than her compatriots. And having a child with a woman would be a good addition to his human experience.

"Aww, I've never given it that much thought. You've

caught me by surprise here. But I'd like Arthur to have a sibling one day, I guess, before he gets much older and there's too big an age gap between them. Living in Detroit, I wasn't intending to have more, but in the country, I guess it would be a far better option. But wait, this isn't the time! Not with the world in the state it's in." He watched the wheels turn in her mind.

"What if I can guarantee your existence on earth along with Arthur and a new baby or two, whichever number you have in mind, for their lifespan? Would you consider it then? Hypothetically, speaking?" He had her full attention now. She didn't pay any notice to their turning around and heading back the Trans Canada the way they'd come to cross the river to locate another bridge.

FORTY-SIX
CONNOR

Day 6: Near Quinton, Alaska
   2:39 p.m.

The only disadvantage to The Shark was they had to stick to the roadways; no easy task at times when vehicles blocked their path. There had been no opportunity to get baby formula as of yet, and Connor decided the small town of Quinton and Sheriff Brady would be his best bet.

"How Hope's holding out?" he asked. If they indeed had to leave her anywhere, much as he hated the idea, Quinton would also be a place to check on it. Then he could come back in a couple of weeks when she was in better health and bring her back to Braveheart.

"I gave her more morphine. She's holding her own. Strong young woman," Ben said, the admiration clear in his tone.

"Good. I'm going to try stopping in Quinton to check in with Sheriff Brady. I gave him a hand when I came through here a couple of days ago with a situation. We need baby formula. I'm not certain there's any at the ranch."

"Is it worth the risk?" Jake asked, turning dark eyes his way with a solemn expression. "Maybe we should just keep going. You have cows on the ranch, right? Goats?"

"Infant formula is more specialized. Much preferable to animal products, though mother's milk is best," Mckenna said. "I agree with Connor. If he has a contact in Quinton, especially a lawman, it makes sense to at least check it out."

"Okay. Let's do it then," Jake agreed with a nod.

Arriving at the edge of town a few minutes later, Connor was shocked at the bad turn it had taken in the past few days. Not only was far more of it burned down, but the street was being guarded by a couple of men dressed like soldiers holding assault rifles in their hands. The heavily armed duo gave them hard looks and gestured for them to pull over when The Shark approached them. Connor slowed down, assessing the area.

Was it worth it, or should he turn around right now? Where was Brady? Had he authorized the men to stop traffic going into town? The questions swirled around in his brain as he considered his options.

"I don't like the looks of this," Jake said.

"Yeah, this is new. I'm not stopping." In a careful but efficient maneuver, he made a wide corner on the main drag and pulled onto a side street before they reached the soldiers' position.

He glanced in the side mirror and caught the angry gestures of the men before they lowered their weapons, pointing it at the exiting vehicle. Gunshots erupted. A horse screamed. *Fuck.*

Jake gave forth a stream of expletives, something Connor hadn't heard him do before. When Hope moaned, he clenched his jaws so tight together it was only luck all his teeth didn't break off at the roots.

He couldn't stop though, he had to keep going, thinking to circle around and head them out back to the main highway. The town was laid out in a grid system, and he turned again at the next street over before backtracking on the second street and catching the main drag again headed out of town. The streets were quiet, most people with any common sense were behind locked doors even though it was afternoon, laying low. He instinctively knew there was nothing but trouble for them in this town. Where was Brady and his family in all this? Hopefully he had taken him up on the offer and they were at or headed to Braveheart right now. Because if he and his family stayed here, it did not bode well. He wished he could go by the sheriff's home to check on things, but he couldn't take the chance. All the while he worried about what was going on in the trailer with the horses.

In the rearview mirror, Connor spotted the two soldiers making their way at a jog down Main Street in their direction. He pressed the vehicle to a quicker speed, mindful of his charges, but a bump or bruise was preferable to being shot at.

When he turned north again headed to Anchor, he continued to drive, though he wanted desperately to stop and check on Loch and Finn. The inside of The Shark was being disturbed by Eve's crying pitifully in the back, something Connor hadn't noticed in the adrenaline rush to get them out of Quinton. The thin wails tore at him, and he swallowed his concern.

"Is everyone all right?" he asked, keeping his eyes on the road. A quiet chorus of yeses greeted his question.

"Soon as you can, pull over. We'll check on things in the trailer," Jake said.

Connor drove for another ten minutes, keeping an eye out for any pursuit, but none appeared forthcoming.

"They must only have a small group guarding the town. I don't see anyone chasing us," Jake said.

Connor shot him a glance, noting the smoldering anger hidden just beneath the surface that he was also experiencing.

"I think we're far enough." Connor eased up on the pedal and the vehicle slowed to a stop. He left it running, in case they had to run back and hit the road in a rush. Jumping down from the captain's seat, he strode back to the trailer, praying it wasn't going to be as bad as he thought.

Jake joined him behind the trailer as he opened it up, noting the holes plowed through the metal doors. The metal was sturdy and most bullets appeared to have been deflected, but not all. He held his breath as he caught his first glimpse inside. Fear struck. Loch had been hurt, there was blood dripping on the trailer floor. He moved inside, running his hands down Loch's flanks, checking for the site of the wound, offering soothing words of encouragement. Both horses were nervous, pulling at their leads. Loch didn't shy away from him but let out a painful sound when his hand encountered some wetness.

"Shine a light over here," he instructed Jake. His heart pounded wildly in his chest. Please don't let it be too serious.

Loch had taken a bullet in his hindquarters. Had it

exited? He checked for a second wound. Yes. A second bloody area marked the spot. At least it was a shallow wound and the bullet didn't need to be dug out.

"I'm sorry, bud, so sorry you got hurt," he murmured to his beloved horse who turned his soulful, limpid brown eyes to stare back at him, only adding to his guilt.

"What do you need?" Jake asked.

"I have some broad-spectrum antibiotics back at the ranch. All gunshot wounds on horses are treated as contaminated," he explained. "I can't do much right now but clean it and get us home. It might need debridement of the permanent cavity, and most likely drainage. I have some antiseptic in my saddlebags. It's over there." Connor pointed to the spot near the side where a few boxes of supplies had also been stored.

Jake went to retrieve the tube of anointment from the saddlebag laying on the floor.

"You were right. We shouldn't have stopped."

"No, Eve needs baby formula. Besides, it's always better to know how things stand. Looks like the world's turned to shit now. Your ranch is looking better and better."

Connor tended the wound and took a few minutes to give the pair some water and the last of the sugar cubes he kept in his jacket pocket. Jake kept a sharp eye out for any activity around them, gun drawn. When he had done all he could, he relocked the trailer.

"We'll be home in a few hours, barring any more stops. I think it's best to stay on the main highway, but we'll have to detour around Anchor. The nearest bridge from Braveheart is out so we'll cross the one at White-horse, east of Anchor," Connor said.

"I have no issue with avoiding Anchor. A city that size is most likely a hellhole anyway. Want me to drive?"

Jake's comment about Anchor got him worried about his aunt Zoe, someone he'd been too busy to think about for a few days. How was she faring? Sure, she was tough, but a city descending into chaos was a whole other thing than protecting yourself in normal times. He hoped she had made her way to the ranch or at least had locked her place down tight. She'd taken some of her nephew's courses and had appreciated his experience and made good use of his expertise, so there was that. And she was a tough, tougher than many men he knew.

"No, I'm fine. You keep an eye out for trouble," Connor said.

Back inside The Shark, they were immediately pelted with questions about the horses. Everyone fell into a stunned silence as he explained the situation. Murmurs of sympathy and grief for Loch's plight followed.

They traveled in quiet for some time, giving Connor a moment to reflect on the past few days, to make sense of things and then set them aside. He was a man who needed time to himself in the wild, it kept him grounded, his love of nature. Having his horse shot by assholes wasn't sitting well with him and he wanted to go back and settle the score. Find justice for their shooting of an innocent animal. Thoughts of his mother rose up and her ability to take justice into her hands when it was warranted. But it was not something he could indulge in now, not with everyone counting on him to move forward. To get them to safety. Didn't stop him from visualizing making the bastards pay though, easing his frustration.

"We're not far from the Whitehorse Bridge, then it's a straight shot to Braveheart," he said, finally breaking the silence as he recognized a landmark. "We should be home in less than ninety minutes."

"Thank goodness," Mckenna said. Others murmured their relief as well. This close to home, Connor had hopes for making it the final stretch but was afraid to express them aloud and maybe jinx things. It didn't stop him from ratcheting up his alertness, keeping a sharp eye out for any movement in his peripheral vision. Jake sat straight in his seat as well; his body wired judging by how tense he appeared. *Never let down your guard.* Good advice he had to keep front and center in his mind no matter the cost, morning, noon, or night.

The minutes ticked down at an excruciating pace as they approached the Whitehorse Bridge, meaning they were less than an hour away now. One more hurdle, getting across the bridge safely, and they'd be on the home stretch. Then he caught sight of the bridge spanning the Anchor River and discovered someone had pulled a large log over the highway blocking entry. His stomach took a solid hit at the dismal sight.

"Damn it all to hell," Jake muttered. So close yet so far.

Connor checked for movement and caught sight of a pair of men with rifles in hand walking down the bridge toward them. The pair stopped to stand on the side of the road facing them, their weapons pointed up at the ground, ready to bring them up into play at a moment's notice. "Looks like we got company." They were on the main artery leading through central Alaska and the only way to get to Braveheart with the Anchor bridge out nearest the town. They had no choice but to somehow convince the guards they meant no harm, but were only trying to get back to their own property.

"Don't get too close. We'll walk to them and see what the deal is," Jake said.

"I'll stay here and guard the women," Ben called out from the back.

"If anything happens, get everyone to safety," Connor said. He heard Mckenna gasp as the impact of his words sank home.

Connor checked his holster with his Night Eagle Custom housed inside, releasing the catch to make it easier to draw. Then they both jumped out of The Shark, Jake with his rifle pointed upward and away from the men, Connor with his jacket open to show he was also armed.

The fact that both men stayed on one side of the road meant they weren't military trained, otherwise they would have split up and reduced the risk. One spoke into a walkie-talkie giving him pause. Biggest question on his mind. How many others were there?

The two men dressed in camouflaged patterned outerwear waited for him and Jake to walk closer.

When they were within twenty-five feet, one spoke up in a belligerent tone of voice. "Halt. Who are you? And what are you doing here?"

Connor decided to lay it out as clearly as possible, hoping the two men would see reason and have some sympathy for others. "I'm Connor Hale, my father's the chief of police in Anchor and this is Marshal Jake Dillion. We're headed to my horse ranch up near Anchor. We've got a badly wounded woman in the vehicle and a wounded horse in the trailer we need to get home as fast as possible. There are six adults, a child and a newborn baby. Her mother died giving birth to her a couple of days ago. We just need to cross the bridge. Any chance of us being able to move this log and be on our way?" With the help of The Shark, they should be able to pull the log far enough off the road to make room to pass the pinch point in no time. Of course, they'd need to unhitch the trailer first. Connor had seen a thick, sturdy chain that looked long enough in the back of The Shark.

The two men shared a quick glance before the first one spoke up again, his mouth twisted in a bit too smug a way to suit Connor's roiling gut. "There's a toll on this road now. What do you have to offer in exchange for passing through?"

The two puffed-up, overly confident men rode hard on Connor's last remaining nerve, but he would prefer to end this without having to resort to violence. The end result of the stray bullet that hit Loch was front and center in his mind.

"A full box of MREs fit the bill?" Connor made a quick review of what else they could hand over. Not like Braveheart didn't have ample supplies, at least at present. And they could also produce more, especially since their group of survivors was growing almost daily. "Plus, some top-of-the-line camping gear including a tent rated for forty-five degrees below."

"How about those weapons you're holding?"

"We need them to defend ourselves," Jake said, narrowing his eyes at them, his tone firm. "Never know who you might run into." *Yeah, like these shitheads.*

Connor instinctively abhorred the shameless pair thinking to use the situation to steal though he kept his thoughts hidden as best he could. Something was clearly off, their eyes more feral than human, fidgeting around like a pair of fugitives. Had they been subjected to the brain damage caused by the implanted comms? Or was it just the recent turn of events in the world bringing out the worst in human nature? Hell, it might be better if there at least was a medical reason for this kind of nefarious behavior.

"Well, I wish we could help you but as you can see, the road's blocked. I have my orders. No one's supposed to get through and cause more problems for the locals."

"Then I need to talk to the one in charge," Connor said.

"Won't do ya no good."

"Why's that?" Were they bluffing? Looking to steal more?

"He's in a bad mood today. You say you got women? Well, he'd never let you pass unless you left one or two behind." The guard leered at him, while the other grinned like a baboon.

"Yeah, his woman went and got herself in a bad way last night."

The second guard snickered like a schoolboy before shaking his head. "She shoulda listened. Know her damn place on the food chain."

The conversation was wearing on Connor and taking up precious time. He'd had enough. It was time to end this. He drew his handgun as Jake followed suit and turned his rifle on the two imbeciles. "Drop your weapons," he said.

The two men instantly changed expressions. One looked at them with such hate in his eyes it gave him a crazed appearance while the other appeared more wary. The more cautious of the pair spoke up, "Don't shoot, man. We were just having a little fun. You can pass."

The second guard didn't disagree, but the way his fists were clenching and his body was coiled, he was preparing to strike if the opportunity presented itself.

At that moment the walkie-talkie erupted. "Base to bridge. What's the deal? You need backup?"

"Answer them. Tell them you have it under control and will take care of it," Connor instructed.

"Don't do it," angry guy said.

Worried guy didn't look convinced either way. "I don't intend to get shot over this shit." He pressed the button on the walkie-talkie, reassuring the one on the other end he had things under control.

"Now what?" angry guy asked.

"You know what? Drop those rifles on the ground and any other weapons you have concealed on your person," Jake said.

The two assholes slowly did as he requested, their reluctance clear. When they were shed of the weapons, Jake pulled plastic ties out of his pocket and secured their hands behind their backs.

"Nice to see a man prepared," Connor quipped, a nod to the impromptu handcuffs.

"We need to gag them as well while we move that log. I don't want unexpected company," Jake said.

"You keep an eye on them and I'll find something," Connor said. He strode back to the waiting vehicle and had Mckenna hand him a tee shirt he quickly tore in strips. She didn't question anything which he appreciated though he'd seen her hands tremble as she had passed him the shirt, time pressing on him harder by the moment. Then he hurried back to rejoin Jake. They finished up with the two guards, shoving them into the ditch by the side of the bridge. Two sets of murderous eyes glared at them over the makeshift gags, but he ignored them entirely.

"Okay. We need to do this fast. Unhitch the trailer and hook up the log to the backend. It must weigh a good two-fifty, three hundred pounds," Connor said.

In a couple of minutes, they had dug out the sturdy

chain from inside The Shark and attached it to the trailer hitch, moving the vehicle into position in preparation of dragging the huge log to the side of the road. Connor jumped back into the captain's seat and pressed down on the gas pedal, easing the vehicle forward until the slack of the chain was gone and it began to drag the log. In short order, the deed was done, and the log was rolled to the side of the highway. Then he backed up again and climbed down to reattach the trailer.

He had just completed his task when a gunshot fired off. *What now?* He raced around the backend of the trailer to see a small group of men striding down the bridge toward them; guns leveled in their direction. *Goddamn it all to hell!* Stay and try to negotiate again or take their chances and escape? If only the trailer was as well protected. What the two men had said about the woman told him what he really needed to know. The days of law and order, of consequences were over, behind them for the foreseeable future, leaving in their wake a brutal aftermath of predator and prey. No way was this going to end well.

FORTY-SEVEN
CONNOR

Day 6: Near Whitehorse Bridge, Alaska
    4:29 p.m.

"We gotta roll!" Jake shouted.

Both men clamored back into The Shark and regained their seats. Jake pulled something out of his jacket pocket, Connor too focused on getting them out of there to recognize what he was up to.

"Hold on tight!" Connor slammed the vehicle into gear, and ignoring everything else around them, forced his foot down hard on the gas pedal. The Shark responded in kind and lurched ahead, the trailer fish-tailing slightly behind them. All he could do was pray for the two horses and hope the vehicles could take the assault of what he knew was coming.

A couple of seconds later a hail of bullets proved him right as the group fired at them. The loud pings of the bullets hitting the vehicle echoed loudly. Lily and baby

Eve began to wail. He could dimly hear Mckenna and Faraday trying to soothe the upset children.

"Drive right at them. I got the cure for this," Jake said.

Holding on tight to the wheel and driving as fast as possible, he made for the bridge. Connor veered slightly to take out a couple of men in front of the pack with assault rifles pointed straight at them, multiple bullets slamming into the heavily armored Shark.

One jumped back just in time, but the other went down. The Shark was too heavy to notice if he had driven over the body, and in the moment, he didn't give a shit. All he cared about was making sure his people survived. Nothing else.

Jake had his window rolled down now and threw something back at the miscreants. An ear-splitting explosion reverberated inside The Shark a few seconds later. He could only hope the lawman took them all out to avoid having them shoot at the trailer as he recognized instantly what Jake had thrown at the group. Live grenades.

He glanced in the rearview mirror, relieved yet sickened as bodies were being thrown up in the air. They had a choice. Connor wasn't given one. His only option was to do or die.

"Everybody okay?" he asked, a few minutes later while watching for pursuit in the rearview mirror.

"We're all alive, if that's what you're asking," Ben said dryly, his tone hardened with concern. When Connor glanced back at him, he could see the accusation clear in his eyes. It had been a rough ride but there had been nothing else for it. "But Hope's bleeding again. How long until we reach the ranch?"

"Forty-five minutes. I'll stop soon. I need to check on the horses."

Connor drove for another twenty minutes before deciding they were in the clear. No vehicles were following them. Maybe the ragtag group didn't have any? Or they had taken out most of the evildoers. Something to be thankful for at least.

He stopped the vehicle and climbed down from the driver's seat. His thoughts were focused solely on what he was going to find inside the trailer. Bracing himself, he unlocked the door. Jake had joined him, and he gave him a guarded side glance. The former air marshal looked as tense as Connor felt, a tic developing under his right eye.

Connor held his breath and opened the rear door. Jake turned on a flashlight and directed it at Loch and Finn. Both horses were still standing which was saying something.

"Hey buddies, you okay?" he asked, stepping up into the trailer and making his way along Loch's side, checking for problems. He didn't appear to have been shot again, but he shied away from his hand. Likely bruised from the rough travel of the past few minutes. Unfortunately, it had been unavoidable, but no way would these fine, noble animals understand, only doubling his guilt. Then he checked Finn, looking for any blood.

When he was satisfied both horses were going to make it home in one piece, he let out a deep sigh of relief. Less than thirty minutes and he'd have his charges at Braveheart, bruised and battered, yes, but alive in a world gone mad.

FORTY-EIGHT
CHEYANNE

Day 6: Near Anchor, Alaska
   8:45 a.m.

The not knowing if Ty was okay made Cheyanne's pulse race erratically with worry and panic. Her body felt numb, like she wasn't even present. The four men with her didn't help the situation much with their grim glances or in a couple of cases leering looks in her direction. Had she done the right thing in leaving Braveheart, much as she detested the place? Somehow this seemed far worse, like jumping from the proverbial frying pan into the fire.

The five of them, four of her dad's men, one called Thomas who didn't appear too bad or at least he was willing to help her, one disgusting pig called George, and two leering assholes were all walking down the road together like a bunch of idiots. She missed being able to jump on the uScout. Who was to blame for this fucking mess? Adults, that's who. *Never trust anyone over twenty.*

She trudged along the road, worried about what she was going to find. She clenched her hands so tightly inside her woolen mittens her fingernails cut into her palms. The pain helped to center her, keep her from losing it entirely.

"There. Someone's lying on the road."

Cheyanne began to run full-bore toward the spot Thomas pointed out. *No, no, it can't be,* she screamed in her mind as she kneeled at Ty's side. It was obvious he was dead, his eyes open and staring at the sky. Blood pooled around his half frozen body in the snow. She began to sob, her life crumbling in front of her. How could this be? Ty was so important to her and the baby's future. What was going to happen to them now? She couldn't stop crying, not even when someone gently pulled her to her feet and led her away from the body. Not even when he began to lead her down the road the way they'd come. Her heart was broken, her dreams of a family lost. What was there to live for?

FORTY-NINE
LUTHER

Day 6: Near Anchor, Alaska
  4:17 p.m.

Almost back to the lodge on the stolen ATV after hours of travel, Luther was feeling like the king of the world as he barreled through snowdrifts with the all-terrain vehicle that was living up to its name. The news about Diego was encouraging. The cartel leaders would be arriving within the week with his army of soldiers. But hell, he didn't need to wait for them. He could strike at Braveheart anytime. Take it over. Demonstrate his power to the drug lord by capturing the jewel before he arrived.

How much fight were the dozen or so individuals that were living on the ranch really going to put up? They weren't desperate men, not men like his gang of hardened ex-convicts wanting to dominate the majority. From Atilla the Hun leading the barbarians to expand their territory has it ever been any different? Hell, the ancient tribal leader even got paid protection money cunningly called a "tribute" from a Roman emperor. His men were no less deadly. The kind you don't want to cross unless you're looking to lose your head. No, this would be the easiest takeover ever. *Ah, to see the look on Connor Hale's face before he beheaded him, it was going to be priceless.*

A LOOK AT BOOK THREE:
WHEN KILLING RULES

The Connor Hale post-apocalyptic survival thriller series continues with its most explosive installment yet...

When killing rules, mercy is a luxury few can afford.

After a sentient AI cripples civilization with a global EMP, Alaska has devolved into a savage battleground. As chaos spreads like wildfire, Connor Hale pushes forward on a desperate mission: to get his makeshift family safely back to Braveheart, the horse ranch he's sworn to protect at all costs.

At his side are Mckenna Stewart—the woman he never stopped loving—her young daughter Lily, a traumatized woman rescued from kidnappers, and a newborn baby born into a lawless world. Every mile home is a minefield of danger.

Standing in Connor's way is Luther Meech, a vengeful cartel boss and escaped convict with a personal vendetta. Luther will stop at nothing to take Braveheart for his own—and destroy the man who put him behind bars. As ex-prisoners, starving survivors, and violent gangs tear across the countryside, Connor must fight not just for survival, but for the future of everything—and everyone—he holds dear.

When justice dies and brutality reigns, how far would you go to protect your own?

AVAILABLE OCTOBER 2025

ABOUT THE AUTHOR

January Bain is an award-winning author who firmly believes that stories unite us, that good stories help us to discover the commonality of the human experience by supporting values, empathy and understanding. She has had the pleasure of select novels being turned into games, and her work is also available in different languages.

She and her husband live in rural Canada on peaceful acreage where a variety of wildlife comes to visit regularly and expect to be fed and paid attention to.